MORTGAGED MORTALITY

J. C. JACKSON

SHADOW PHOENIX PUBLISHING

Mortgaged Mortality

J.C. Jackson

Copyright © 2020 J.C. Jackson

Published by Shadow Phoenix Publishing LLC

ISBN-13: 978-1732283565

Cover designed by J. Caleb Design

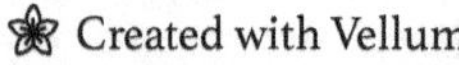 Created with Vellum

For those who have wanted a fresh start.

1

THE ROADS WERE both wonderfully and woefully empty as I drove back to the main office. Wonderful as this was the first time I had ridden my motorcycle home. Woefully because it made the roughly two-hour drive feel longer, though the autumn colors were stunning. I popped the visor on my helmet for a moment to get more airflow. The cool air hitting my face was refreshing.

I was more than capable of riding back, but I had always left the purple, white, and black bike at my adopted parent's house. I had finally gotten around to getting my tag to bring it onto the grounds for the main office. I had put it off for years for one reason or another.

I picked up speed as the twisting mountain paths gave way to straight open road through a valley. I hoped the weekend break would help me come back fresh to my search for necromancers.

Not that Silver had been any help the past several months. He was always away on other business for the Terran Intelligence Organization. He barely acknowledged my existence in passing anymore. He never bothered to respond to my messages. Some partner he was.

I had to slow as I approached Blessing. *Almost back.* I navigated my way through the small town, ending up behind an enclosed black truck with a TIO license plate. I was curious about who I followed in the fleet vehicle. Those who chose to live in town had their own vehicles so it must be someone who lived in the on-site housing like I did.

Whoever the driver was, they certainly took their time getting through town. I could not get around them with the amount of traffic on the roads. *Too many tourists for the autumn festivals.*

It felt like an eternity to get to the road leading to the main office.

I hung behind the truck for a bit as we got away from the town. As soon as Blessing was out of sight and the road was clear, I put my signal on and started to pass the truck.

Glancing to see who the driver was, I saw a familiar male Elf with long, braided silver-white hair. *Silver. Why am I not surprised? He does tend to be cautious while driving.*

He shook his head at me as I sped by. I wore a full-coverage helmet with a dark visor and my hair hidden under it, a neck warmer, and my jacket. With any luck, my size would not give away my identity.

Out of spite, I kept my increased speed once I got back into my lane, leaning down over the tank, tightening my legs around it. I took the turns much faster than I normally would, increasing my distance so I could be out of the parking garage before he got there.

The sheer exhilaration at driving like this pushed me to keep going. Why had I not done this before? I could not resist the smile that came to my face at the excitement.

Apparently, I had been cooped up with desk work for too long.

Silver's truck continued to get smaller in my mirrors. I shifted gears and increased my speed. I barely slowed entering the final curve before reaching the main office, leaning the bike more than I was used to. The wind pulled harder against my clothes.

Those riding courses I had enrolled in over the summer out of sheer boredom were coming in handy.

I slowed back down as the gate came in view. I stopped at the barrier and the tag on my small windshield caused the light on the panel turn yellow, showing it was recognized. I pushed up the visor so the guard could see my face. Half of it anyway. Just enough so he could make sure the tag matched the driver.

"Nice ride!" he shouted, waving me through as he raised the arm across the drive.

I waved and closed my visor, proceeding more slowly onto the grounds. The tighter turns would slow a larger vehicle, but despite my previous entertainment, I did not feel like pushing it. The adrenaline rush of speeding down the road had worn off.

Finding the parking area set aside for motorcycles, I walked it back into a space at the end. Once I had set the kickstand down, I rested on the bike, drained from the ride. I needed to do that again some time. Maybe tomorrow if the weather was nice.

I had been numb to most things for the past month or so. My initial frustration at being stuck on desk work only for months on end had given way to hopelessness. Eventually that turning into simply going through the motions of my day-to-day life. It had not helped that both friends and family had become too busy to have much time to talk.

After taking a couple of minutes to calm down I got off and gathered my bag off the back.

Silver walked up through the garage toward me as I got the chin strap on my helmet undone. Damn, I had wasted too much time. I still had the visor down so with any luck he had not and would not recognize me still and just keep walking. All the time I spent trying to communicate with him and now I was hoping he would leave me be.

He glared at me as he passed. "You know, you remind me of my partner. Damn reckless and constantly risking her life," he spat. He had not even slowed.

I frowned as he continued walking toward the elevator. I tore my helmet off and shot back at him, "It's nice to know how you feel."

Silver stopped and turned, looking at me with wide eyes. His mouth worked, but no words came out. "Ketayl?" he finally managed to say softly.

I narrowed my eyes at him. This conversation was over. I hiked my bag further up my shoulder and raised my hand. Then I teleported myself to my quarters.

NOTHING FOR MONTHS. Absolutely nothing that even resembled the presence of a necromancer. Added to that was I had been chained to a desk. I had not even been sent out for any training.

The excitement of my ride earlier gave way again to the numbness.

The halls were always quiet at this time of night. I had taken to training during off-hours. It mattered little when I did things. Being stuck on limited duty only gave me a lot of pent up energy. I could see no reason that I had not cleared the psychological evaluation to be able to return to the field.

I tossed my sweatshirt to the side of the room, not caring where it landed, and hit the switches. The lights came on in quick succession, illuminating the large testing bay. Targets hung at the back, but I was not frustrated to the point of wanting to be destructive with magic. Not yet anyway.

As I strode across the hard floor to the center, I yanked the shrunken staff out of the holster on my thigh. I needed to feel something again. Something more than frustration.

It would have been better if I had not known Silver was back. There was nothing I could do about it now other than avoid him.

He had been traveling for the past few months. I saw him less and less as they sent him out more frequently for reasons that he refused to talk about. Then he stopped talking to me at all unless I caught him in passing and those were brief. He certainly never came into the office anymore. Why bother trying to have a conversation with him?

I hesitated, blowing dark auburn strands out of my face. I tucked them behind my ear as much as I could.

Even Kitteren was too busy with her new dog to talk much. Everyone else was rarely available. It would take days to get replies to my messages if I heard anything back at all.

My shoulders slumped. I was alone. Hopefully the weather would hold so I could go out on more rides. I might have brought it up too late in the season, but it had remained warm so far.

Pressing the button to release the staff, it made a satisfying soft metallic sound. I moved hard and fast through a sequence of swings and thrusts, going from one set of movements to the next without pause. I had done this so many times I did not have to think about it.

Unfortunately, it left me alone with my thoughts. What was I doing wrong? What had I done to drive everyone away? I could not even figure out why the doctors held me back from being able to go out into the field. I had run the tests, taken the classes, sat through more appointments than I cared to count... and still nothing.

I swung my staff for an overhead strike, reversed it, striking the same imaginary target from below. Switching direction, I attacked another point behind me.

What did I need to do to fix this? I kept myself composed. I put more effort than before into all my work and training. I followed all of the rules. What more did I need?

The physical exertion helped me keep the facade I showed everyone. I hated being this helpless to fix my situation.

I heard the door open and turned enough to see who it was out of the corner of my eye. My curious glance turned to a glare. "If you're here to patronize or insult me, you can leave. I certainly don't need a lecture on my recklessness," I shot at him, still aggravated about earlier.

Silver crossed his arms. He wore his armored jacket. Seeing what could be considered his uniform jacket only annoyed me further with the reminder. He was still a useful part of the TIO.

I turned away from the person I still considered my friend despite the strain on our relationship. I had no patience to deal with his coddling or his lectures. I needed action, not empty promises of ending this current torment.

Silver came over and stared at me, his face unreadable.

I sighed. Unused to his silence I asked, "How was your trip?" If he sought me out, I could only hope that maybe he was willing to talk. Maybe I would not feel so isolated for at least a little while.

"Taxing my patience as usual. Had a debriefing and an important meeting back-to-back," he said matter-of-factly.

I clenched my jaw at the mention of work. At least I had the satisfaction of knowing his dislike of meetings were second only to how much he hated desk work. I walked away from him. Something stirred in me at him being here. Annoyance, frustration... I remained unsure. It all ran together after a while.

"Prove to me that you're ready to return to the field," Silver said, his tone even.

I stopped and turned sharply. "What?" Then I noticed he wore all of his armor. How had I missed the heavily textured, plated material on his legs and the metal coverings over his boots?

"You heard me," he taunted with a smirk on his face.

I scrunched up my nose at him before sighing and shrinking my staff. "What's the point? You're not the one who can make that determination." He could not clear me for the field.

"No, but you can, so fight me," Silver demanded. His shield appeared on his arm.

I shook my head and continued to go get my sweatshirt. He obviously did not understand the situation. What would he know? He had not been available to even reply to my messages.

"If you leave, I'm going to assume you quit."

I spun on my heel and growled at him. "I'm not quitting! I wouldn't still be here if I was."

"That's a lie. You'll put yourself through Hells and not complain."

"What do you want from me?!" I yelled at him. Immediately I bit my lower lip and looked toward the floor. Damn him for making me emotional. I wanted to at least be content to feel something else, but him pushing me was not what I had in mind. "You won't even respond to my messages and now you want to spar?" I shook my head.

"I want you to fight me," Silver said evenly. "Or should I start looking for a new partner?"

I clenched my teeth. "If that's how you feel then maybe you should." I shoved the shrunken staff back into the holster on my thigh.

Even Silver had given up on me. I clenched my fists to keep from shaking. I needed to get out of here.

I caught movement out of the corner of my eye and reacted instinctively, putting my hands up, casting my shield spell. I grunted at the impact of Silver's thrown shield against mine. "What in the Hells are you doing?!"

He caught his shield easily as it came back to him. "Not letting you leave until you fight me."

I growled at him. He drew his sword.

"Don't you have more important things to do?" It was my last-ditch effort to get out of this. As much as what he said hurt, I refused to fight him. Solo practice was one thing, but I did not trust myself to maintain my composure against an opponent. Not like this. Not while I remembered the thrill of the ride earlier.

"No."

"Well, go find something. I'm sure you have a long list of duties to take care of. You're probably about to head back out on assignment," I spat. I turned away from Silver and took a deep breath. I needed to calm down. Letting him rile me up would not help my situation. If he thought of me like this now, how much further would our relationship change when I finally managed to get off limited duty and returned to the field? Having been held captive for weeks earlier in the year had already done enough damage.

Before I could take another step, a transparent golden wall formed up in front of me. I turned. Silver held his sword up behind his shield.

He narrowed his eyes at me. "I already told you: I'm not letting you leave until you fight me."

I let out an exasperated breath. "No. Can't you see that's only going to make things worse?"

"Maybe I want to see if you've still got that fire in you. Your reckless driving doesn't count. Fight me."

"Stop. This is ridiculous." I put my hand against the wall and pushed. Maybe it would drain him the same way it did mine.

"Fight me and you can leave. It's a straightforward solution."

I yanked the shrunken staff out from the holster before teleporting behind Silver and extending it to hit him in the back. He turned in time to take the strike on his shield. My distraction failed.

Silver swung his sword and I rolled backward out of the way, coming to my feet, my staff in both hands, aiming to connect across his stomach. He blocked my attempt with his sword, all the while grinning as if he knew something.

Baring my teeth at that cocky grin of his, I pushed at the block. There was no chance of me physically overpowering him, but I had let my frustration take over. I cast a spell to give me a boost, jumping back several yards. I needed to rethink my strategy.

Silver threw his shield again and I dropped to the floor to avoid it. This was it, he was too determined to have this fight for me to back down or escape. He often found our sparring fun, but something was off about this.

I used a flight spell to propel myself forward, bringing my staff down in an overhead swing before his shield could return to him.

"Are you angry?" Silver asked calmly, blocking my strike with his sword, catching his shield with his other arm. He backhanded me to the ribs with his shield and I flew a few yards, hitting the hard floor and rolling.

I rolled to my feet, growling at him. I held my ribs. He hit harder than he usually did when we trained, though we had not trained together in months. "I've played by the rules and I'm still stuck on limited duty. I'm frustrated." *Stay calm. You won't get back into the field if you lose your composure now.*

"Angry. You passed frustrated a long time ago. Are you upset that I can see past the mask you put up?" Silver walked slowly, keeping his distance. His grin never left his face as he spoke.

"What do you know?! You haven't been here!" I threw a strong wind spell at Silver, knocking him back several feet, which caused him to drop his sword in the process. I sprinted across the distance, again bringing my staff down in an overhead swing.

He rolled out of the way, swinging his long legs, kicking mine out from under me. I hit the floor hard, my staff falling from my hand.

I rolled to pick up my weapon. Silver grabbed me from behind as I stood up. I managed to shift my stance and used all the strength I had, kicking a foot out from underneath him before I flipped him over me. I threw him down as hard as I could on the floor. I shuffled a few feet away, falling into a ready stance. *Silver is provoking you on purpose. Don't go too far.*

Silver grinned broadly as he scrambled back to his feet. "That's new. You've gotten better." He flexed his left arm, his shield reappearing.

Now he mocked me. I bared my teeth at him. I was done playing nice. I slid into a wider stance, knees bent, staff at the ready. "You still drive slow," I shot. If he wanted to trade insults, I was ready.

He shrugged. "At least I'm not likely to smear myself on the roadway. Now to answer your question about what I know: I know a lot. Care to narrow down your request?"

I growled at his cocky attitude and launched a series of attacks. Silver countered most and only took glancing blows on the rest. He ignored his sword on the floor. Occasionally he would taunt me, asking if that was all I had or if I was still angry.

He continued to defend, never seeming to tire, never giving me an opening. Occasionally, he hesitated. Whether he was uncertain or luring me into an opening, I could not tell. I used it to catch my breath instead of taking the potential bait.

After several minutes a large space formed between us. I tired of this mockery. "Enough!" I conjured a fireball in my hand within a split second and threw it at him. Flames engulfed my opponent, blocking him from view. My eyes widened as the satisfaction of putting an end to our fight changed to fear in an instant. I had gone too far.

The spell dissipated before I could react, showing that Silver had brought his shield up in time to block it. The force of the blast had pushed him back several yards. He looked at me with wide eyes from over his shield, scorch marks marred the floor leading up to and around him.

I stared at him, covering my mouth with my hands. The sound of my staff hitting the floor echoed loudly. What had I done? I could have seriously hurt or killed him with that fireball. I stood frozen.

Silver quickly closed the distance, grabbing me and pulling me against him.

That broke me out of my shock. I brought both fists up and hit him in the chest. "Let me go!" I yelled, my voice high-pitched and I pushed at him as hard as I could. I had to get away. I was dangerous.

I could not concentrate enough to teleport and he held onto me so becoming invisible was pointless. Where would I go? He had an uncanny knack of being able to find me no matter what I did.

Silver brought his shield up behind me and held me tighter. I was trapped. I hit him again, doubting he felt it through his armor since he had not even flinched with my previous strikes. Damn him. I knew he was far better in combat and I let him provoke me.

"It's not fair!" I pounded his chest again, but I could not hit as hard. "I've done everything everyone asked of me and more." I rested my forehead against his chest to hide the tears I could no longer hold back. My legs gave out, too tired to continue the fight.

Silver sat down on the floor with me. His large rough hand stroked my hair; his pin eventually turned into a hug. His shield hid me from the world.

I hit his chest again, barely moving my hands. He simply held me through the torrent of tears, continuing to stroke my hair. I stayed where I was. It was warm being held by Silver.

Eventually I calmed down, exhausted. "Not fair," I muttered. The events earlier in the year had come to the forefront of my mind.

"What's not fair?" Silver asked softly.

"Arcanist."

"You can't blame what you are."

"Would never have gotten the system working. Never been used as bait to get the orb back. Never would have gotten you dragged into it. *You should have let me die.*" I whispered the end in my dialect of common. I would have taken our captors and the ship down with me if he had not stopped me.

My friend made gentle shushing sounds, stroking my hair.

Eventually I moved away, wiping my face with my hands. "Sorry."

Silver gave me a soft smile. "Don't be. It's good to have you back."

2

I RAN a hand over my hair as I sat on the edge of my bed, still worn out from the confrontation with Silver last night. That was not even counting his words to me earlier about my driving. Though he only proved himself right about my recklessness. I could have killed him with that fireball.

Never before had he frustrated me to the point where I stopped thinking about my actions. I rubbed my face - this train of thought was getting me nowhere. At least he should be busy for most of the day so I could avoid him. Even so, I would take extra precaution to stay away from where he would likely be.

I batted the mouse lightly on the computer to wake it up. My schedule was open last I checked, but something could have been snuck in. The doctors had been notorious for it over the last few months.

I raised an eyebrow at a meeting scheduled this morning. I needed to report to my office and Silver was also listed to attend. Was this about last night? Had someone seen what happened between us? I should have been more careful.

My heart sped up. Was I being replaced? The fireball alone would have gotten me into a lot of trouble. I had never thrown one at someone in a training session before. It was simply too dangerous.

Silver would not explain his words about having me back. He also spoke about finding a different partner. I had no idea which way to think.

I hurried to get ready for the day, my mind attempting to make sense of what was going on.

It had to have been because of last night. Why else would I get scheduled for a meeting like this?

Would I have to train my replacement? I never got training for it. How would I even explain what I did? Not that I had accomplished anything in the last several months.

I had a few personal items at my desk in the office. Perhaps this was simply to collect my things.

I paced around my quarters and stopped. How much time would I have to pack up here? Not that I had much. Would my adopted parents let me live with them until I could find something else? Why should they? It was plain to see how dangerous I was.

Should I beg for another position here so I could stay? Would there be anything I could do? Was there anything I would want to do? I cringed at the thought of forever being tied to a desk. When had my preference changed? I used to need to be pried away from desk work and would balk at the idea of going into the field.

I shook my head and grabbed the bag I carried daily. I paused to look at it for a moment. Did it even matter if I had it? There were only a few items in it and none of it essential.

It does. Even if it's the last time.

WALKING down the halls like this created a strange sensation: it was both comforting and frightening at the same time. Normally I would not think anything of it, but I had no idea if it would be the last time. It was probably the last.

I stopped outside the door and looked around. No one else was here and no one was coming down the hall. I glanced at my watch and found I was almost a half hour early. I rolled my eyes - I should have paid more attention to the time.

I reached for the hand scanner and stopped. Then I sighed and leaned back against the wall to wait. My habit of getting to meetings early failed me this time and I was not ready to go in. I had nothing I needed to go over or prepare. Nothing to keep me busy once I entered.

It was irrational to think that if I put this off it would never happen, but for the moment it helped.

Time ticked by slowly. I went from leaning against the wall to shifting back and forth from foot to foot and now I paced. My thoughts spiraled farther downward with each turn.

This was my fault. I lost composure last night. I should blame Silver for provoking me, but the fact he could do it so easily only showed I was incapable of staying in control anymore. That I was reckless.

I stopped and looked at my watch again. It was almost time and no one was here. Should I go in? I bit my lower lip and stared at the hand scanner.

"What are you doing out here?"

I jumped at the sound of Silver's voice. "Um, I..." I trailed off. I bit my lower lip, not wanting to explain my reasoning. Even I found it ridiculous.

"Let's go." Silver stood over me.

Rolling my eyes, I put my hand on the scanner. I took a deep breath to prepare for the final time I would enter my office.

I hesitated with my hand on the door. Silver shoved it open and prodded me into the office.

Lockonis leaned against the center table watching us. I cringed. This could not be good if she was here waiting. Especially with how early she had to have gotten here for me not to have seen her.

The fiery red headed Elven woman looked from me to Silver and back. "Ready for some action, kid?"

Action? I blinked and tilted my head. The words were not adding up in my head. "I'm not being replaced?"

My boss raised an eyebrow at me. "Replaced? Where did you get that idea? Oh, yeah, last night." She laughed lightly. "Nope, had your partner push you to get you cleared. You're stubborn."

"I'm what?" I looked up at Silver who turned his head away. He had called me reckless and now I was being called stubborn. I folded my arms and glared at him.

"The doctors wanted to see some sort of emotional reaction from you about what happened with the pirates," Silver said quietly, "They weren't too happy about what I did."

I frowned. He never said that when he was picking the fight, but technically he never lied - he just had a horrible habit of giving only the information he wanted to.

"Okay, enough of that. Let's get you caught up." Lockonis walked over to the wall screen, waving at it to wake it up. Files were already spread out. "A couple months ago we were drawn into a meeting with First Union, a large bank in Human Territory in this region." She pointed at the south east region of the map. It was dotted with peninsulas and islands. "It was being handled by the Sola branch, but it escalated to here."

I strode closer to the screen and tilted my head. "A bank?" Why would a bank come to the TIO for something? "Why us?"

"They're claiming there's a necromancer involved getting people out of debt. What was it, killing people and bringing them back once the account had been written off? Is that the rumor?" Lockonis looked to Silver.

Why had I been left out of this one so far? I had been running in virtual circles for months with nothing to show. I clenched my hands into fists at my sides.

"Pretty much. I've been collecting information from the the bank, but there's no pattern we can discern. It's a mix of people who are doing well and paying on time and people who are struggling," my partner added.

I paused at the thought. I had stopped calling him my partner months ago. Frowning at the distraction, I went back to chewing on the information. There must be some common thread.

"It's good to see her going again," Lockonis said, sounding amused. "The short version is, you're both going to need to go out there. Piecing it together from here hasn't worked and the bank has been more or less unhelpful. The most the cyber team has managed is to hear whispers of someone called 'the necromancer.' He or she never appears calling themselves that so there's nothing there at the moment."

Silver folded his arms. "It's difficult to say if this person even exists other than there have been quite a few unexplained deaths with no bodies..."

"A necromancer would be a possible reason for it," I finished. "But not the only one."

"Exactly," Lockonis said. "Take your time and familiarize yourself with the case file. I'm in no rush to get into a fight with the bank again. Also, Ket," she paused until I looked at her, "you'll be reporting in regularly."

I rolled my eyes and groaned. There had to be a catch to getting me back out in the field.

"I know. I know," Lockonis said. "Silver, you also need to keep an eye on her."

My partner nodded and I frowned. I just knew he was going to be a pain about it.

"Once you're ready to go, I'll assign someone from the cyber team to you. Okay, I'm done. Later!" My boss left. Typical Lockonis.

I glanced up at Silver before heading to my desk. "Guess I've got some reading to do."

I SAT BACK at my desk, rubbing my eyes. I had been going over the basic information in the main case folder for hours. I glanced at the wall screen and the files still sitting up there. Maybe a change of view would help.

"Let's take a break," Silver said.

I shook my head. "I'm good."

My partner got up from his desk. "Come on. You don't need to jump on this full force. Besides, I'm bored."

I sighed. His words meant he was going to annoy me until I caved. "Fine." I also understood my status: I was on probation.

As he held the door open for me, he asked, "What's your take so far?"

"Mostly that I have no real understanding of how banks and financial institutions actually work." I sighed. "I want to come back and use the wall screen to see if I can find a pattern. I thought I saw a couple, but I'm not sure."

Silver stroked the small patch of hair on his chin. "How you do something in a few hours that others haven't managed in months always amazes me."

"I don't actually have anything," I said. "I thought I saw a couple of patterns. Not that I have."

"We'll see." He sounded rather confident about it. "I arranged travel to the headquarters for First Union."

I stopped. "Isn't that a little fast? We don't have anything. We should have a direction first." The TIO never gave us a hard time about extended stays somewhere, but I wanted to exhaust my offsite options first and form a plan.

Silver turned to look at me. "We should go talk to them. We won't leave until late tomorrow evening. Plenty of time."

I sighed and shook my head, catching back up to him. My partner expected the impossible.

"What about searching for the necromancer the same way you did when you found the one using the werewolves?"

"Hm?" I glanced up at Silver. "Maybe, but I doubt there will be any news articles in relation - it doesn't sound like it has made it to the media. Might be able to cross-reference documents from the bank though." I chewed on the idea.

Silver put his hand on my head. I batted it away. He laughed. "It's good to have you back. Been lost without you."

"I'm sure you've been doing fine without me," I grumbled.

"You know I hate desk work. They were hoping maybe you'd open up if I wasn't around as much, which is why I've been traveling so frequently."

I shook my head. The whole situation was more complex than I previously figured. Too complex.

"Ketayl," Silver said softly, pulling me aside. "I'm still worried. You won't talk about what you went through. You've given facts, but not how it affected you. And what you said last night..."

I closed my eyes for a moment before turning away from him. "I shouldn't have reacted like that."

He grabbed my arm before I could take a step. "I'm quite good at pissing people off. I picked the fight with you to get you to react because we both know I can get a rise out of you. If you hadn't, we wouldn't be having this conversation."

I clamped my mouth shut. I wanted this conversation to end.

Finally, he released my arm. "You've gotten really good with your staff."

"I've had a lot of time to practice," I muttered and moved away from him.

Silver stepped in front of me. "Ketayl, wait."

I sighed, folding my arms, refusing to look up at him.

He leaned down so he could whisper, "Kela, I won't let you die."

I clenched my teeth. He used that name with me rarely. I noticed mainly when he wanted to get my attention. "You should have. You would have been doing everyone a favor," I snapped, keeping my voice down.

Silver grabbed my chin and forced me to look at him. "No. Knock it off or I'll pull you off of this assignment."

I pulled away from him roughly. "You'll what?"

"You heard me."

I growled at him. "Can you make up your mind if you need me or not?"

"I do, but you need to take care of yourself more. I need you."

The last few months certainly seemed like he did not need me. I stepped back away from Silver. "We should finish our break so we can get back to work. This is cutting into the remaining time we have here."

Silver sighed and led the way to the dining hall. Of course he was hungry and he likely wanted to make sure I ate also.

I FOLDED my arms and stared at the wall screen. Tilting my head did not help make what I thought I saw any clearer. It did not match up with what the people before me had been working on.

"You've got something?" Silver asked.

I bit my lower lip. "I don't know. It's like there's two different people."

"We haven't heard anything beyond the one."

I turned to look at Silver who flung a pen at the ceiling. "I didn't say I was right. It just looks like two. Could be the same person who happens to be targeting both ends of the spectrum and leaving the people in between alone. What I don't understand is why would someone who is doing well paying off their debt want to go to a necromancer? Were they in any danger of falling behind?"

My partner got up to collect the pens on the floor. A couple stuck in the ceiling tile. I frowned at his childish habit.

"Not that I could tell. I've got a fairly decent handle on how the system works, but I'm no expert and no one has seen an obvious reason they would seek out the services of a necromancer. Could be personal I guess."

"Run any backgrounds?"

"The cyber team has, but I haven't heard anything."

I scrunched up my face. No wonder no one put anything together yet. The information was all separated. I had more work ahead of me than I expected. I rubbed my temples with my fingers - my first day on this case was quickly turning into an all-nighter.

Turning back to the wall screen, I stared at the information before me. I needed to go deeper. Link all of this together. I took a moment to breathe before returning to my desk. The only way it would get done was to do it.

"What do you need?" Silver asked.

"To gather all the information together. There's got to be something deeper linking all of this."

"It should all be in the case file. I thought it was organized."

I formed my mouth into a thin line. "It's fine. I've got it."

Silver opened his mouth to say something when his phone rang. He frowned at me before answering it and walking back to his side of the office.

I ignored him and delved into the file. No wonder no one got anywhere. It was a mess. Files were dumped in with little attempt at organization.

This had definitely become an all-nighter.

I force-cleared the wall screen from my computer so I could get started. Time was lost to me as I tagged files and rearranged them into folders. All the while getting a better picture of what was going on. How had I not noticed this mess sooner?

Pursing my lips, I wondered if I could find out if other banks in the area had seen a similar pattern, but on a smaller scale, and had not reported it. Or at least not made the connection a necromancer was involved. How had First Union decided a necromancer was involved? And if they had not, then who had?

I searched through the files, looking for the initial report. First Union contacted the local law enforcement office who conducted a preliminary investigation into the claim. The term necromancer was used as far back as the first report.

Then it passed onto the Human Territorial Investigative Agency. Little information came from them as well. Both seemed to have let the case sit.

Finally, First Union took their petition to the Terran Intelligence

Organization who then took over the case. It had been with the Sola branch not even a week before it was pushed up to us. Part of me wondered if it was simply no one wanted to deal with the crazy idea that a necromancer was involved and passed it off to someone else. I had no idea why a necromancer would want to get involved with banking. Most of the ones I had dealt with were separated from the majority of society.

This was getting me nowhere again. The first question was who made the connection and was it accurate? No bodies did not necessarily equal a necromancer.

I rubbed the bridge of my nose. It would not have landed with my team unless they thought it a serious threat.

Or they wanted to keep Silver busy.

Now I had no idea.

"Ketayl, it's time to call it a day. You've been at this for hours," Silver said.

I glanced up and more pens were in the ceiling. How long had I been at this? "Have you done anything?"

He pointed up at the ceiling. "Pretty much just that."

I rolled my eyes and returned to what I was working on. Granted he needed to wait for me to catch up on months of work. I wished he had given me more than two days though.

A pen landed on my desk. "Hey!"

Silver smirked. "Shut it down - it's time to go."

I threw the pen back at him before returning to what I was reading. *Child.*

Out of the corner of my eye, I caught Silver preparing to throw another pen. Once it was airborne, I sent it back at him with a weak flight spell, my eyes never leaving the screens in front of me. I heard it ping off of one of his metal bracers.

"I'm not sure if that's fair or not," Silver said.

"When you keep interrupting me, it is."

My partner laughed. "Okay. Okay. You win, but it's time to go. You can come back to this tomorrow. I didn't expect you to do as much as you have."

I sighed, rubbing the bridge of my nose. "I haven't done anything."

"Sure you have. Been watching you organize the case file and you've been searching for patterns all day."

I shook my head. "I'm going to be here all night. You don't have to stay."

"Ketayl..." Silver got up to stand over me. "You're done for now. If you keep this up, you'll get too buried in the details and not see the bigger picture."

I glared up at my partner.

"I'm also not letting you overwork yourself on your first day on this. Come on. We can talk about what you're seeing so far over dinner. Is that acceptable?"

My hands hovered over the keyboard, conflicted between ignoring him and following his suggestion. "Fine." I locked my computer and got up. His earlier threat of removing me was still fresh in my mind.

3

————

EVEN THOUGH IT WAS AUTUMN, it was warm when I got off the plane in Sola. I breathed in the ocean air for a moment to calm my nerves. Close to a full day with an overprotective Silver in a small jet was not my idea of relaxing. Even Lexi, who had been assigned to us from the cyber team, seemed to have noticed the tension. Either that or werewolves did not do well being confined in a plane for an extended period of time. I had caught her pacing often while I read.

I followed the two through the airport, feeling wholly out of place not being the one with the information for transportation and lodging. Not the one taking lead. Had I really gotten so used to the position? It had been the better part of a year since the last time I had even been out on an assignment and then it was just me and Silver.

Once we loaded into the loaner vehicle, Lexi leaned forward, appearing between us in the front seat. "Just drop me off at the hotel. I want to get set up."

I nodded. Lexi had a fair amount of equipment with her and she had been unable to get started on the flight here.

Silver looked up into the review mirror. "You're coming with us to the meeting at First Union."

"I need to start my virtual hunt as soon as I can," she argued.

"It's a good idea," I said, hoping to end the conversation. If Lexi did not want to go, I was not about to make her. I would rather not be a part of these meetings either.

"We'll be visiting the Sola office after," Silver said, "The whole team needs to be there."

I sighed. There went my hope of ending the rising conflict. I wished I knew why he thought we all needed to be there.

"I need to do something after that flight." Lexi's voice sounded tight. "Dragging me to meetings I don't need to be at will only make it worse."

The creak of Silver's fingerless gloves sounded through the cab. "You're going." His voice was firm.

Lexi let out a low growl. She shifted forward more, her shoulders were in line with the backs of our seats. I had known Lexi from a case a year ago, but I had never seen her act like this. She was usually even-tempered if not timid.

"Silver, we have plenty of time. Head for the hotel and let her get started. Those meetings don't need all of us," I reasoned.

My partner shot me a look out of the corner of his eye. "You're not driving. We need to make a showing."

I sat up straighter, staring at my partner. *What about my driving?*

"A showing of what?" Lexi's volume had begun to rise. "We need to show progress and you'll be holding me back if you don't let me get started. And don't you dare disrespect Ketayl like that again."

I pinched the bridge of my nose. The argument was only getting more heated. Lexi was right though that Silver's plan made no sense. What had happened here in Sola previously that he felt the need to push this issue?

"I'm not disrespecting her. We're all going," Silver said, matching Lexi's volume.

I could sense an energy build up from the back seat. Was Lexi pushing for dominance? What was happening here? Why were they fighting over something so minor? And worse, why I had gotten dragged in as a topic of contention?

Silver pulled off into the nearest parking lot so he could turn and face her. "You don't have seniority."

"And you don't either. Ketayl does."

"Enough!" My voice echoed with a tiny bit of my power.

Both of them stilled and stared at me with wide eyes.

"This isn't how a team functions." I turned to stare at my partner.

"We need to go check into the hotel anyway and the better showing will be to have answers sooner rather than later. I'd rather not see the list of dead get any longer."

Silver tried to stare me down. He turned away first. "Alright. Maybe we'll get lucky and Lexi will find something while we're out," he said before resuming driving. His body was stiff, but at least he was seeing reason.

Lexi shifted so that she could whisper in my ear away from Silver, "Thanks."

I let out a breath I had not realized I had been holding. If this was happening before we even got started, I worried about how the investigation itself would go.

WE GOT Lexi settled at the hotel with her equipment and headed back out.

"You're awfully quiet. Even for you," Silver commented as he drove us to First Union.

"Just thinking." *What am I doing here? I'm barely familiar with this case. Not to mention what already happened between Silver and Lexi. Was it right of me to have stepped in? If I hadn't, the fight would've gotten worse. I don't think either of them would've backed down.* I bit my lower lip, staring at the tablet in my lap.

"About?"

I shook my head. "Doesn't matter."

Silver sighed. "It does matter. You've been edgy since we left. Everything will be fine. Just let me do the talking since I've been working with them."

"Yeah, sure." I preferred it when Silver did the talking, but this still sat wrong with me.

Silence fell between us for a few minutes. I read through the case file while he drove.

"Can I ask you something?" Silver asked quietly.

I raised an eyebrow at him. His tone concerned me more than his words. "What?"

He tugged on his braid with one hand. "Well, um, I know it's a bit late to be asking, but when did you get a motorcycle? I didn't even know you could ride."

I let out a light huff. It never occurred to me he was unaware of that. "A few years ago. It's how I get around Great Tree when it's just me. I just hadn't gotten my tag to have it at the main office until now. Spent weekends over the spring and summer doing skill work. Haven't had much else to do."

"I wish I could take back my words. I'm sure it's different from your perspective," he mumbled.

I shook my head. "You were being honest."

"Doesn't make it right."

I shrugged, dropping the conversation and hoped it stayed there. Silence followed for a couple of minutes.

"Do you think it'll be better to track down the ones with debt problems first?" Silver asked.

I nodded. "There's no discernible pattern to the ones who don't have problems that I can see right now. It'll be easier to find someone who may be desperate enough to seek out the necromancer if there even is one. Let me keep reading and see if something pops out otherwise."

Silver thankfully left me alone the remainder of the ride. My nose stayed in my tablet most of the time.

I started to think I needed more knowledge of how all of this financial stuff worked. It made no sense to me. *How did anyone come up with such a convoluted system?* Worse yet was how did anyone else make sense of it all? I was definitely out of my element here. Science or the arcane, I could do, but not all of this strange movement of money. I doubted my involvement in this case as the main headquarters of First Union towered over us. *Why am I here?*

"Ketayl?" Silver asked quietly as we walked through the grand doors of First Union.

I took in the intricate stone and metalwork. The ornate wooden desks. The leather seating. I clutched the strap of my bag tightly with both hands. I belonged here even less.

"Hey." Silver pulled me aside gently. "What's going on?"

"Why am I here?" I asked, keeping my voice as hushed as possible. My words were out before I could stop them. "I could've analyzed the data from the office. That's all you really need me for, right?"

"No, I need you here. I can't do this alone. Especially not if we're potentially facing an actual necromancer."

What was he seeing in the information that I had not? I could not confirm or deny a necromancer's involvement.

I shook my head and signaled for him to continue. All I had to do was stay quiet and gather information. I only needed to look for a pattern, right? Find the person involved. While I was still technically on desk work, at least I would have a different view and people to work with.

We were escorted to the top floor of the tower and into a large conference room overlooking the city below. How much more did I have to take of this flaunt of wealth? I knew this was the headquarters of a large banking institution, but it only reminded me of how out of place I was.

The view of the city was impressive from here. Cars and people crowded the streets below. Sola was such a busy place. This was not somewhere I would want to live. I had never been fond of crowds and had become less and less so over the past couple of years.

I glanced at Silver. He stood next to me along the windows while we waited for the people meeting us. My partner wore his armored jacket over his business attire, but oddly enough it did not seem out of place. Perhaps his confidence overrode the strangeness. Most people would not know his jacket was armor anyway.

I shifted uncomfortably in my business outfit. Looking the part did not mean I belonged here. At least Silver left me alone for the moment.

"Ah, wonderful of you to come, Agent Blaise, though we hadn't expected you back so soon. I see you brought someone with you," a Human man about my height said as he entered the room. He was followed by two other Humans - a man and a woman.

"This is my partner, Ketayl," Silver said as he took a seat at the table.

I bowed quickly and followed his lead, knowing I could not duplicate the ease in which he greeted these people. Not with as nervous as I was. It took everything I had to keep from fidgeting.

The Human man who spoke bowed in response. "It is a pleasure, Agent Ketayl. I'm William Marks, the CEO of First Union. Allow me to introduce my colleagues Karen Lockheed, our COO, and Joran Sol, our CFO."

I nodded to them and sat gripping my tablet tightly in my lap. I should not be here. Not in a room with these important people. I tried to figure out if they were more intimidating than the Alpha

Prime of the werewolves. I mentally kicked myself for getting distracted.

Once everyone was seated, William said, "It's been quiet since we last spoke."

Silver toyed with the end of his braid. "Well, I was here only a few days ago. I'd be concerned if something had happened."

I opened up the notepad function on my tablet and dug out the pen for it. I needed to keep from doodling. I had gotten into the habit over the last several months.

"You okay, Agent Ketayl?" Karen asked softly. She sat across from me.

I forced a smile as everyone's attention turned to me. "Long flight. I'll be fine, thank you."

"She spent most of it going over the case file looking for a pattern we could use to track this person," Silver said.

"Good to know everyone is on-board," William said. "Let's get back to the matter at hand. The necromancer is costing us a lot with our CDOs and CMOs."

What are CDOs and CMOs? The acronyms were foreign to me and likely the full names would make about as much sense. The terms being thrown about only made it much more pronounced how much I was out of my element. If only the conversation would come back to something I understood.

"Who determined it was a necromancer?" I asked before I could catch myself. I bit my lower lip, hoping there would be little conse-quence for speaking out.

William sat up straight looking at me. Then he turned to Joran.

Joran sat with his hands folded in his lap. "We did. Uncommon, yes, but one of our financial advisors, Tae Kim, has a family history with them and he was the one who first saw the pattern of behavior. At least that's how he explained it to me."

It rationalized the use of the term at least. Whether it was true or not still needed to be determined.

"We," Joran said, signaling at the three of them on that side of the table, "remain speculative, but we have nothing else to go on and he made a convincing case for it. He's one of our best financial advisors and not a man known to flights of fancy."

I tossed a sidelong glance at Silver, raising an eyebrow at him.

"We can talk with Tae," my partner said.

I nodded, jotting the name down. Information this financial advisor had could also prove useful in searching for other necromancers.

"Unfortunately, we sent him to a conference in Haven over the weekend. He'll be back tomorrow. I'll have him come directly to the office. Let me pull up his itinerary," Karen said. She had her tablet out. "I apologize for the inconvenience."

I forced a smile and shook my head. "It's okay. It'll give us some time to gather together questions."

"The best route we're figuring to be able to track down this individual is to find someone who may be desperate enough to seek out a necromancer's services," Silver said. "Can we get a list of people who are having issues paying off their debts?"

"That's confidential information," Joran said sharply. He sat up straighter and stared at Silver. "The privacy of our customers takes precedence. You'll need the proper paperwork to obtain that information."

"Confidential information going to an organization who deals in confidential information," William countered. "I think we can make an exception here. Unless you want us to lose even more money. Our customers will end up somewhere else if this gets out."

Joran stared at William for a moment and then held up his hands defensively. "I'll have my team arrange something. Don't expect details"

"We don't need much information or any details regarding the debt," Silver clarified. "I think a dozen or so of your worst cases should be sufficient."

Joran nodded, writing on the notepad in front of him. "That's acceptable."

I tapped the side of my tablet with my nail. A dozen was a small window to take a chance on. I would have wanted to throw a wider net, but in all reality, would it be any better? There were too many variables and we would be drowning in information.

Facial recognition software could help on the deceased though. A person may be "dead", but if they "came back" after the debt was written off as claimed, it would still be the same body. I jotted the idea down on my tablet. We might be better off chasing the dead.

"Tae Kim can be back in the office tomorrow morning about 0930. I'm afraid I can't get him in any sooner," Karen said.

Silver nodded. "That'll be fine. Thank you."

"I'm curious, Ketayl, what brought you on-board for this case?" William asked. "Do you have a financial background?"

I sat up straight and looked at him with wide eyes. How was I supposed to answer this? "I... uh..." I bit my lower lip and stared at the tablet in my lap.

"She's an arcane investigator," Silver answered. "The reason she hasn't been here until now is because she was injured on a previous assignment and was on limited duty."

My partner really walked the line with his statement. He technically told the truth, but my physical injuries had healed months ago. I should have been released back to full duty then.

"Ah, I'm glad to see you recovered. Though I am curious - an arcane investigator?" William said. "I would have expected someone with a financial background."

I sat completely still; my hands clamped around the edges of my tablet.

"Our team was built to deal with necromancers. You couldn't ask for someone better to find one than her," Silver said with a smile.

I bit my lower lip. My partner gave me far too much credit.

Karen watched me carefully while the men continued to talk. I shifted uncomfortably, focusing on the device in my lap instead.

The meeting did not last much longer. Silver spoke with the men as they walked out the door. He had such an easygoing attitude in dealing with these powerful people. They were laughing at something - I had blanked out on the conversation since it was unimportant.

"Agent Ketayl, can I have a moment?" Karen said.

I nodded stiffly. "Just Ketayl is fine."

She lowered her voice. "I apologize if I'm overstepping my bounds, but you seemed... tense during the meeting. Was there something else?"

I shook my head. "I apologize. It's a personal matter."

"I understand." She held out a business card to me. "Give me a call if you need anything. Since this potentially deals with personnel, it falls under me."

I accepted the card and bowed stiffly, catching up to Silver. I tucked the small piece of paper into my pocket as I got on the elevator. I needed to focus and get to work.

4

Silver drove us to the Sola branch office after our meeting. The building appeared similar to the one in Ocean's Edge: a brick exterior, with a few floors, and large mirrored windows. At least this was more familiar.

I silently followed my partner upstairs after checking in at the front desk.

"Just a warning," Silver said while we were in the elevator, "Frank Barrass is mad about the case being shifted to us. I'll deal with him if he starts anything."

I raised an eyebrow at my partner. "Should I ask what he's done?"

"It's minor. Usually just mouthing off. Ayda, who heads this branch, pulled him off of it and sent it up to us when she caught wind of a potential necromancer being involved."

The elevator doors opened before I could ask more. It certainly sounded like more than that, but Silver's behavior had been down-right odd. I wondered if I really knew him. I had no idea what he had been doing while we were separated.

A strong arcane presence broke my train of thought. Why had my partner not said there was a mage here?

"Oh look, Silver's back," an older Human man grumbled. He sat at a desk nearby. "You bring your girlfriend along? Thought to have a nice vacation in Sola?"

Heat rose to my cheeks. Why did people automatically assume that?

"Shut up, Frank," a male voice from the back yelled.

A female Elf poked her head out of an office. "What's the commotion about?" Then she saw us. "Hey, Silver, welcome back. What can we do for you?" There was the mage.

"Ayda, this is my partner, Ketayl," Silver introduced me.

I looked up at the taller woman. Her dark brown hair was neatly braided back.

She gave me a formal Elven greeting which I returned. "It's a pleasure to meet you finally. Silver's been telling me about you. Oh, and where are my manners? I'm the head of this branch." She leaned closer before whispering, "And don't mind Frank. He's like that to everyone. Try being his boss."

"We have one more with us from the cyber team, but she's back at the hotel working. I wanted to introduce Ketayl to the branch in case she needs something," Silver said.

Ayda nodded. "Absolutely, our branch is at your disposal. Let's talk in my office."

"Jerk, case-stealing fairy," Frank muttered.

I cringed at the racial slur and looked to the others to see if they heard it, but it appeared I had been the only one. Now I understood Ayda's words. How did she put up with it if he was like this all the time? Were they supposed to put up with this all the time? I thought there were rules about racism and discrimination.

Should I tell someone about what he said? Then I questioned if I had even heard him right. I decided to hold my tongue on the matter - there was no point in creating more problems. We were here for a case, not a personnel issue.

Ayda waited until we were seated in her office. "Alright, let's get down to business. You said you had another?"

Silver nodded. "Alexis Thorton."

"Oh, Lexi. I spoke with her on this when I pushed it up the chain. I'd ask if she would rather work here, but Frank could pose an issue."

Silver continued. "She's still new to the TIO, but Lockonis wouldn't have sent her if she wasn't good. And we've both worked with her during another assignment."

Ayda crossed her arms and looked at both of us. "Didn't realize she was new. I'd love to meet her sometime. Let her know she's free to come here if she needs something."

"We'll be fine working out of the hotel for the most part. I don't want to interrupt operations here unless we have to," Silver said.

My partner wanted us all here and now he wants us to work out of the hotel. Could he make up his mind?

The head of the Sola branch eyed me. "You're rather quiet, Ketayl."

Silver laughed. "She usually is. She's the arcane investigator for our team. She's fairly close to finding a pattern."

I bit my lower lip. "I'm not sure. There's really nothing connecting the opposite ends of the spectrum. It's almost as if it's two separate people still."

Ayda raised an eyebrow at me. "I sensed a strong arcane presence from you. It also sounds like you're better caught up than I figured. Silver said you hadn't been brought in yet when he was here at the end of last week."

Silver grinned. "She likes puzzles. I've had to tear her away from it a few times already."

I glanced at him out of the corner of my eye and scrunched up my face. "I'm sitting right here," I muttered.

Ayda raised an eyebrow at us. "I know your team is autonomous, but, again, if you need anything, let me know. I'd like to keep track of this one if you don't mind. A potential necromancer in my territory? Can't say I like that much. You've dealt with them before?"

I nodded.

Silver spoke. "Yes. Our team was formed after dealing with one since they use both the divine and the arcane at high levels."

Ayda frowned. "Good thing it went to you then. I don't think anyone here could handle it. Even as good as Frank is, he'd be in over his head." She stood up. "I'll let you two... three get to it then. Good luck."

I bowed to Ayda and followed Silver out the door.

Frank glared at us as we left. I hoped he would not pose a problem.

"Do you think it will work?" Silver asked.

I bit my lower lip. I had not completely thought the idea through. "It could. I mean, facial recognition was how Rathal tried to find me in Mystic Port after he lost track of me."

Silver crossed his arms and looked at me. "He said you went undetected."

Maybe he had a point. I sighed, not wanting to give up this idea. "I did, but that's because I avoided cameras. Looking for someone who has been 'dead' for a while might be easier. We can check publicly posted images as well. People are always taking pictures and it's hard to avoid it for a length of time."

Lexi sat next to me, nodding and typing. I glanced at her screens - she flitted from one thing to the next too quickly for me to keep track of. She had been outright avoiding looking at or talking to Silver since we returned. After their disagreement in the loaner vehicle, I could understand, but we needed to work together.

I pinched the bridge of my nose. I really did not want to be a mediator between them.

"Wouldn't they change their hair and other features to avoid being spotted?" Silver asked.

"Yes, but not their facial structure, which is how it works," Lexi said, her words clipped as she finally responded to him. "Not unless they went through an expensive procedure and then we'd still find a trace of them."

Silver held up his hands in defeat. "Okay, you two do your thing. I'm going to head out and see if I can't catch a rumor or two."

I raised an eyebrow. That seemed like a poor strategy. This city was large and it would be a shot in the dark. Unless there was something he was following from a report I had not read yet.

"Hey, Lexi," I said quietly after Silver left.

She paused in her typing and looked at me.

"I know this is strange to ask, especially now, but how come you went to the cyber team?" I remembered her telling me she was good with computers, but I had never imagined this.

"Heh, um... Yeah, I guess this is a weird direction for me from what you saw. I was Sasha's assistant only when she needed me, which was really only when we had visitors. Other than that, I was part of a group that maintained the internal network for all the packs and I ended up being one of the techs for the Alpha Prime's pack."

Now I felt worse about essentially stealing her away, but she had wanted to join the TIO of her own accord.

"Sorry to bother you. I was just curious." I sorted through my things, trying to appear busy until I figured where I wanted to start. Unlike Silver, I preferred to have some direction.

"Silver was making you uneasy," Lexi commented after a minute.

I raised an eyebrow at her. Could she read minds now?

She touched her nose.

I shook my head and returned to what I was doing. "I've been away from werewolves for too long. I forgot about that."

Lexi laughed lightly.

"Alright, let's get to work." I picked up my tablet and got comfortable, prepared to be deep in the case file for a while. I was unsure of how long Silver would be gone. Even Lexi remained quiet while she worked.

I had not heard the door before Silver knelt in front of me and pushed down the tablet in my hands. "Come on, let's get out into the city for a bit. Sola is rather nice."

I raised an eyebrow at him. "I'm months behind in this and you want to go out?"

"Yes. Look, we're at something of an impasse until we get more information one way or another. I doubt you'll get much more out of the case file than you already have."

I pursed my lips. While I had gotten the sense I was rereading the same information over and over again, there must be something.

"Go on without me," Lexi said, "I want to see if my search can turn up anything other than partials. Just bring me back something."

I raised an eyebrow at the young Human-looking woman who had her brown hair pulled up in a messy bun. "Are you sure? You should probably take a break too."

"Yeah, I'm good. Even a virtual hunt is satisfying for me."

"Come on," Silver said, "It'll be good to get out and stretch our legs."

I closed my eyes for a moment, took a deep breath, and reminded myself to play by the rules. Silver would not make unreasonable demands. He was more likely to hold me back.

"Besides, it'll give us a chance to catch up."

I bit my tongue. I wanted to snap at him for ignoring me over the last few months, but reminded myself he was under orders to do so. Maybe they were right and I should not be back in the field.

I heard a faint growl from Lexi.

"Hey, what's going on?" Silver asked, his temper audibly rising.

I shook my head. "Let's go." Preferably before another argument started between them.

Silver raised an eyebrow at me before moving away.

I silently followed him through the hotel. I could sense his eyes on me.

As soon as we were alone in the elevator, he asked, "Did you contact your family?"

I hesitated for a moment. "No."

"Not even Kitteren?"

"She doesn't have time to talk anymore," I said quietly, my words clipped.

"I doubt that. You went to Ocean's Edge to visit once or twice."

I sighed. "Riva takes up most of her time outside of work. Not to mention her relationship with Rathal." Of all the situations, I was ignored because of a dog. The boyfriend I could at least understand.

"I'm sure once Kitteren gets her trained better she'll be back to her regular calls. Though I thought Riva was well behaved already." Of course he would push. Why had I expected otherwise?

"She is with me for some reason. She gives Kitteren a hard time."

Silver laughed. "Riva is really your dog."

"She's a dog. She can probably pick up on my arcane capabilities and is afraid of them." It was a common enough occurrence.

Silence fell between us again.

Once we got outside my partner spoke again. "Okay, what's going on? You're not happy about something."

"What gives you that idea?" I muttered.

"Ketayl..." Silver sighed. "Look, I've known you long enough to know when something isn't right. You didn't even fight me about going out."

"If I did, you'd take me off this assignment," I said flatly. I was not about to bring up the headache I was sure to get if he and Lexi got into an argument again.

"Is that..." He paused. "Okay, so maybe I set that tone before we left the main office, but no. I want to make sure you don't overdo it. Doesn't mean you can't be yourself."

I turned my eyes to the ground. Months of being alone and I even questioned who I was anymore.

Silver took my hand in his and squeezed it lightly. "I know of a good place to get something to eat that's nearby. We can walk since it's a nice day."

I nodded. Better to agree than possibly upset this balance.

"You know this case hasn't been with us for months, right?"

I raised an eyebrow at Silver, vaguely recalling the timeline.

"It didn't get to our team until a few weeks ago. Lockonis kept you out of it because she didn't want to interrupt whatever you were working on."

"To you," I corrected. I wished Lockonis had asked. I would have told her I had nothing.

"Us. Our team. I already told you I can't do this alone and I don't want anyone else for a partner."

How could he say that after asking if he should look for someone else? He was impossible to keep up with. I went to pull my hand away, but Silver held it firm. I sighed and stopped fighting. *Just put up with it.*

"It came to the Sola branch not long before that," he said, seemingly ignoring my effort. "Most of the time I've been away I've either been training or conducting trainings. Took some time to visit places also."

"Oh." I feigned a lack of interest. Where he visited did have me curious, but I refused to ask. Not after he ignored me for so long, orders or not.

Silence fell again.

"I heard you spent some time at your parents. Do anything interesting?"

I shook my head. "Outside of the skills classes? Helped Father with a few things and tested out of classes for this semester."

"They're letting you test out again?"

I nodded. "Given everything that occurred, they agreed to allow me to test out rather than take time out."

"Why would you take time out?"

I flattened my lips. "It was considered part of limited duty even as loosely connected as my work to get a rank assigned is."

"I'm sorry."

"Figured everyone gave up on me," I muttered.

Silver let go of my hand and wrapped his arm around my shoulders. "I never will."

"What about..." I shook my head and shut my mouth. Bringing up our fight could make things worse.

"When I picked a fight with you? Like I told you before: they wanted some kind of emotional reaction out of you and I knew I could do it. Needless to say, they weren't happy with my methods, but I got you back." Silver squeezed my shoulder. "And since when could you flip me over?"

I shrugged. "I don't think I could do it again."

"Yeah, you were pretty pissed. I'll admit, it was a lot of fun, though I wish we could have sparred under better circumstances."

I rolled my eyes. I almost killed him and he thought it was fun.

"Oh, come on. I know you hate physical training, but you usually find a creative way to beat me."

I gave a short laugh. I had missed training with him despite how much I complained about it. He continually forced me to come up with more imaginative ways to come out on top.

As Silver said, we were close to the restaurant. And quite a few other shops and places to eat. I had not noticed how close we were to other things.

"Would you like to wander after we eat?"

I nodded. Perhaps a break was in order.

5

Never. Never did I want to work in finance or investing or whatever it was Tae Kim had just bored me with for the past two hours. Our loaner car coming into view was a welcome sight.

"What's your take on the information?" Silver asked as he opened his door.

I took a deep breath, sorting through what Tae had told us as I got in. "If you ignore the financial aspect, he didn't give us much."

Silver made a face at me before he started to pull out of the parking spot. "I don't think you can ignore that. It's why we're dealing with First Union."

"When we're trying to figure out if we're dealing with an actual necromancer or not, you need to. I get why he thinks that way. The story about Tae told us his great grandfather being in the Racial War and having to clear fields of bodies in case there was a necromancer around who could reanimate them is nice, but I don't see how it applies here," I countered.

"Imagine having to fight your best friend who you watched die or have to fight an enemy you already killed. That's..." Silver trailed off and shook his head. "I don't think my imagination is strong enough for that horror."

"That's beside the point here. These people are dead. We have death certificates for all of them. The concerning point is that there are no bodies. No funerals. No memorial services. Not even an obituary. It's far more likely they got a new identity and left the area." I needed to focus on the case, not the history lesson we got with all of the financial babble. "If they're dead, or rather presumed dead, then they don't have to pay back the bank."

He glanced over at me quickly. "Tae could have something with thinking that we're dealing with a necromancer. Ketayl, what is going on? You're normally more open-minded about things than this." He sounded concerned.

I scrunched up my face and stared out the window. "We just wasted how much time for seemingly no reason and you certainly weren't helping any asking him about acquiring property," I snapped.

Silver tightened his grip on the steering wheel. "First, I apologize for getting off topic during our conversation. Second, how can you think this was a waste?" His voice was even.

"Because I don't even know why we're here. The second someone says 'necromancer' we get called? Right now, I don't see any evidence to support the theory." What was wrong with me? Normally I would let it be and do the job whether we were really needed or not. I would simply let the truth unfold for me.

"There's nothing to not support it either," he shot back. He sighed. "Arguing like this isn't getting us anywhere."

It was the first sensible thing I had heard out of him since we left.

"And really, I am sorry I got Tae off on a tangent about property. You should have stopped us."

"How could I with you two talking over me?" I muttered.

Silver growled at me.

I glared at him. We should not be arguing with each other while he was driving, but here we were, and I refused to back down.

"Alright, fine, let's get back to what we got," Silver said, "I noticed you jotted down the word 'bait' on your tablet. I never thought I'd see you write that. Not after you've been used as bait a few times now." His words were clipped.

I sighed and rolled my eyes. At least it sounded like we were back on track again. "I don't want to be bait again, but I don't know if it's possible to set up a struggling account as bait - something to attract the necromancer. Enough to make contact."

Silver stroked the small patch of hair on his chin. "Maybe, but something tells me the struggling accounts are finding the necromancer rather than being searched out since there's no real pattern to them. We couldn't do it with a high-grade account. Not without causing further issues for First Union."

"The struggling accounts wouldn't cause them more problems?" I would assume any account defaulting would cause them problems.

"I have no idea. Probably. I understand this financial stuff about as much as you do."

I bit my lower lip. The bait idea was likely out. "What about talking to the survivors? The people who would have personally known the account holder."

"As soon as I get a list, I can do that," Silver said.

I rolled my eyes. "What about me?"

"You're helping Lexi make the list."

I rolled my eyes. At least it felt like I had a decent direction now. This whole case still did not sit right with me. I hated being this much out of my element.

"How hard would it be to find survivors of the deceased?" Silver asked once we got back to our suite.

Lexi crossed her arms and hummed. "Survivors? I assume you mean friends and family of the account holders." She paused for a moment, rocking side-to-side in her chair while staring at the wall. "It shouldn't be too hard. There's a cache of the social media accounts held by the deceased. I can see who they were around frequently and extrapolate a routine from their family or friend's account." She turned around and got to work before either of us said anything further.

There was nothing to do but let her work. A question crossed my mind. "Isn't that an invasion of privacy?"

Lexi gave a short laugh. "Are you kidding? People post so much stuff publicly they pretty much monitor themselves. Like this guy here," she said, pointing at her screen. "He frequents a night club not too far from here. I mean, he did me one better by tagging the place in his photos. At a quick glance we would be taking a shot in the dark if he would be there during the week, but going into the weekend he hasn't missed one for the last few months from what I can see here.

He also posts a ton of vacation pictures. It looks like he had been in the Northern Isles this past spring."

Thumbnails appeared on one of her screens along with his ID photo. The pictures Lexi had pulled up were mostly of him with various women - they either had red hair or were Elves it seemed. I squinted at the name under his ID photo to read the name.

I bit my lower lip. There was nothing striking about Matthew Nefield: dark hair and eyes, average height and build for a Human man. The only thing that stood out was his creepy grin in the thumbnails with the women.

"A night club?" Silver leaned down to see her screen. Then he turned to me. "Think we should try to catch up with him?"

I bit my lower lip. "Depends how close he was to the deceased."

"They seemed to have been really close friends. He called him a brother quite a few times," Lexi said, "but they aren't related. It's not too common to refer to someone as a sibling like that and not have a close relationship."

Silver stood up, grinning. "Sounds like a good enough place to start while you find more. Ketayl, we're both going to have to go shopping to fit in there."

"Where?" I wanted to make sure I understood exactly. He could not seriously be considering dragging me to a night club.

"The night club," Silver said flatly.

I shook my head. "Why don't we catch up with him somewhere else?" There had to be an easier place. And quieter.

Silver crossed his arms and looked down at me. "Because I'm hoping alcohol will loosen his tongue."

"You really don't need to go shopping, Silver," Lexi commented.

"Why not?" Silver's question had a demanding tone.

Lexi looked at him for a moment. "Just wear your normal clothes with your shirt untucked and show off your chest a little. You'll fit right in. Ketayl doesn't have anything that will work. At least not with what I've seen you wear so far."

"What's wrong with what I wear?" I asked. I doubted I owned anything which would normally be worn at such a location, but surely I could get away with something. Wait, why was I thinking of going? It was a horrible idea. "You should go instead of me."

Lexi shook her head. "I used to go clubbing on occasion before I was changed. Now it's too loud for me not to mention the smells. I don't know how other werewolves stand it. It's total sensory overload for me."

I frowned. "We need to come up with a different plan. Find somewhere else or even someone else. I don't see this working out. We won't be able to rely on the information if he's intoxicated."

"No, we're starting here since we have a name and a pattern of behavior," Silver ordered. "Go figure out something appropriate to wear."

"I'm going shopping with Ketayl!" Lexi exclaimed, getting up and gathering her things.

I glared at Silver.

He grinned at me.

"This is a bad idea." Having Silver as lead kept putting me into tough positions.

Silver crossed his arms and leaned back against the table. "You'll be fine."

I FROWNED, disliking being stuck as bait again. Silver should have known better than to even suggest it, but of course this guy would have a thing for redheads and Elves and I conveniently happened to be both. Lexi tracks down a survivor of one of the deceased and I end up sitting at a bar in a night club waiting to see if he showed up. Why did I get stuck somewhere I would never go on my own with loud music and far too many people? The bright flashing lights bothered me.

Not to mention the smell was awful. Silver owed me heavily for this. I sighed. I could not turn down the order either - not if I wanted to stay on the case. I squeezed my glass of water. I hated having that held over my head.

Silver also knew I had a certain distaste for crowds and the people staring at me made me even more uneasy.

My partner moved around the club, seeing if he could find our contact rumored to frequent this place. At least I found a corner to observe from that lessened the effects of the lights. Not that it worked to hide me from the crowd as well as I wished it would. I had already gotten an earful from Silver for hiding in the bathroom earlier.

How we could even hear each other through the earpieces in this place was beyond me.

Yes, I had a job, and this was my protest of it. I fiddled with the ear cuff Lexi had made me wear.

"Quit fidgeting, Ket," Lexi said, her voice coming through the earpiece I wore. She was watching the club through the cameras.

My face felt strange wearing makeup and I itched to rub it off. Better would be to disappear into the bathroom and wash it off. Lexi had far too much fun dressing me up. It was going to be a wonderful feeling when we got back and I could be out of all of this.

The bartender dropped off another glass of water. I nodded my thanks and put my hand on the front of my shirt when I reached for it, uncomfortable with how low cut it was. Added to it was leggings and short high-heeled boots. Why had Lexi insisted on making me wear this? I felt like I stood out despite the similar outfits other women wore. At least I had convinced her away from skirts.

I listened absently to the chatter from Silver as he turned down another woman asking him to dance. It was either that or the men and women who approached him wanted to have drinks with him. He had been walking around with the same drink for a while now.

I could only guess the thoughts of the other two as I turned men and some women down.

"Our man is here. He just entered," Lexi said calmly.

I turned to scan the crowd. With all the people here, I could not spot him. I sighed and went back to my water. Silver could hunt him down. This place was draining.

"Ketayl, go find him," Silver ordered.

"No." I was not moving from this spot until I could leave.

"He's heading toward the bar," Lexi said. "Looks like he's searching for someone."

"I lost track of him," Silver replied. "Dammit, Ketayl, you know your role."

And if I was ideal bait, he would find me. I refused to budge.

There was a long pause before Lexi spoke. "He's moving along the bar talking with people. He's heading your direction, Ket."

"Ketayl, get up and go talk to him," Silver ordered.

I glanced to the side, not wanting to be obvious, but I could not spot the person we were looking for. There were too many people and the fast-moving colored lights made it worse. The pounding music was giving me a headache. "No," I said flatly. "I can't even see him."

"It'll make things easier if you make the first move," Lexi said, her tone gentle.

I gripped my glass of water tightly. I was close to leaving as it was. I did not care how much trouble I would get in for it.

"That's no way to enjoy an evening," a male voice said a moment later. The heavy smell of alcohol followed and I scrunched up my nose.

I tensed up as the Human man came up on my right side. I rolled my eyes. *Not another one.* I glanced up and it seemed our target found me.

"Well, at least he decided to talk to you," Lexi said.

He had a broad smile on his face. "Can I at least buy you a real drink?"

I shook my head. "Thanks, but I'll stick to water."

"A shame. A little alcohol makes this crowd a bit more pleasing to look at, though definitely don't need it for you. My name's Matt." He slid into the open seat next to me.

I heard Lexi snickering.

I forced a smile. "Ketayl," I said flatly. *Where is Silver?*

"Ket, at least look like you're interested in talking with him," Lexi said.

Matt ordered himself a drink. It smelled like he had already been drinking, but he was not slurring his words and seemed coherent. Silver was hoping alcohol would loosen his tongue, but I thought he might be too intoxicated given the smell. Either that or he had an unfortunate accident with a drink before he got to me.

"*He's drunk,*" I said in my dialect of common, "*This isn't a good time to get information.*" I did not care how crazy I looked talking to myself.

"What did she say?" Lexi asked.

"Ketayl, just talk with him. He might be more willing to give up information like this," Silver ordered.

"I'm going to take that as a greeting." Matt kept grinning at me and leaned on the bar. "Hm... gorgeous red hair and that accent. Northern Isles?"

I blinked. I had an accent? "Um, yes."

"You flirt like a dead fish," Lexi commented, and I wanted to tell her next time we were switching places. She could learn to tolerate the noise and smells instead.

"Ah, a friend of mine and I were planning a trip up there. Hear it's absolutely stunning in the summer. What brings you to this tiny little hole in Sola?"

I took a sip of water, coming up with something to keep him talking. "Helping a friend. Insisted I come here." If I could have glared at Silver right then I would have. Lucky for him I could not see well in the direction I assumed he was because of the flashing lights.

"It's certainly my lucky night." Matt gently touched my wrist. "A beautiful redheaded Elf comes to my favorite haunt with a most delightful accent. And I do love redheads."

I moved my hand away. I wanted to shove him away and teleport back to the hotel room. I contemplated dumping my water on him.

"Relax, Ketayl. You can handle this," Silver said calmly.

Easy for you to say. At least I knew he had eyes on me and could intervene if needed. It gave me some level of security.

"You canceled your plans?" I asked before I gave into the instinct to run.

"Sort of." Matt picked up his drink and downed it in one shot. "A guy being dead makes it hard to plan a vacation."

"Oh, I'm sorry." That was what I was supposed to say, right? "What happened?"

Matt signaled for the nearest bartender to bring him another. It was a different Human man than before.

The bartender shook his head. "No one should've given you that one."

"Come on! Things are getting good here."

"They'll get worse if you keep it up. And if you harass my *good* customers, I'll have you tossed out." The bartender turned to me. "I think the Moon Water would be to your tastes, miss. Let me know if you'd like to try it."

Moon Water? It took me a minute to remember the poster in the bathroom. It was a signal to the bartender to intervene in some fashion if someone was being harassed.

I forced a smile. "I'll think about it." I had my own backup, but I appreciated the gesture.

The bartender nodded and left.

"Ket's right. We need to abort this - he's too drunk," Lexi said.

"No, Ketayl can get the information. Would you help her out?" Silver replied.

"Silver, if a bartender is cutting him off, what he says is going to be garbage," Lexi argued.

While they went back and forth in my ear, I sat frozen. I had no idea what to do. I wanted to run, but I was ordered to stay.

"I just had a brilliant idea. You could show me around the Northern Isles when I go visit. Joey's taking too long to come back to life," Matt said. He stroked the back of my hand with a finger again.

With an idea like that, he had to be drunk. I tightened my grip on my glass and moved away from him again.

Just a little longer. Focus on the information. "How is he coming back to life?"

Matt gave me a lopsided smile. "Magic. Though there's magic you and I can create tonight if you're interested."

"Silver, call it off," Lexi argued. "This guy has nothing like this."

"No, we need more. Ketayl, you've got to get confirmation," my partner ordered.

"He's too drunk - we can't rely on the information. You just heard his grotesque pick-up line," Lexi countered.

The instant Matt put his hand on my back, I got up, swiping my glass to make it look like an accident, dumping my water on him. I did not turn around to find out what kind of mess I caused as I hurried for the door.

I dug the earpiece out as soon as I was free. Hearing both of them calling me only contributed to the headache I had.

Once I got away from the crowd outside the club by the door, I leaned against the wall and took a deep breath to calm myself. Why had I not fought more against this plan? I got my heeled boots off, needing to be able to run if Matt followed me.

"Ketayl!" Silver called, running up to me. He reached for my arm.

I stepped out of his reach, glaring at him. "Don't. Don't you dare touch me right now. You can finish this stupid plan yourself." Then I turned on my heel and left, moving as fast as I could barefoot.

6

DEAD END after dead end after dead end. Who was this necromancer? A week later and I still had no answer. Lexi had found a few more survivors, but they had nothing to tell us. Or rather Silver. He went out on his own for the most part. After what happened at the night club, he had decided to not bring me along on his searches.

It gave me a break from the headaches the two of them caused. Silver would say or do something Lexi disliked and there would be another dominance contest. More than once I simply left to go somewhere else within the hotel.

"Give it a rest," Silver said. He had gotten back not long ago from talking with another of the survivors. He had been quietly sitting on the couch fiddling with his phone.

I sighed. I wanted to keep going, but I remembered his words earlier this week about making sure I kept from overdoing it. Not to mention I was certain my position was much more precarious after I disobeyed his orders. I got up and plugged my tablet in.

Even Lexi had gone out for a walk, needing a break.

"You're not putting up a fight?"

I flattened my lips. "I know my position right now."

"Kela…"

"Look, if this is the best I can manage at the moment then I have to deal with it. You have your orders and I have a job I want to keep." I kept my back to him and held my hands to my chest to hide how hard I was squeezing them together. I wanted to fight back - give him a hard time about needing to find some sort of lead. Keeping the peace between us was more important.

Silver squeezed between me and the counter. He put his hands on mine. "Stop. This isn't right. Dammit, this isn't you. You don't have to hide from me."

I stood still, turning my eyes to the floor. "I can't put you in that position."

"What position?"

Taking a deep breath, I corrected myself, "I can't jeopardize your position."

Silver grabbed my shoulders. "Screw my position. I need you back. I should have ignored the orders to limit contact with you, but the fool I am bought into their reasoning and I wanted nothing more than to get you back. And dammit, Lexi was right that I should have called it off as soon as we saw Matt was drunk. I should never have let you go through that."

"Okay, enough of this. Did you get anything?" I moved away from him. I had asked him when he got in, but he had only made a noise I could not translate.

Silver frowned and crossed his arms. "No, or rather the same information we got before. We have solid confirmation of the necromancer and that's it. No contact, no description, nothing. Just the ones who had struggling accounts were expected to come back someday."

I sighed and leaned back against the counter. "I'm not having much luck getting more information about necromancers. It's as if history glossed over their existence. I'm barely finding notes of them existing in arcane texts."

My partner stroked the small patch of hair on his chin. "It's a tarnish and the people who write the history books get to say what goes in. What about other sources?"

"Folklore seems to have the most information, but how accurate it is I would consider questionable, but there is a common thread about raising the dead or draining people's life essence."

Silver took the desk chair and sat across from me. "Okay, you've been cooped up here too long if you're reading through folklore for information."

"I figured there's got to be some truth behind the fiction. It's just a matter of separating it," I argued. It might be far-fetched, but I was willing to try.

My partner stood up and took my hand, tugging lightly to signal he wanted me to stand up. Sighing, I did so, crossing my arms as soon as I was at my full height.

"Let's go out for a bit. You really can't stay holed up in here," Silver said.

I frowned. "I've been going out for food." Sola was otherwise too busy for my liking.

"That's not enough. Come on. Maybe inspiration will strike while we're out," he reasoned. "It's about time you stepped away from it for a bit."

I rolled my eyes.

Silver gave me a broad grin. "We could always go back to the club instead."

"No," I said quickly. "I ran out of polite ways to turn down offers for drinks and companionship."

Silver grinned broadly. "I kind of want to see you not be polite now."

I scrunched up my face. "You already did. You make me go again and I'll dump my water on you."

"Okay. Okay. Well, we need to go now then." He gestured toward the door.

I raised an eyebrow at him. "Are you planning on going back to the club tonight?"

Silver tugged lightly on his braid. "Thinking about it. There's got to be information floating somewhere."

I bit my lower lip for a moment. "I don't think you'll find it there. Not enough points converge on the club."

Silver paused and raised an eyebrow at me. "Points?"

I took a deep breath before elaborating, "Not everyone went there. There are also people from hundreds of miles away with no connection who have been reported as dead with the same pattern."

"Yeah, you've been cooped up too long."

Silver let me collect my things before he ushered me out the door. He held my hand again.

"Why do you hold my hand?" It was a curious action he had been doing since we came to Sola.

My partner looked down at me. "Oh, um, well, it's easier for me to keep track of how you're doing. Usually you've got my hand pretty tight in public, but when you start trying to crush it is when I need to do something."

I pulled my hand away from his and crossed my arms. He needed to leave me be.

"Ketayl?"

"I'm fine," I snapped.

Silver sighed. "It helps keep me grounded also. I..." he paused and reached for my hand, but stopped. "I need to know you're okay. That you're here. I won't ask for more. I'm sorry I've made you uncomfortable on a number of occasions."

I eyed him for a moment before I let out a soft huff and took his hand. "What a pair we are." Apparently, I missed how all of this had been affecting him. Given how busy Sola was, holding his hand also kept us from getting separated.

He squeezed my hand lightly. "Indeed."

My partner found us a quiet restaurant for lunch. Or it had been quiet. A couple of women were seated nearby about 10 minutes after us and chatted loudly about seemingly everyone they knew, making unkind comments about them over their overpriced salads.

I never thought people actually talked like that. It hurt to have to listen to. At least it had distracted me for a bit from feeling like someone was watching me.

As we left Silver asked, "How would you feel about walking around the market district a bit? It's the middle of the afternoon during the week. The crowds should be thinner."

I nodded. "I'd like to find something for Kitteren."

"Have you contacted her?"

I shook my head. "I don't want to be a bother." That was all I was. In my desperation for some contact I had become selfish. I needed to fix that.

Silver toyed with the end of his braid. "Is it possible she was given the same orders I was?"

Biting my lower lip, I considered the possibility. "I don't know, but she always seemed pretty focused on her dog. Not to mention she and Rathal have gotten quite serious."

He hummed for a moment. "I don't know what to tell you. You could always ask her."

I shrugged. "Maybe." It might not be worth it.

We wandered in and out of many shops. I was unsure what to get my sister. I had not realized how lonely I had become with everyone limiting their contact with me.

I had been here a week and out of spite told none of my family. Even when I had been down at my adopted parent's house, they always seemed too busy when they were there. Mother had been traveling a lot because of her business and often Father went with her if he had no other commitments.

My thoughts were not enough to keep the sensation of being watched at bay. It had been that way since we left the hotel, but I kept silent, unsure if I was jumping at shadows.

"Ketayl?" Silver asked.

I shook my head to clear my thoughts. "Remind me to message Kitteren later."

He raised an eyebrow at me. "Yeah, sure."

I bit my lower lip. I had no idea what to get my sister. I saw hair accessories in a window as we walked by. Kitteren had started growing her hair back out.

"Come on. It'll be something different." Silver tugged on my hand, heading for the door. "Besides, it'll be a break from the crowds."

I bit my lower lip. "I don't know..." I cringed at the sound of the doorbell going off.

"Maybe you'll find something for you."

I rolled my eyes. "This is a little too much for me."

"But not Kitteren? The two of you look almost identical," Silver pointed out.

"It's her personality." I gently held up a crystal butterfly hairclip to examine. "As rough as she can be, she does love to dress up."

I heard a clerk approach Silver. "Is there anything I can help you find?" the Human man asked.

"We're just browsing, thanks."

Thank goodness my partner deflected the clerk for both of us. I hoped he would not be pushy.

"Hm." Silver moved about, looking at the various displays of jewelry and hair accessories.

Grinning briefly, I teased, "Are you looking for something for yourself?" I forced my expression back to neutral.

"What?" My partner turned and looked at me with wide eyes. "Why would I want something here?"

I shrugged. "You're a bit eccentric. Not to mention I know you keep spare hair ties on you."

He quickly put back what he had been holding. "Not like this. And those are in case I lose one."

I hid my amusement behind my hand.

A soft smile graced Silver's face for a moment before something caught his attention. He reached around me to the display I had been standing in front of. I missed what he picked up before he held it to the back of my head. "I think this would look nice on you."

I turned to see what he was talking about. It was a silver crescent moon hair clip. Small, delicate looking chains with crystals hung from it. "A moon?"

Silver shrugged. "You're kind of my opposite so why not? Besides, you said you don't like gold." He grinned broadly.

"Please don't make that joke again. It was bad enough the first time," I warned. My face had started feeling warm at the memory.

"You laughed pretty hard at it though. I mean, you must like 'Silver' if you don't like gold." My partner gestured at himself.

I rolled my eyes and groaned at the bad pun. I turned my attention back to the display. Maybe the butterfly one I first looked at?

A Human woman entered the shop and headed directly for the counter. I took a deep breath and let it out slowly. Just another shopper.

"Has it sold yet?" the woman asked, keeping her voice down.

"No, I'm afraid not," the clerk said.

"Can't you guys just buy it off of me? I really need the money."

The conversation now had my attention. Silver followed me as I made my way to another display where I could listen to them better.

The clerk sighed. "It's not within store policy. I'm sorry."

"Please? Just this once?"

"No."

The woman's shoulders slumped.

The clerk eyed us. "Look, I understand your situation. I may have another solution for you. If you don't mind coming to the back?"

"Okay."

The clerk called for someone in the back to come up front.

Silver leaned down to whisper, "I'm going to get this and see if I can't catch them out back."

"I'm better at hiding," I argued.

"I'll take this one. You're still undecided in here anyway."

"What am I supposed to do?"

"Keep an eye out in here." Silver patted my shoulder and moved to the counter with his purchase. I never saw what he bought.

I sighed. He must not trust me to be able to pull it off. Was it worth arguing with him about later? I wanted to do something in the field. He had dragged me all the way out to Sola after all.

Silver came over, tucking the small bag into a pocket inside his jacket. He leaned over and kissed my cheek. "Take your time. I'm sure you'll find something she'll love." He spoke at a normal volume. "I'm going to get some air."

I stiffened up at his movement. What was he thinking kissing my cheek like that? I touched my cheek and watched as he left the store.

"You've got a sweet boyfriend there," the female clerk at the counter said.

I felt the heat rise to my cheeks. "He's something else." *Something else as in not my boyfriend.*

She laughed lightly and went back to what she had been reading.

"Do you get a lot of consignments?" I asked after a minute or so while I browsed.

"Hm? Oh, yeah. We have a lot of local crafters who sell here. The owner started this store to sell her own and it evolved from there. It's hard to bring home a paycheck sometimes." She laughed lightly. "Many of them are very talented. Sometimes we get some unique vintage items in for consignment."

I forced a smile. "I'm glad I stopped in then."

"Looking for something specific?"

"Just a gift for my sister. She's not easy to shop for."

The woman at the counter smiled at me. "I know how that feels - mine is next to impossible. Take your time."

I lost track of how long I browsed until something caught my attention. The hair pins reminded me of the gold and silver feather necklaces Kitteren insisted on buying for us at the festival in Mystic Port. There were gold and silver hair pins here I thought would match. Maybe it would even be a reminder to her.

I picked up the gold one. The three metal feathers hung by small chains a few inches from the base of the pin, each one longer than the last.

"Thank you so much. I'll definitely contact him." The woman from earlier said.

"It'll cost, but it'll be your final payment," the male clerk said. He went over to a display and picked up a solitary brooch. "Here, you might be able to use this to bring down the cost or keep it."

She clutched the brooch to her chest. "Thank you." Then she quickly left.

"I'm going to head to the back and remove that from the system," he said to the female clerk and then disappeared.

I glanced at the time on my phone and messaged Lexi to see if she could pull footage from the area and get an ID on the woman I just saw. I also mentioned the store clerk she had spoken with.

It might not be a lead, but it was worth a shot.

A few more people came in. They were being loud and the clerk greeted the group, chatting lightly with them. I bit my lower lip. I really wanted to leave, but I was unsure if I should get the hair pins.

"Hey, are you okay?"

I jumped at the voice, not immediately recognizing it as belonging to Silver.

"No, you're not," he observed quietly, taking my hand.

I squeezed his hand hard. "Sorry, I think I'm done with crowds."

"It's okay. I didn't see them come out the back. Did you have any luck?"

"Yes." And that was all I was willing to say at the moment.

Silver smiled down at me. "Then let's get out of here unless you saw something you wanted to get."

"I don't know. It's hard to guess what to get for her."

He looked past me to the display I stood next to. "Hey, these look like those necklaces I saw you and Kitteren wearing at that festival."

Part of me had hoped he had forgotten about that time, but I should have known better. "This might be a poor reminder."

"Nah, get them. She might not be here, but I think she'd like having something to share with you."

I sighed and took one of each color and went up to the counter.

As soon as we left, the feeling of being watched returned right before a familiar male voice called to us. "Out shopping? I thought you had a case to work on."

Silver growled and turned around. I followed his line of sight and Frank stood there with his arms crossed.

"Maybe you should leave this to those of us with experience and dedication," Frank spat.

"You're one to talk. Have you been following us?" Silver accused.

Frank stood upright. "I don't need to follow a couple of young bloods like you."

"Yeah, and you just happened to be in the market," Silver shot back.

I stepped in front of Silver knowing he would not relent unless I convinced him to drop it. "Hey, we got a lead. Let's go back and see what Lexi turns up."

Frank looked at the store we had exited. "A lead, huh? Here?"

"Just stay out of our way," Silver said firmly. "This isn't your hunt."

Silver took a step forward and I changed tactics, putting my hands on his chest and pushing him to get him to walk away.

"Yeah, listen to the fairy girl," Frank said.

I turned, letting my power rise with the anger at what he had called me. I glared at the man. "It would be wise of you not to call me that. Leave us be."

Frank took a step back, his eyes wide.

"Ketayl..." Silver said quietly. "Your eyes."

"I don't care. Let's go."

"A NETWORK?" Silver asked after I explained my theory.

Lexi tapped her finger on the table she had set up on. "It makes the most sense. Various points of contact all leading to the source so there's no other single commonality among those who sought the necromancer's services. It may even be a chain before someone gets to the source."

I leaned back against the table next to Lexi's computer. "This one sounded like she was on the struggling end of the spectrum. Tae was talking about something else regarding the high-grade accounts that I honestly couldn't follow."

Silver laughed. "Yeah, it took me a bit to catch on and I still have a hard time keeping up with him. Basically, the ones who are high-grade, so not seen as in danger of defaulting on the debt, are sold to investors or something like that. I'm not sure what happens after."

I raised an eyebrow at him. "It might be the clue we need."

My partner's shoulders slumped. "Okay, okay. I'll look into it. You two trace the network."

"Just waiting for a return on the facial recognition," Lexi said, smirking and leaning back in her chair.

I bit my lower lip, feeling useless. "I'll compile a list of potentials in the meantime." Not that I thought it would help.

"Yeah, you two talk over my head," Silver muttered.

I rolled my eyes.

The computer beeped. "Looks like we've got information about the store clerk," Lexi said.

I turned to see what had come up.

"Oh?" Silver came over to lean over my shoulder. I stiffened at his presence.

Lexi snorted. "He's supposed to be dead."

"I figured that's how the network worked." The idea had been brewing in my head for a while.

"What do you mean?" Silver asked.

"One person deals with the necromancer and then passes the information onto others. If it kept branching out like that, I don't know how far it would go. It could go far past dealing with just First Union." I bit my lower lip considering the possible size and connections this necromancer might have.

Silver turned me to face him. "Hey, figure out what you can. Both of you. I'll get this packaged and mailed, okay? See if I can find anything else while I'm out." He held up the gold hair pin I purchased for my sister.

I nodded.

"Don't forget to message Kitteren," Silver said before closing the door.

Oh right, that.

Sighing, I picked up my phone and typed up a quick message letting her and my parents know I was away from the main office. What more should I say at this point? Were they given the same orders?

The whole set up was far more complex than I cared for.

No sooner had I put my phone down on the desk, it rang. Rolling my eyes, I picked it up and groaned at the name: Kitteren.

Lexi laughed lightly while she typed.

"Ket, where are you? What's going on?" Kitteren asked the moment the call connected. I held the phone away from my ear at her volume.

I sighed. *"Sola."* I spoke in our dialect of common. With Lexi in the room, I wanted to keep it as private as possible.

"What in the Hells are you doing way over there?"

I pinched the bridge of my nose. Now she was curious about what I was doing. *"Working."*

"Working... oh. They sent you out?"

I sighed again and took a seat in the comfortable chair in the corner. This would likely take a while. I heard a whine in the background.

"Quiet, Riva. I'm talking to Ket," Kitteren said softly.

"How's she doing?" I asked, changing the topic.

"Still a right pain in the ass sometimes. She misses you. I was thinking of seeing if you wanted to come back out here soon, but... Why are you in Sola?"

"Working."

"You said that."

I took a deep breath. *"Kitteren, listen, I'm on probation and I'm not really doing much other than trying to track down someone from the hotel suite. Silver's doing most of the legwork and Lexi's here also."*

"Ket, I'm worried—"

"Are you really?" I snapped at her, my patience gone. *"You haven't seemed to care the last few months."*

Silence was on the other side of the line. Then it went dead.

What have I done?

I jumped when my phone rang again, this time requesting a video call from Kitteren.

Hesitantly I answered. *"Hey,"* I said softly, *"I'm sorry."*

Kitteren's wide-eyed expression softened and she looked down. Riva nudged her way into the video feed. *"Yes, Riva, it's Ket."* She rubbed the black dog's head. *"I should be the one apologizing. I wanted to give you space so you could focus on healing."*

I rubbed the bridge of my nose. Everyone thought they knew

what was best, but no one stopped to ask what was actually needed. Or at least listened.

"*Ket, forgive me, please?*"

I flattened my lips into a line, closing my eyes for a moment. Kitteren sounded both desperate and sincere. I let out the breath I held and turned my attention back to my sister. "*There's nothing to forgive.*" I forced a smile.

"*You're too kind,*" Kitteren said softly. "*I hope I can make it up to you in time. So, Sola?*"

I shrugged.

"*Is it nice?*"

I shrugged. "*Haven't been out much, but you'd probably enjoy it. Too busy for my tastes.*"

Kitteren laughed lightly. "*Yeah, Sola is known for that. Maybe you could try the library or something. Being cooped up isn't good.*"

"*You sound like Silver.*"

"*Ugh, don't insult me like that.*"

I hid my amusement behind my hand. It never took much to break her out of her gloom.

Kitteren's face turned solemn. "*You probably won't believe me, but I've really missed talking to you.*"

"*Were you also under orders to limit contact with me?*" I had to know.

Kitteren's eyes went wide for a moment and then she looked down. "*Yes.*"

"*It's okay, I understand.*" Understood, yes, but it did not make the months of loneliness any better.

"*Was he also ordered?*" Kitteren asked quietly. "*Silver that is.*"

I nodded.

"*I was wondering how you found out.*"

Silence fell between us. I could not bring myself to look at her at the moment. Not until I figured out what to do with the information.

"*I take it he's not around.*"

I shook my head. "*It's just me and Lexi.*"

"*How are things between you and your partner? I know it was strained the last time we talked.*" I noticed she kept from using his name this time.

"*It's been... awkward. I can't put him in a position to get in trouble, but it really ties my hands.*" I really had not thought about it until now.

Being stuck here trying to help from a distance when we were so close to where everything was happening was torture.

"Then get him in trouble."

I sat there with wide eyes, staring at my sister.

"Seriously, he's probably not going to care as long as you don't do something stupid or reckless. You know he won't report it if you're doing your job."

"You talking to Ket?" a male voice asked. Rathal stepped into view a moment later. "Hey, cutie."

I felt the heat rise to my cheeks when he called me that. Kitteren elbowed him.

He laughed. "Good to see I can still get a reaction out of you. Just wanted to say hi before I left. Later."

"Bye," I said quietly.

Kitteren toyed with her loose hair. "I should probably get going also. Some of those newbies need a lesson in humility and I better plan for how to do it."

I nodded. "Okay. I'll talk to you later." How soon that would be was another question. This reconnecting with everyone was horribly awkward.

"Damn straight you will. Later, Ket." The connection ended.

Lexi smiled at her computer.

"What?" I asked.

Lexi glanced at me quickly. "I haven't seen this side of you before. Heard you mention my name."

I shrugged. "Kitteren gets worried so I tell her who I'm with."

"Ah. If you don't mind my observation, it doesn't seem like things have been the same between you and Silver like they were in Ghost Forest."

"It's complicated." Perhaps things were irreversible.

"Isn't it always?"

She had a point. "How much do you have on the store clerk?"

"I'm back tracking to when he 'died' and the issues he was having. I got a hit on the woman."

That got me out of my seat. "Can you send the information on her to my phone? I want to check out the situation."

Lexi tilted her head at me. "Sure, but don't you want to wait for Silver?"

I shook my head. "Frank from the Sola branch office has been tailing him. I don't think he can stand giving up the case. His focus is probably on Silver, but if he decides to follow me, I can lose him."

"Good idea. I'll get the information forwarded and track her down. I should have her routine shortly. I'm hoping she's a creature of habit."

"Thanks, Lexi." I grabbed my bag and headed for the door.

"Wait."

I turned to see what she needed.

Lexi tossed a small device to me.

I raised an eyebrow at the earpiece. It was bigger than the one she fitted us with for the night club.

"It'll be easier to direct you verbally," she said.

I smirked and turned it on before fitting it to my ear. "Good?"

"Go find her."

7

As soon as I left the hotel, I felt eyes on me once more. *Probably Frank.*

I fidgeted with my phone for a minute, searching around until I spotted him with a book in his hands at the bus stop nearby. His unassuming demeanor almost had me overlook him. He obviously had experience doing this.

Silver could probably learn something from him if they were not at odds with each other.

I led Frank a block away and down a quiet alley before turning to face him, which made him pause at the entrance to the alley. I crossed my arms and waited for him.

"Is that Frank?" Lexi asked.

I kept my voice down. "Yeah."

"I'm not sure if I'm old or you're good," Frank commented as he approached. He stood over me.

I frowned, glaring at him. "Time will tell. Why are you following me?"

He narrowed his eyes at me. "I want to know what in the Hells you are."

"Annoyed is what I am," I muttered. I must have hung around Silver too long if I came out with an answer like that.

Lexi snickered in my ear.

Frank glared at me. "Don't give me that load of crap. I checked your file. You're an arcane investigator and you were on limited duty until that bastard brought you in."

I bit the inside of my cheek in an attempt to keep my expression neutral. "Silver is my partner. Has been for years." *Years? Has it really been years already?* Only a couple, but longer than it felt.

"What about that thing with your eyes? Don't tell me it was a trick of the light or some other sort of excuse," Frank said, "I may be old, but I'm not blind."

"You pissed me off. It happens." Not that I could lie knowing I let it happen to scare him. "This interrogation is over." I turned and walked away.

Frank grabbed my arm.

"Oh crap," Lexi said, sounding worried.

"You'll want to let go," I said flatly. The area I led him to was quiet, but hurting him at all would only land me in trouble.

"Answer my damn question: what in the Hells are you?"

I closed my eyes, coming up with a plan to get away from him. "Gone." I teleported a short distance behind him and used my invisibility spell to hide, flattening myself against the wall.

"What in the Hells?" Frank looked around frantically for a moment. "Dammit. I should've just followed the other one." He put his hands in his pockets and left.

I let out the breath I had been holding and stepped away from the wall, releasing my spell. I debated reporting this to Ayda, but what good would it do other than possibly land me in trouble for being confrontational? I was on such a fine line already.

"Nice. Information incoming," Lexi said.

My phone dinged and I pulled it out, smiling at the information Lexi sent. Now I could do something useful.

LEXI HAD SENT me a detailed schedule for Patrice Rollins right down to which trains she took and at what times. Apparently, she would go into the consignment store daily on her lunch break to check on the sale of her item which was when Silver and I came across her. If I hurried, I could catch the same train as her. I would rather catch her en route home than have to possibly deal with her other family members.

Quickly paying my fare, I hustled down into the station. I scanned the crowd. Had I beat her here?

I checked the information on my phone again. The board overhead told me which train was coming in next and it was not the one she normally took. "Did I miss the train I needed?"

"Nope. I'm impressed - even with the delay you got there early," Lexi said.

I frowned and crossed my arms, leaning back against the wall. "I'm concerned about Frank interfering with us like this. We could miss something."

"No kidding. Any idea how to get him to give up on the case?"

"Not yet." Not that I had given the idea much thought. I assumed Silver and Ayda would handle it, but Frank seemed to be beyond their control. There had to be something.

I breathed a sigh of relief when the train rolled in and the crowd thinned out. Even as focused as I was on finding Patrice, the packed station made me uneasy.

The board changed, the letters clacking loudly as they flipped around. Patrice's train now showed.

People filtered down into the station quickly and it filled faster than I was prepared for.

Thankfully Lexi had eyes out. "To your left near where you came down. Your target just showed up."

I wove my way through the crowd to get closer, but the train arrived faster than I could get to Patrice. What was I going to do when I caught up to her?

We ended up on opposite ends of the same car and I looked around while trying not to touch anyone. I had never felt claustrophobic like this before. I needed to focus on keeping track of the woman. Focus on my task. Maybe I could strike up a conversation with her as a lost tourist? I lacked creativity on how to learn more information.

"Hey, you okay?" Lexi asked.

"I'm not fond of crowds," I said quietly hoping she managed to hear me over the noise.

"It won't be too long."

Before I could come up with a plan to talk to Patrice, I had to follow her off the train. I kept my distance, not wanting to alert her. She clutched a piece of paper in her hands as she walked. Lexi fed me directions whenever Patrice was out of my line of sight.

The crowds thinned and I moved closer. I ducked into an alley.

"What are you doing? She was heading straight down the street," Lexi said.

"I can't follow her in the open much longer and using my invisibility spell out on the street would draw attention."

Lexi sighed. "Okay, I'll keep track of her. Just hurry."

That had been my plan. It did not take me long to catch back up.

As I followed her onto quieter streets, I heard her whispering: "I can do this." "They're better off without me." "I don't want to lose them." "It's better this way." And the cycle would repeat.

"She sounds desperate," Lexi commented.

I bit my lower lip as I could not reply without being heard by Patrice. Should I be worried that she would do something rash? The best thing I could do right now was follow her at least until I was sure what her words meant.

The houses began to appear more run down the longer we walked.

"Pat!" a woman called. She waved at her from a fenced yard with two young children running around her legs. Twins?

That caught the attention of the children. "Mommy!" they shouted repeatedly, jumping up and down at the fence.

Patrice smiled and waved back.

"Any luck today?" the woman asked.

Patrice shook her head. "I was hoping the locket would have sold, but..." she trailed off.

"But?"

Patrice clutched the paper tightly to her chest. "I may have another option, but I couldn't ask you to take on more than you already have."

"What do you mean?" the woman had put her hands on the children's heads gently, stopping their bouncing. "Hey, can you two go inside for a bit so auntie can talk with mommy?"

The children pouted, but did as they were told.

As soon as they were gone, the aunt folded her arms and asked again, "What option?"

"Death."

"Oh no. Hells no. You aren't leaving these kids. They need you. Just because your asshole of a husband racked up a ton of debt and then got himself killed doesn't mean you have to go and follow him."

"What am I going to do? I can't find a decent paying job to pay the banks back and loan sharks was how all of this began. I'm going to lose the house and..." She trailed off and hung her head.

I put my hand to my chest as it tightened. I should leave and not overhear this conversation, but I needed to. I had to know what was on that piece of paper.

The aunt shook her head and then pulled out a cigarette and lit it. "We'll figure it out. Just don't go leaving me and your kids, okay?"

Patrice took a deep breath. "It wouldn't be permanent. Just long enough for the banks to write the loans off."

That sounded exactly like what the necromancer was doing. I inched closer.

"What?"

Patrice handed the woman the paper she had. "He apparently can bring the dead back to life. It takes a while, but I'd still lose you and the kids. Maybe in time..."

The woman smoking looked at the paper before making a face and setting it on fire with her lighter.

"Wait! Don't!" Patrice tried to stop her.

I reached out, but pulled my hand back quickly. My lead burned up right in front of me. *Dammit.*

"Oh no..." Lexi said quietly.

"No making deals with demons," she snapped. "We'll get through this. Besides, the kids like auntie time. I'll make some calls again - there may be something new. We'll make it work, sis."

I took a deep breath and walked away. There was no point in staying. The lead was gone. I should have done something, but who was wrong here? There was a mention of loan sharks, but the banks sounded just as bad and they were legally allowed to do this to people.

As I wandered, I found a quiet place to release my invisibility spell. "Lexi, I'm going to take a break. I'll come back in a bit."

"Yeah, take your time. I'll see you when you get back."

I tore off the headset and powered it down. I looked it over, snarling at it, before clenching my hand around it, drawing back to throw. I stopped and lowered my arm in defeat. I shoved the headset in my pocket. I had been so close to finding the necromancer, but was it worth it? Was it worth the hope these people had?

Wandering for a bit longer, I took a seat on a nearby bench in a peaceful park. If only I had the nerve to talk to Patrice, I could have gotten the information. I was useless. I could try to get information from the same person she had.

Right now though, I had nothing to go back with. I may not be struggling financially, but having a chance to start over like Patrice had been offered... I might take it.

The problem was, I would still remember. All the pain, all the joy. How could anyone make a decision like that?

Taking a deep breath, I turned my eyes to the small pond in front of me. It was nice here. Not like the hustle and bustle of the city center. "A fresh start doesn't sound so bad, but I'm not sure I could give them up," I muttered.

"Give who up?"

I jumped at Silver's voice. "What are you doing here?"

"I could ask you the same question. Or rather I should be the one asking you that question as I came to find you after Lexi said you went out on a lead." Silver sat next to me on the bench.

I leaned forward, pinching the bridge of my nose between my thumbs. I screwed up. I knew every decision I made was being evaluated and I chose to pull this.

"Ketayl, talk to me."

I shook my head. "Nothing to talk about. I missed my chance to get more information."

"So you came to the park?"

I shrugged. "I wanted to think."

A large hand stroked my back.

I sat up to glare at him, but Silver took his hand away before I could say anything. Staring out over the water I asked, "Have you ever wanted to start over?"

Silver shifted and sat back, stretching out his long legs. "Sure, plenty of times, but I have a feeling you might be thinking more all-encompassing. What happened?"

Taking a deep breath, I explained what I witnessed.

Silver stroked the patch of hair on his chin. "It does make one think, that's for certain. It also gives us a perspective on the people struggling and who might take up an offer like that."

I had not considered that. "How can we quantify how likely a person would be to take up such an offer? How do you factor the variables for how much they have to lose?"

"How do you take an off-hand comment and turn it scientific?" Silver asked with an exasperated tone.

I smirked and glanced at him out of the corner of my eye. He was smiling at me. I turned my attention back to the pond. The lights around the area were starting to come on now that the sun had set.

Silver shifted, leaning forward on his knees. "You asked me if I ever wanted to start over."

"Yeah." I knew little of his past, but it sounded like there had been some things he would have liked to have forgotten. Starting over would not have erased what had already happened though.

"I haven't been doing a good job of it these past several months, have I?"

I bit my lower lip for a moment trying to figure out what he spoke of. Then I recalled when we were back safe from the pirates of him asking if we could start things over between us. "You had your orders. You probably still have orders. Should I ask how much trouble I'm in for taking off like that?"

"You're doing your job. I don't see any trouble with this. One of us knew what you were doing and could keep tabs on you. It's all I ask."

I shook my head and stood up. "We should probably head back."

"Yeah."

We walked for a bit before I realized we were headed to the trains. "You didn't drive?"

My partner tugged lightly on his braid. "Lexi gave me the directions for the train. I didn't even think about it when I was following your trail."

I shook my head. Too often I could not figure out how he thought.

Silver silently sat next to me on the mostly empty train. He fidgeted with his hands and kept his attention on them.

I sighed and reached over, putting my hand over his to get him to stop. When he looked at me with wide eyes, I said quietly, "You need this, right?"

"It's okay. I know how..." Silver trailed off when I took his hand.

"Can't work on starting over if you never start." I forced a smile. He was trying to make things right and it was only fair if I put in some effort also.

"Ketayl…" Silver said quietly. "You don't have to do this."

I looked out the windows across from us, not that there was much to see. "I vaguely remember someone once telling me that the Gods work through people. I may not have much in the way of faith, but it couldn't hurt."

Silver stared at me for a moment and then laughed. "Never thought you'd be the one to give me a faith lesson." He squeezed my hand. "And giving me back one of my own on top of it."

I shrugged. "At least you know I was listening."

He brought my hand to his mouth, kissing it lightly. "M'lady."

I rolled my eyes. "Ugh. Don't start that far back."

8

LEXI TAPPED the side of the keyboard with her nail. "Ketayl's right. I don't know how you would quantify something like that. I mean, you've got the loners who might be easy, but what about that other guy? He and Matt were planning a trip to the Northern Isles, but we don't know what his financial problems were specifically. And then there's Patrice who was desperate enough to consider it despite having young children and family."

"I'm not sure if what Matt said about the trip was true or if he was just flirting with her," Silver countered. He muttered something under his breath.

Lexi gaped at him openly, but said nothing.

"Um..." I started since the conversation had died. Both of them turned toward me. "This is a stupid question, but do I really have an accent?" It had been nagging at the back of my mind since Matt commented on it.

Lexi shrugged. "It's usually barely there. I tend to hear it on specific words. Though it was thicker that night for some reason."

Silver smirked. "It usually gets thicker when she's tired or stressed. It's the couple of instances I hear it more. When you take her to the Northern Isles it's all you hear. Or when I mess with her enough to get it to come out. Granted, she's usually mad at me."

"Wait, what?" When had he done that?

Lexi laughed quietly, trying to hide behind her hand.

Silver grinned at me and shrugged. "I can't help it. I like hearing it."

I rolled my eyes and shook my head. "Let's get back on topic." Even though I was the one who started it. In the long run it mattered none, but now I knew to stay alert for when Silver decided he wanted to pry it out.

"Well," Lexi started and paused. She blew the strands of hair that had fallen from her messy bun out of her face. "I can give it a try, but our sample size is too small to have a decent chance of this working."

"I'll see about getting more," Silver said.

I bit my lower lip, unsure of where I could be of use. "I can help with sifting through information."

"Don't forget to check in," Silver reminded.

I rolled my eyes. So far, I had been able to get away with messages, but eventually the main office was going to want a video call. "I know. I know."

Silver patted my head and I swatted his hand away.

"By the way, nice handling that guy earlier," Lexi said. "You were far nicer than I would have been."

"What guy?" Silver looked at me, crossing his arms.

I cringed. Why did Lexi have to say anything? "Frank followed me. I lost him."

My partner frowned. "You should have told me. We need to report this to Ayda."

I shook my head. "It's not hard to lose him. He's been following you also."

"Not just you two," Lexi said quietly. "I've smelled someone following me so I'm assuming it was him, but I think he gave up when he realized I wasn't going out on the case."

I frowned. Frank was becoming a problem. If it was only me, then it would not matter as I could easily lose him. Lexi could outrun him, but Silver stood out and was oblivious to his presence.

"You and I are going to talk to Ayda tomorrow." Silver looked directly at me.

I sighed. This would likely get me in trouble.

"Okay, I'll deal with him," Ayda said, sitting back in her chair and crossing her arms. "I know he's been poking into your personnel files, but I assumed it was harmless given how limited his access is."

"Could he have gotten deeper than the general information?" Silver asked.

The Elven woman shook her head. "Frank may be a damn good agent in the field, but I have to fight with him to get him to submit his reports electronically. The only reason I know he was in your records was because I helped him. Thought maybe it would put his mind at ease knowing more about the people who had taken over the case."

Silver and I looked at each other and shrugged. It was a good idea on Ayda's part, but apparently not effective enough to deter Frank.

"I don't even know what's in mine," I admitted. "But he knew I had been on limited duty until recently."

"The trouble is I don't have any cases for him right now to keep him occupied. This area tends to need people who can follow a digital trail and that's not Frank," Ayda said. "Let me talk with him and I'll be looking into my options on how to deal with him. If nothing else, I can tie him up with trainings."

Silver stood. "We appreciate it."

I bowed to Ayda.

"Ketayl?"

I turned back to Ayda. She was now leaning forward in her chair.

"Frank came back muttering about you being scary. Is there something I should know about? You didn't cast anything against him, did you?"

I shook my head. "I told him he was pissing me off and left."

She forced a smile and waved us out the door. Dammit, I should have been more careful.

Silver remained silent until we were back in our loaner vehicle. "What really happened with Frank?"

I sighed. "He followed me, I caught him, we had some words, and then I lost him."

"Don't make me have Lexi show me the footage," Silver warned.

I took a deep breath. My answer should have been sufficient. "He followed me. I caught him. He wanted to know what I was because of what I did during our last encounter. I refused to give him the answer he wanted. He grabbed my arm and I teleported away from him and hid until he left."

My partner frowned. "Still rather summarized, but at least there's enough of a description now to explain why he thinks you're scary. You probably should have kept your power in-check the first time."

I raised an eyebrow at my partner. "I ran away. Wouldn't that make me a coward?"

Silver shook his head. "It's better to pick your fights."

"This coming from you?" What had I missed in the past few months? Just when I thought things might settle back to the way they were, something new came up.

"I never said I was any good at it." Silver flipped the tail of his braid back and forth with one hand as he drove. "It does bother me that Frank is following all of us."

I bit my lower lip for a moment. "I'm more concerned he might get in over his head. If we're dealing with an actual necromancer, he would be sorely unprepared for it."

"Another reason to get him to leave us alone. Tell me about that lead you followed again." Silver flipped the end of his braid back and forth.

I bit my lower lip. Silver would bring up my failure. "Her sister burned the piece of paper with the information. Patrice has two small children and she was desperate enough to try and convince herself this was the path to take. I was thinking about catching up with the person who gave it to her."

My partner hummed for a moment. "I'll stop by the store again and see if I can't come back with something. I assume it was her children she was having a hard time giving up."

"Yeah. Likely her sister also. No husband. Apparently, he had left her in a dire situation financially." Her situation was not even of her doing.

"He was the one who caused all the financial problems? Is he alive?" my partner asked.

"No."

"Well, there goes the idea of chasing him down," Silver pouted. "Granted, it wouldn't be our hunt, but it could have proven entertaining scaring him into taking responsibility."

I raised an eyebrow at him. "Sometimes I wonder about you."

Silver laughed. "Only sometimes? I've been slacking."

9

"Lexi, have you gotten anything else on the store clerk?" I asked when we returned.

She turned to look at us. "Oh, hey. Not exactly, but I was taking a look at the death certificates. They're filled out almost identically depending on the group. There's only a few different people who have signed off on them and I thought you'd find this interesting." She turned one of the larger screens toward us.

I bent down to see and Silver leaned on me. I turned to look at him. "Really?"

My partner just smirked at me.

"Pain in the ass."

"Exactly." He sounded far too happy about it.

I rolled my eyes and returned my attention to the screen. It was a spreadsheet with the information. It was right there: all of the struggling accounts were signed off under one name and the high-grade accounts had three different people signing off. Each one corresponding to a particular region.

"We need to talk to these people who are signing off," Silver said, standing up. "Figure out why they look so similar."

Finally. I stood up and glared at my partner. I may be significantly shorter than him, but he had been pushing it.

Lexi bit her lower lip for a moment. "There's a problem with that idea at the moment."

I raised an eyebrow at her.

"I can't find them. Frankly, I'm not sure any of them actually exists. I'm still exhausting all of my avenues."

I bit the tip of my thumb for a moment before looking up at Silver. Maybe he had an idea.

He shrugged. "Are they being signed out of a particular facility? I could go check it out."

Lexi handed over a piece of paper. "This is for the struggling accounts. I don't think there's anything there though. Looks like warehouses."

I pinched the bridge of my nose. "It would be warehouses," I muttered.

"You are definitely not going now," Silver said.

"What? Why not?" I put my hands on my hips.

"I think we both remember Mystic Port," he said.

"Hey, I was right about there being something going on. I can be of help," I argued.

Silver shook his head. "Not this time. Especially not if Frank might be following us. Can I count on you to create a distraction for him while I go check out the area?"

I scrunched up my face. "You're better at causing a distraction. I can lose him easily."

"I'll cause a distraction for you if you don't stop arguing with me," Silver snapped.

I stood up straight, clenching my hands by my sides. Was he really going to play that card? We stared at each other for several long seconds. "Yes, sir," I ground out and went to my room.

"Wait, isn't she..." Lexi started.

"Not now. Give her some time," Silver said softly.

"No. Hells no. Whatever it was you did was horrible. You know I can smell people's emotions and... and..." Lexi paused, sounding upset. "I'm going out."

"Lexi, wait!" he called after her.

The door opened and closed sharply.

I stood in the room I shared with Lexi, facing away from the door, my hands still balled up into fists. I was shaking and I could not stop it. I wished Lexi voiced what she could smell from me. Then at least I would know what I was feeling because I could not make sense of it.

I jumped when strong arms wrapped around me from behind - one across my shoulders and the other across my stomach. "Let go of me," I warned.

Silver rested his head next to mine. "Not until you hear me out."

"I don't need to hear you out. You made yourself perfectly clear." I attempted to wiggle my way free, but he held on tighter.

"In the worst way possible," he countered. "I know how much the incidents in Mystic Port affected you. I'm not going to drag you along on a possible ghost chase when I don't have to. All I plan on doing is driving by and seeing if it may be worth looking into further."

My shoulders slumped. "You should have said that to start."

"Yeah, well, I'm good at pissing people off and look, I got my whole team at once." Silver continued to hold onto me. "I'm so sorry. You should be the one leading the team, not me. You made it look so easy and I thought I could give you the break you needed this time."

I sighed and then a thought crossed my mind. "What if we invite Frank to help us?"

"What? Where did that come from?" Silver finally let me go. He turned me around to face him. "By the grace of the Gods, I'm so sorry." He gently wiped my face.

I had been crying? I shook my head and walked away from him, rubbing my face on my sleeve. "If he's this obsessed with the case, why not use him instead? He's supposedly good at hitting the streets and gathering information and he knows this area far better than we do. If you can stop fighting with him, I can't see why not."

Silver grinned. "I think I can behave." He stroked my hair. "Let me make a few calls. I'm going to transfer lead back to you. I hope you don't mind."

I shrugged. The title meant little to me. Being able to actually act meant more. I knew I would still be doing a lot of desk work, but I would not be tied down.

He ruffled my bangs and I swatted at him. I really did not get him sometimes, but at least we stopped fighting. Now I needed to get my team pulled back together.

"While you do that, I'll track down Lexi," I ordered.

"Yes, ma'am."

"Don't start that again." I brushed past him. Tracking down a werewolf might prove difficult. I pulled out my phone and sent her a message, hoping she responded to me. First the team and then the case. I could do this.

FOLLOWING the directions Lexi sent me, I caught up with her at a fence along the water overlooking the harbor. "Are you okay?" I asked.

She turned to me with a forced smile. "I should be asking you that."

I shrugged and stood next to her. "Silver can be a jerk, but we ironed out the problem."

"You forgive me if I don't believe everything is fixed. Not with the way he's been acting this whole trip." Her words were clipped.

I sighed and pinched the bridge of my nose. "I wouldn't say everything is fixed, but... He should have said he wanted to do a quick scouting of the location before bringing me with him. He's also transferring lead back to me."

Lexi huffed. "I thought you were lead this whole time. He certainly doesn't act like one."

I pursed my lips. "It's complicated as to why our roles were reversed."

"At least I know you're okay, but... I can't believe he threatened you like that. I'm not even sure what exactly he was threatening you with."

I ran a hand through my bangs. "It doesn't matter what. He's being overprotective in the wrong ways. I think not working together for a while has us both off. I'm sorry you got caught in the middle of it."

Lexi shook her head. "Just know I'll back you."

Silence fell between us as I contemplated her words. While I appreciated the sentiment, I needed the team to trust each other.

"So, what's the plan from here?" Lexi asked.

I ran a hand over my hair. "I'm having Silver bring Frank onboard."

"Seriously?" she asked, her voice higher pitched than normal.

"If he won't leave us alone, we might as well use him. It'll be easier for us to make sure he doesn't get in over his head. The three of us have dealt with a necromancer before - he hasn't, and he'll be woefully unprepared for it."

With no warning, Lexi hugged me. "Thank you."

I froze for a moment before forcing myself to return the gesture. I trusted Lexi, but this still felt foreign to me. "For what?"

"Just being you." She pulled away and I noticed she was blushing. "You find a way for people to help even if they are annoying."

"You better not be thinking of yourself that way." I smiled and then turned back to look out over the harbor, leaning on the railing.

Lexi followed my movement, looking out over the water. "What do you need me to do?"

"Can you see if there's something unusual with the other locations that the death certificates have come from? I'm hoping maybe you'll find other death certificates with the same pattern that might have come from different banks in the process."

Lexi nodded. "It didn't look like much at quick glance and they're pretty far apart. I'll get a search running, but without names, it could take a while."

"Was there anything else unusual about the death certificates?"

She shook her head. "Nothing else other than circumstances of death were unknown and they died at their home address."

I bit my lower lip for a moment. "Those are places where it would not likely prompt an investigation. Is there a way to track back to where the certificates were entered?"

Lexi looked at me with wide eyes. "I hadn't considered that. I'll get on it." She turned to leave and I grabbed her arm. I let go immediately, unsure why I stopped her that way instead of with words.

I forced a smile. "How about we get something to eat first? We haven't talked much since you came to the main office."

Lexi smiled. "I'd like that."

As we were walking back from dinner, Silver sent me a message asking for me to meet him at the Sola branch office. I stopped and rolled my eyes.

"What?" Lexi asked.

"We need to go to the branch office. Ayda probably wants to see us about us requesting to have Frank on the team," I said.

She shifted from one foot to the other. "I can head back to the hotel and get started."

"No, come with me. It'll be good for our whole team to be there so Frank can understand his defined role in this. Provided he agrees of course. I don't suppose you can pull up his personnel file for me on the way there." I hoped she did not take my decision the same way she took Silver's before when he wanted all of us as a show of force.

"Oh, that's easy." Lexi pulled out her phone and fiddled with it as we walked. She deftly avoided people who would have walked into her and other obstacles.

I laughed lightly.

"What?"

"Just watching you navigate while having your nose in your phone."

She grinned broadly. "I can hear and smell most of it. I'm keeping track of you on the rest."

"It's still impressive."

"Here." Lexi handed me her phone as we got on the train. Then I noticed she stood between me and the crowd.

"Thanks."

She simply smiled at me and held on.

As stated before, Frank had an impressive record leading up to the technological revolution over the last decade or so. He started to become a problem and had gone through multiple partners after losing his long-time partner.

Lexi commented. "He's kind of a lone wolf, isn't he?"

"Yeah, but the chance to work on this case might make him more cooperative. Especially if we give him the right tasks." I handed her back her phone. "He did have a long-time partner though." And it had been a male Elf which made his use of racial slurs all the more confusing.

"You're always so kind."

I shook my head. People seemed to misunderstand my motivations. "Just delegating. You might be dealing with me more if I can get the men out into the field."

"That's fine by me. I'm not ready to forgive Silver yet." Lexi frowned.

I sighed and ignored her last comment. "I really want to go back through the information we have. I need to get a better idea of who we're dealing with."

Soon enough we were at the Sola branch office. Silver waited for us in Ayda's office along with Frank who stood watching us with his arms crossed.

"You surprised me with the request," Ayda said. "Especially after our previous conversation."

I shrugged. "It sounded like a better idea than butting heads the entire time and he knows the area better than we do."

Ayda raised an eyebrow at me. "Can't argue with that logic. You in, Frank?"

The man sneered. "Only because you have my case."

I stood in front of him. "If you join us, you take direction from us. No arguments. I won't risk someone against a necromancer. I've looked over your personnel file and you have no idea what you're dealing with if it is in fact a real one."

Frank raised an eyebrow. "I thought he was team lead." He jutted his chin toward Silver.

"Ketayl is better at managing a team," Silver said. "She filled in as head of the Ghost Forest branch and I've never seen someone else maximize the talent at her disposal. No offense, Ayda."

"None taken. You haven't been here enough to watch us," the Elven woman replied, "but I have been struggling to find a place for Frank. Maybe I can learn a thing or two."

"What do you want me to do?" Frank asked. "I need to know before I fully commit to this."

"I want you out there helping us find leads. Your personnel file suggests you excel in that area. You'll be coordinating with Silver."

Frank sneered. "I don't like him, but I'm in."

Most people seemed to have a problem with Silver lately. That was a different problem I was likely going to have to deal with sooner or later.

Ayda sighed in what sounded like relief. "Thank the Heavens," she muttered. "First thing tomorrow morning, report to them. Go on, head home, Frank."

Frank brushed past me and I turned my head to watch him leave.

"Ketayl, may I have a word in private?" Ayda asked.

I nodded and signaled for the other two to step out.

As soon as we were alone, Ayda asked, "Frank has a point. I thought Silver was lead."

I took a deep breath. "He was, but he transferred it back to me."

"Why?" She sat back in her chair and crossed her arms. "Not that I'm complaining. In this short meeting, I definitely got the sense you're better suited to it, but there had to have been a reason he gave it up now."

"We had a misunderstanding. It's cleared up." That was as much as I wanted to say.

She raised an eyebrow at me. "Obviously there's more to it, but I'll leave it alone. I'm surprised you brought Lexi with you."

"We had been out grabbing something to eat when Silver messaged me. I also thought it would be a good idea for Frank to understand that this is a team. I noticed he has had problems with working with others."

Ayda smiled, but it did not reach her eyes. "Yeah, he hasn't been the same since Tef transferred. I've just been letting him ride this out until retirement. He doesn't want to go anywhere else either - Sola's been his home his entire career. Though with this... you do have a way with people. Not many could head the Ghost Forest branch. Especially on as short of notice as you had."

I raised an eyebrow at her.

She raised her hands defensively. "I couldn't help it. After Silver called me with the idea you had, I had to look."

I laughed lightly. "It's okay."

"Good luck keeping Frank in line. Let me know if you need any help."

I bowed. "Thank you."

10

"So, you want me to hit the streets with this guy," Frank spat as he thumbed at Silver, "and interview people who knew the deceased account holders to see if we can get a lead?" He leaned against the wall in our hotel suite, looking at the three of us.

"Yes, Lexi has provided Silver with a list to work from," I said.

"The list is mostly people who knew the deceased, but I've been able to track down a few who are supposed to be dead. I'm still running facial recognition," Lexi chimed in.

Silver crossed his arms and looked at me. "And as much as you're not going to like it, I want to check out the facility Lexi found. Nothing more than preliminary scouting."

I nodded. After our meeting with Frank last night, Silver had decided to push it off. We also had that store clerk to catch up with.

Frank stood up fully. "What facility?"

Right, I needed to catch him up fully to where we were. "It's a building the death certificates for the struggling accounts originated from. Lexi, are you still tracking back the file origin?" I could at least give him this much and hoped Silver filled in the rest.

She sighed. "Whoever it was knows how to cover their tracks. I've asked for some backup from the rest of the cyber team. I'll let you know when we've got something."

I frowned, but there was no helping it.

"And what are you going to do little lady?" Frank asked looking directly at me.

I raised an eyebrow at him. "I'm going to keep piecing together the puzzle from our files. I may have another direction for the two of you to pursue. I'm still getting the feeling we're dealing with two separate people - one handling the struggling accounts and the other for the high-grade."

Lexi pursed her lips and sat back in her chair, crossing her legs at her ankles. "It does seem that way with how the death certificates were handled."

"One more thing," Frank said. "I need to know the people I'm working with. You hide it well." He pointed at me. "But you two I can tell are something else beyond a divine investigator and part of the cyber team."

Silver rolled his eyes and flexed his left arm, his shield appearing. "Paladin." Then the shield disappeared and he crossed his arms, staring down at Frank.

Lexi and I looked at each other. "Um..." she started. "I'm a werewolf."

Frank stopped and stared at her. "Interesting combination." He pointed between her and her setup.

Lexi ducked her head.

I took a deep breath as Frank turned his attention to me. I looked at Silver. There was no way out of this. "Arcanist."

Frank stood up straighter, narrowing his eyes at me. "What now?"

"It's the reason I cast at a high speed with little need for incantations. I used a set of spells to lose you," I admitted.

"So why the lot of you?" Frank asked.

Silver spoke before I could. "The three of us have dealt with necromancers before. Since they are casters of both divine and arcane, Ketayl and I are the team who deals with them. We'll pull on others as needed and Lexi's skills were required for this one."

Frank raised an eyebrow. "Well then. It seems like I'll get something out of this venture after all. Let's go, boy."

My partner stopped and looked at Frank and then us before turning back to our newest team member. "You know I'm about your age, right?" he pointed out.

"Still look and act like a kid to me. Let's get to it," Frank said firmly.

Silver looked at us and then at Frank who was heading out the door. "What did you get me into?"

"Get going." I waved for him to follow our new team member.

Lexi snickered at Silver shut the door behind him.

"Shall we?" I asked Lexi once it was just the two of us.

She grinned broadly. "Let's put them to shame."

I settled down with my tablet and got to work. I lost track of time until a message came in from one of the doctors from the main office. I rolled my eyes and switched over to it, noting I had been at this for hours with nothing new so far.

The message told me a place the doctor wanted me to go to and take an exercise class. The time and location were listed out. *Why now? Why this?* I knew better than to ignore them, but I would still mentally curse at them for interrupting me.

Part of me wondered if it was because of something Silver reported. The idea hurt to think about, but could I truly be mad at him if he was following orders?

I hung my head. They really wanted to interrupt me in the middle of the investigation. I had begun treating it as two separate individuals and started getting a better idea of who we were dealing with on the struggling side. The high-grade accounts I still could not get a good grasp on.

Sighing, I got up to plug my tablet in and noticed Lexi was gone. *She probably went to get something to eat.* I gathered my things and left with no note. *I shouldn't be long. Maybe I'll get back before her.*

I considered bringing my tablet with me so I could keep working, but I had no idea if I would be able to store it safely during this class. They might be able to tear me away from being able to access the case file, but it would not stop me from going over the information so far in my head.

Or at least that was how I wanted to justify turning this forced break around. My mind however kept wondering if it was because of Silver. He seemed content with the changes I made yesterday. *It could have been my fault. I've only been down to the pool a few times. The doctors would have noticed the lack of activity in my reports.*

I WALKED out of the class with Karen Lockheed, the COO of First Union. The encounter had been unexpected for both of us.

"Just don't tell Will and Joran I teach these classes on the side - I'll never hear the end of it." She laughed. "There are days I swear if I could do only this, I would. In any case, I'm glad you dropped in."

Once we reached the area where I had stored my things, I bowed to her. "I quite enjoyed your class, thank you." It was much different than the similar ones at the main office. I picked up my small bag.

Karen followed me. "I'm so glad to hear it. I'll also refrain from asking anything about the case, but I know the other two are anxious for an update."

I bit my lower lip for a moment. "I'll let Silver know, though I'm not sure what we have managed so far is worth taking time out of your day."

Karen laughed. "I wouldn't mind. And as for the other two, the only thing you'll probably take them away from is putting golf balls around their offices. Don't get me wrong, they do a lot for the company, but I've caught them a few too many times. Though as long as that's the worst of it, I can't complain."

I smiled. "Silver throws pens to try and stick them in the ceiling when he's bored. I need to find him something less destructive."

"Talking about me when I'm not around?"

I stopped and turned to see Silver sitting in a chair in the lobby. "What are you doing here?"

Silver frowned at me. "We went back to give you an update and you were gone."

I bit my lower lip. "Sorry, I thought I'd be back before anyone noticed."

Karen laughed. "Anyway, it was a pleasure having you in my class. Feel free to come back any time. I normally teach nights and week-ends, but I needed to fill-in for someone who is out sick."

I bowed to her. "Thank you again." I silently followed Silver out the door. It seemed no matter what I did, I found myself in trouble with someone.

Once we were a distance away, Silver growled at me, "What in the Hells was that?"

I bit my lower lip. "I was ordered to come to this class by the main office. It was a coincidence I ran into her."

"And what did you tell her of what we're working on?" he snapped.

I stopped and stared at my partner's back. What was going on here? "Nothing. She only told me that we should consider scheduling a meeting to give them an update soon."

Silver stopped and turned, glaring me down. Then he sighed and dropped his arms to the side. "Okay, I get it. Just leave a note next time or something. Lexi was so worried about what happened to you she had pinpointed your location and was heading out the door when Frank and I got back."

"Sure." I caught back up with him. "Update?" I hoped a change of topic would ease the tension.

He tugged on his braid. "The store clerk is in custody but isn't talking. As for the location we scouted out... there was a lot of death at that place."

I raised my eyebrow at him.

Silver showed me a picture on his phone.

I could see all the way to the ceiling in the image and the back of the warehouse. Stalls of fish on ice were in neat rows. "A fish market? Any chance there was some place they could have hidden something there? Extra rooms or a basement?"

Silver shook his head. "Frank is really good at collecting information - you were right to bring him on-board. No extra rooms and the floor is completely cemented. There is nothing which looks like an outside entrance to a lower level, not that they would want to build below because it's all water underneath."

I pinched the bridge of my nose and groaned. A dead end. I held out hope that someone could get something out of the store clerk, but I wondered how long we could hold onto him given that he now existed under a different identity.

"We checked out the surrounding warehouses, but there was no hint of something hiding there," Silver continued.

I folded my arms. "Well, the certificates didn't originate there. I hope it's simply someone's twisted sense of humor using that place."

Silver grinned. "Probably. I thought about bringing something back, but Frank said he didn't want the fish smelling up his car."

I rolled my eyes. *Ever the child.* We walked for a minute in silence. "Where's Frank?" I asked.

Silver tugged on his braid for a moment. "We decided to split up to cover more ground. Apparently, I call unwanted attention to myself."

That was not what I wanted to hear. "We shouldn't let him go off on his own. It will likely be dangerous if he goes too far."

Silver continued to tug on his braid. "We had a long talk about the dangers. He promised only to find leads and report in, but he's going to want in when we go to arrest the necromancer."

I blew out an exasperated breath. That put me in a precarious position - I did not want anyone from the Sola office in the line of fire. As it was, I wanted to leave Lexi behind as well.

"I know, I know. It was the best I could come up with as a compromise to keep him relatively safe. It's going to be a pain babysitting him when we go after the necromancer." He tugged even harder on his braid and I put my hand over his to get him to stop. I had never seen him this stressed out. My leaving for the class without any notice only added to it. He needed a break, but how to get him to take one?

I huffed. "Maybe we should take Lexi along as well. She could keep him in line."

Silver stroked the small patch of hair on his chin. "That's a good idea, actually."

"Good timing," Lexi said as we walked back into the hotel suite. "We finally were able to track the death certificates for the struggling accounts all the way back to the source. Still working on the high-grade accounts."

"Where?" I asked, putting my bag down on the counter.

"An electronics shop on the other side of town." Lexi pulled up an image of the store.

My partner folded his arms and smirked. "At least it's conveniently located for us."

"Silver, find Frank and do a preliminary scouting of the area. Do not engage. Lexi and I will work on what we can from here," I ordered.

He smirked and bowed before heading out without a word.

I breathed a sigh of relief at the lack of argument from him before I turned to Lexi. "Alright, what can you get me on this place? Employees, hours of operation, anything you think is important."

"I can get you right down to their bathroom breaks if you give me enough time," she said flatly.

"Okay, maybe not quite that detailed."

Lexi laughed.

I stood up and put my hands on my hips. "In any case, I doubt there's a necromancer hiding in an electronics shop, but I'd rather not take any chances. I'd prefer to involve as few people as possible."

Lexi pursed her lips for a moment. "I think it's a hacker who is killing people in the system and giving them new identities. On the off-chance he really is killing some of them, if I can get on scene, I can search for the bodies. Provided he's dumb enough to kill at the store."

I took a deep breath and prepared myself for the possible argument I was going to get from her. "You're going with us, but you're not going to like your task."

She sat up straight with wide eyes, bouncing lightly in her chair. "Really? I can go? What task?"

I took a deep breath. "You're going to have to keep an eye on Frank."

"Ugh." Lexi dropped her head back. "What'd I do to make you mad at me?"

"Nothing, but I don't have anyone else to make sure he stays safe and out of the way. Sorry." I cringed. I disliked putting her in this position.

"Fine. At least I get to go." Lexi pouted.

I laughed lightly. "I guess I should file the request for a search warrant."

"Um..." Lexi paused and looked down. "I may have overstepped my position, but I already put in the request with Lockonis since we had enough evidence."

I stopped and stared at her. "Good work. Thanks for doing that."

She looked up and smiled broadly at me. It seemed to take little to make her happy.

"I guess all that's left for me is to inform Ayda." That meant I was heading right back out the door.

"And form a plan."

"I need information first." I pointed at her computer.

"Of course."

I picked up my keys and my bag.

"Um..." Lexi started. "Crap, I don't know what to do here."

I raised an eyebrow at her. "What do you mean?" I gave her clear instructions.

She bit her lower lip. "It's something Silver asked of me. He didn't want you going out on your own. While I would ignore him, he made a valid case."

I rolled my eyes. "Seriously?"

Lexi nodded slowly, her head dipped down.

"Overprotective, childish, complete obnoxious pain..." I muttered in my dialect of common, trailing off the other thoughts that came to mind. I had an idea of what would happen if I ignored Silver's request. I also needed to keep Lexi out of trouble.

"That didn't sound nice." Lexi giggled.

I sighed. Maybe I could bargain. "Listen, I'm just going to the branch office to talk to Ayda and let her know we're going to be taking action soon. Track me if you need to."

She bit her lower lip. "Can you wait until we have a plan in place? You might as well save a trip."

I dropped my bag and my keys, putting my hands up defensively. "Okay, you win. You'd be able to hunt me down anyway."

Lexi smiled. "It's not as easy as you'd think if you don't have your devices on you and if you teleported. I'd have no trail to follow - virtual or physical - and would have to circle out."

"Alright, enough. Get me the information." Most of my team was being overprotective. It was making it difficult to get anything done.

"Yes, ma'am."

11

"THE PLANS for the electronics shop shows a full basement," Lexi said. "From what I can gather, the owner, Gregory Cummins, goes downstairs after the shop closes. He's usually there for a couple of hours. Sometimes longer."

"He could be working on repairs," I said.

"True, but he's met with people after hours. Another interesting fact is he worked for First Union in the IT department up until about a year ago. That's when he opened this shop." She sat back in her chair and looked at us.

"Could have just wanted to open up his own business," Frank pointed out. "Some people like being their own boss."

Lexi nodded, bringing up more information for us. "That's true and I can't tell you what it was like working for them, but with their salary and benefits package, it's hard to see anyone wanting to leave that."

"He could have been forced to resign," Silver offered.

I sighed. "This is getting off-track. Have you gotten information on who he's met with?"

She shook her head. "Not yet anyway. I'm still running facial recognition, but I don't know how well that's going to work. Many of his after-hours clients wore hoods, hats, or scarves and never looked directly up at the cameras. He has no cameras for downstairs. The best I'm hoping for is a partial at this point."

Frank folded his arms and leaned back against the wall. "We need better evidence before we barge in there. Never liked going in on suspicion of activity."

Silver looked as if he wanted to argue.

I cut him off. "While we have confirmation that this is the location, I agree. If we can get at least one person on the list who met with him, I'll take it. Otherwise, we'll have to start looking at the other employees."

"The hard part is whatever computer this person is using to generate the death certificates and give them new identities is offline most of the time. Only reason we found him was he popped on recently. They managed to gather some digital evidence, but he's got Hells of an encryption on his files and they haven't broken it yet," Lexi said, "but at least we know that the system that created the death certificates is in this building. Or at the very least, they used this location."

"I'm not sure how much time we're going to have if this person finds out the cyber team found them." I pursed my lips and looked at Silver. "Should you and I still go in first?"

He nodded. "I don't want to chance anyone else on the assumption that he's not also an actual necromancer as much as this seems otherwise."

"Alright, let me know when you get a hit on facial recognition," I told Lexi. "Any chance he's onto us?"

She shook her head. "Not likely. Lockonis was the one who found him and she can be silent when she wants to. Granted, most of the time she likes to fry the other person's computer."

My boss confused me sometimes, but it was good to know she was the one who found him.

I SAT SILENTLY in the passenger seat next to Silver while we waited for Lexi and Frank to get in position by the back door. The store was going to close up shortly and we figured it would be the best time to do the search and not scare any customers, provided he was not expecting after hours clients. Without knowing Gregory's likely reaction, I wanted to limit potential issues.

"Can I scare him?" Silver asked.

I sat up straighter. "What?" *Where did that come from?*

My partner grinned broadly. "Can I scare him? It might make him easier to deal with."

I rolled my eyes. "Save it for the interrogation room, please."

"Where you won't be."

"Exactly." I would probably watch, but I learned while we were in Ghost Forest to not be in the room with him.

Silver laughed lightly. "So how do you want to handle this?"

"Try to get in by being a last-minute customer and then show him the papers?" I offered. "Then at least we'd be inside."

My partner made a face. "You lie to him then. I'll follow silently. What if he resists?"

"Glass store-front. I can see enough to teleport inside." I pointed at the building.

Silver grinned. "Ah, the thief shows her face."

I frowned and turned away from my partner. "That wasn't funny."

"Sorry." Silver ran his hand over my hair. "I only meant to tease you."

I took a deep breath. "I know, but…" That hit a little too close to home and he should have known that.

"Hey, remember that if it's from me, there's no malice behind it."

"We're in place." Frank's voice came over the line.

I breathed a sigh of relief. "Let's go." I got out of the vehicle without waiting for a reply. I needed to focus on the here and now, not the past.

Gregory approached the door and I hustled to get over there before he could lock it.

"Hey! Could you help me?" I called out to him.

"Sorry, lady, I'm closed for the day." Gregory's eyes darted behind me where I heard Silver approaching.

"It'll be quick," I pleaded. It looked like playing the last-minute customer might not work.

Gregory shook his head. "Come back tomorrow."

Frowning, I held up the paper. "This says I can come in now."

Gregory pulled the door shut and by the time he got the lock, I had teleported in. He turned and froze when he saw me sitting on his counter.

Silver stood outside the door grinning before violently shaking it. "Our target is running. I'm locked out, but Ketayl is inside." I heard him say over my headset.

"That wasn't very nice. You know doing that could get you in trouble, right?" I tilted my head at him. I was enjoying this too much. I needed to be more professional.

Gregory charged, shoving me. I fell backwards off the counter. He ran for the door to the basement.

As I hit the floor, I heard Silver ram the door. Metal groaned loudly and glass cracked at the impact.

I rubbed my head as I started to sit up. Lexi pulled me to my feet. "Go let Silver in and secure this floor," I ordered. "I'm going after him."

"Wait, you can't go alone," Lexi said.

I had made my way to the door to the basement. "Silver will back me up."

Frank shook his head and had already moved to let Silver in who punched the door, causing it to shake violently. "He pissed her off, kid. He's got to deal with her now."

I pushed my way through the door to the basement. I ran down the stairs after Gregory. While the storefront was not overly large, the basement was. It was partitioned off. I was unable to see around the corner where I heard someone.

When I sensed Silver come up behind me, I held up my hand for him to stop. Gathering arcane energy in my hands, I slowly crept along the wall, peeking around the corner.

Gregory typed quickly at one of the computers in the area. Information scrolled past on the six screens mounted to the wall at a dizzying speed. Why not run? What was so important he ran to where there was no exit?

There was a tug on my leg and cylindrical metal object was placed in my hand behind me. I turned and looked down.

Silver had put my shrunken staff in my hand. "You need that," he whispered in my ear.

I sighed and let go of the gathered arcane energy from my hands. Time to get this over with. I stepped out from where I hid. The soft metallic sound of my staff releasing caused Gregory to turn around.

Gregory grabbed a large weapon he had sitting on the counter next to him and turned sharply, pointing it at me. It had three claw-like protrusions around a large barrel and was big enough he had to hold it with both hands. He shook as he looked at me.

"There's no need for that," Silver said calmly. He took up a place near the wall we had hidden behind, blocking the only exit. He wore his full armor and had his sword and shield out.

"Don't you understand? I'm helping people. Can't you just leave me be?" Gregory kept alternating which one of us he aimed his weapon at.

"You may be helping people," Silver said, "but you're still breaking the law."

"Enough of this," I muttered, drawing arcane energy to my free hand.

Gregory turned to me and fired. A blue orb came flying at me. I froze. All I could see was the blue orb the pirates forced me to use over and over. Repeatedly being stuck in that system until Silver broke me out. Always wondering if it was the last time he would be able to free me.

The next thing I knew, Silver stood in front of me, a golden shield surrounded us. "Dammit, snap out of it, Ketayl! It's not the same!"

I shook my head and clenched my teeth. I ran at Gregory, transforming the energy in my hand into electricity.

Gregory managed to dodge me at the last second and I hit his computer. Screens exploded and the smell of burnt circuitry rose while I turned my staff on him. He fell to the ground, his back into the corner.

I held my staff near his throat, electricity sparking along it.

Silver grabbed my shoulder, pulling me back. I struggled to remain where I was until he got between me and Gregory. "Stop. He's down. You scared him enough to make him wet himself."

I lowered my staff and took stock of the whimpering wet mess on the floor before me. This guy was the necromancer? Something was wrong here.

Silver eyed me carefully before pushing a button on his headset. "Frank, can you call in a request to pick this guy up and take him back to the office?"

"Already did. Their ETA is about 5 minutes," Frank replied.

"Thanks." Silver turned to me. "Go over by the wall."

"Why?" I snapped.

My partner glared down at me. "Because I don't need you scaring him enough for him to soil himself too."

I sighed and did as he asked. I had just made my position much more precarious. When had I become so short-tempered?

Silver grabbed my arm as I went to walk away. "We'll talk about this later." His voice was even, making it impossible to gauge his thoughts. "Now go."

I lowered my head as I retreated to the wall. Coming here had been a mistake.

AYDA and a few others from the Sola office took Gregory away.

Lexi frowned as she looked at the system I had damaged in the fight. "I'm not sure if I can recover anything from this."

I hung my head. "Sorry. It's my fault," I whispered.

"Do you two mind collecting evidence down here. I need to talk to Ketayl privately," Silver said.

"Yeah, sure. There might be something I can find," Frank replied.

Silver waved for me to head upstairs ahead of him. I knew I was done for at this point. There was no rationalizing my way out of my rash behavior.

The backroom was small and overloaded with electronics in various stages of repair. I headed for one of the chairs in the room.

Large hands on my shoulders stopped me and Silver turned me around to face him. The next thing I knew, I was being held in a tight hug. "I'm sorry," he whispered.

"What?" What was going on here? I had expected a stern lecture at the very least.

"I saw the same thing you did, but I wasn't the one who was abused daily with that Gods-forsaken orb on the pirate ship. I should've stayed closer to you down there."

I shook thinking about it.

Silver stroked my hair. "Let it out. I'm not going anywhere."

"I... I..." I clenched my fists, refusing to give in. "The job isn't done yet. I'll deal with it later."

"We both know you won't." Silver's voice was flat.

I took a deep breath and repeated, "The job isn't done yet. I'll deal with it later."

"Exactly. The job isn't done, but you need to take care of yourself otherwise you won't be able to finish."

"I hate your logic sometimes," I muttered, tears already forming.

Silver laughed lightly. "You've told me that before. Just let it out. We've got more to talk about still." He rubbed the back of my neck. I had not realized how much I missed this. How much I needed this.

The tears fell and continued for a while. Silver held me silently.

I sniffled. "You're going to have to report this, aren't you?"

"This right here? No. How you reacted during the fight, yes, but I can keep it factual. Besides, I doubt anyone actually pays attention when I submit reports."

"You're not calling it in?" What was he doing ignoring orders? Was it ignoring orders? Knowing Silver, he was walking a fine line.

He shrugged. "I don't see a reason to, but we do need to talk about it."

I sighed, moving away from Silver, rubbing my eyes. "Sorry. And if it makes you feel better, I read your reports."

He smiled softly. "You're probably the only one then outside of direct requests."

I took a seat on the chair in the room and hung my head. "I suppose now is when you have to come down on me."

Silver squatted down to be more at my level. "I'd be a hypocrite if I did. I wanted to kill him, but we need him alive. You managed to literally scare the piss out of him before I made a move."

I pinched the bridge of my nose. "I wasn't trying for that. I damaged our evidence reacting the way I did."

"Let Lexi and the cyber team work on that. She'll dismantle it and send it back."

I took a deep breath, bringing my focus back to the case. "I assume you want to interrogate him."

"Of course." Those words sounded far too excited at the moment. "Now I have to at least scare the piss out of someone to match your intimidation levels."

I raised an eyebrow at Silver. He snorted and we both started laughing. I tried to hide my amusement behind my hand.

"Okay, let's go see how they're doing downstairs," Silver said.

I shook my head. "I'll be down in a little while - I'm probably a mess."

Silver shook his head. "You've had enough time to clear up." He strode toward me and took my face in his hands, wiping away whatever was on my cheeks. "There. Good to go."

"Thanks." I tried to force a smile but did not have the energy for it. Then I followed Silver back downstairs.

"Well, I found a ledger," Frank said as we arrive. "He made good money off these people. It looks like he was getting into weapons development also, but if he sold anything, I can't find anything about it."

"Gregory does have an engineering background as well as IT. It's weird though that he kept his records on paper instead of electronically," Lexi commented.

I tilted my head, considering the reasons one would do that. "It'd be easier to hide paper."

Frank put the bagged ledger in a box. "Girl's got a point."

"So, instead of a mortgaged house, these people decided on mortgaged mortality?" Silver asked.

I pursed my lips. "I assume it would be a one-time payment. Gets rid of all of their other debts and gives them a chance to start over. I wonder how far he went in creating new identities for these people."

"Some were payment plans, but pretty much one last payment, yeah," Frank said.

I bit my lower lip. "Okay, let's see what else we can find. How's the system?"

Lexi frowned. "I'll have to send this back. I don't have the tools here to attempt to recover anything."

I bit my lower lip. "I should probably cut back on using electric-based spells."

"At least around sensitive systems," Lexi tossed back, her words clipped.

I hung my head. "Sorry." It was another mark against me.

Silver came over to me with a smirk on his face. "It was worth it seeing that guy piss himself."

"Okay, okay. Back to work. We need to follow up on the other death certificates still." There was work to do and what Gregory said still bothered me. He begged for us to leave him be, but how much of his belief in being the good guy was an act? Without looking at the ledger, it was hard to decide on who preyed on these people more: him or the banks.

I found myself again wondering what it would be like to have a fresh start. It was common enough for Elves to have multiple careers over their lifespan, but I remained unsure if I could leave.

1 2

GREGORY KEPT SHIFTING in his seat, his eyes darting around the room. I stood on the other side of the one-way glass. Silver refused to let me in the room. I could have argued with him since I was team lead, but I also disliked being in a room when he interrogated someone. Even watching could get uncomfortable.

Part of me had wanted to let Frank interrogate him, but I gave it to Silver since he was my partner.

At least the Sola agents had given Gregory a change of clothes before we got back, though now he looked like a prison inmate.

I looked at my watch. "How long are you going to make me wait?" I asked, knowing Silver would hear me through the headset I wore. "Too much longer and I'm going to find Frank and take him with me to get this started."

"Someone's impatient," Silver replied, his tone teasing. "I'll be there shortly."

Lexi had dismantled the parts of the system she needed and was currently sending them off. Frank was busy going over the other evidence. I was the only one left with nothing to do. I fiddled with the headset - at least I could directly contact Silver without Gregory knowing about it.

Silver entered the room a few minutes later and took a seat across the table from Gregory. I could see both of their faces. My partner crossed his arms and leaned back in his chair, silently staring at the Human man. *He seems to be taking a calmer approach this time.*

Gregory fidgeted.

"Why do this?" Silver asked after a minute of silence.

"Why not?" Gregory answered, his words clipped. "The banks just take and take with no regard to whatever situation someone might be in. They give them no help to get back on track. I offered these people an out."

Silver raised an eyebrow at him. "You previously worked for First Union. A little hypocritical?"

"Okay, look, I was tasked to deal with these files of dead people. High-grade accounts. I came across some files I shouldn't have and I needed to leave before they found out. I took the idea of killing people to get them out of debt and used to help people who were struggling. I didn't literally kill anyone - just in the system. Give them a new identity and a new life. I think it's fair."

I raised an eyebrow at the information. He gave that up too easily. I jotted what he said down on my tablet. That would be the reason I thought there were two people. The one on the high-grade accounts bothered me though and I was unsure if we could get Gregory to talk further. *"Does he know anything else about the high-grade accounts?"* I asked Silver through the microphone, using my dialect of common.

Silver's eyes slid over to the window before he slammed his hand on the table. "And yet you exploited them for large sums of money to do it."

Don't tell me he didn't understand. I crossed my arms and frowned at the window, knowing no one else could see me. "Ask about the high-grade accounts," I restated.

Gregory jumped back in his chair. His hands being bound to the underside of the table was probably the only thing that kept him from falling over. "I... It was their last payment. I need to make money too."

"You had a store and it looks like you were developing weapons. Were you planning to sell those as well?" Silver snapped.

Silence filled the room again as Gregory opened and closed his mouth several times. "Lawyer."

"Yeah, you would go that route." Silver got up and left.

"Hey! Hey! You can't just leave me here like this! Hey!" Gregory yelled over and over.

After about a minute of that, he settled down again.

A few minutes later Silver entered the room with me. "At least he gave us something before he shut up."

I glared up at him. "You should've asked about those high-grade accounts. Something tells me he was less concerned about us know about them than the weapons he was developing."

"I know. I'm sorry. I got carried away on my train of thought. Though it looks like your instinct about there being two separate individuals was right." Silver tugged on his braid. "I'll try him again in an hour or so. Let him cool down, but I doubt he'll talk more."

I bit my lower lip. "I'm concerned the next one might be an actual necromancer."

"It could just be another guy like this." Silver waved his hand at Gregory who still sat chained to the table. "He said he first came across it while working at First Union."

"Possibly, but someone at the bank is obviously involved. It sounds like it might be a team effort." I folded my arms and stared at Gregory through the window.

My partner crossed his arms and turned his attention into the interrogation room as well. "Yeah. I think we need to have another talk with Tae. He might be able to shed some light on this."

"What can he possibly give us that he hasn't already?"

Silver tugged on his braid. "With the struggling accounts out of the way, we can focus on the high-grade. He might be able to see a pattern that neither of us would given our lack of a financial background."

I sighed. "Okay, call him."

———

"I can't really think of a reason anyone here would want high-grade accounts to fail." Tae sat back in his chair, folding his arms. "It's like asking to lose your job. If the bank fails, we're all out of work." They had been talking for a while again, but finally came back around to why we were here.

"Hm..." Silver looked over at me. "Any reason someone outside of the bank would want them to fail?"

Tae sat forward and tapped his finger on his desk. "Maybe, but it would be far-fetched. They could have taken a short position on the securities then relied on government insurance to collect big on the failure. I just don't know if it would be worth it in terms of monetary value because of the stability on these accounts. Investors want to make money. If it doesn't stay above the high-water mark, showing poor performance, they will lose on their investment - it's a gamble for the most part. Some people are good at reading the market. Personally, I prefer more stable options."

I rubbed my temple at the terms Tae tossed out. My head still spun in an attempt to make sense of what I just heard. *How has anyone figured out how to make money this way?*

"Collection from the government insurance would be a lump sum up front though, right?" Silver seemed to have a better grasp of how this worked than I did.

"True." Tae nodded. "It's excessive to set up a failure. Not without some other reward for the effort."

"Thank you for your time," Silver said, standing up. I followed his lead.

Tae shook his head, also standing. "I'm glad the last one was just some computer guy and not an actual necromancer. I wish I could have been of more help."

"You'd be surprised how much you gave us that we can use." Silver shook his hand and we left.

I chewed on what we heard on the way to the elevator. Tae said excessive, but if this was a team effort instead of just an individual, they would have more resources. Gregory had only been able to do so much by himself.

"Okay, what are you thinking?" Silver asked as we got to the elevators.

I bit my lower lip for a moment. "I think we need to see if we can find out who was working with Gregory before he left First Union."

Silver crossed his arms and looked down at me. "I think that's a question for Karen. Should we go up and see if we can get an appointment with her?"

I shrugged. "I doubt she'll be available." Though I was certain they would give us priority.

"Can't hurt to go talk to her secretary." Silver pressed the button to go up. "I'm sure she'll make the time. The bank is highly invested in this case."

I fidgeted with my hands as the elevator took us to the top floor. Silver put his hands over mine.

As we got off the elevator, Karen was at the front desk, talking to the receptionist. She looked at both of us. "Oh, hello. You here to bring us good news?"

"News at least," Silver said. "We wanted to schedule a meeting with you. We're going to need more information for this next stage."

Karen raised an eyebrow at us. "If now would be good, I can get the other two." This was a different Karen from the Karen who taught that class. I wondered if it was because of the setting.

Silver and I looked at each other. "We're already here," he said.

I nodded.

"Come with me. Those boys are probably doing nothing but putting golf balls around the office." Karen first showed us to the conference room we were in previously and left to get the other two.

A few minutes later, the CEO walked in with a big smile on his face. "I hope your being here is good news."

"In a way," Silver answered. "We found the person who had been taking advantage of the people with struggling accounts."

Karen folded her arms. "By your wording, we aren't out of the woods yet."

I shook my head. "This individual had previously worked for First Union in the IT department. He was using his skills to 'kill' people in the system and setting them up with new identities."

"For a price," Silver added. He could not seem to let that detail go.

"Wait... he worked for us?" Karen sat forward. She grabbed a nearby notepad and pen. "Who?"

"Gregory Cummins. He left the bank about a year ago," I paused and looked at Silver. How much should I be saying? We needed more information, but we were going to have to give to get.

Silver nodded at me.

I took a deep breath. "He informed us that he was tasked to deal with accounts of dead people and he had caught wind of what they were doing with the high-grade accounts. He decided to quit before they found out what he knew. Is there a chance we can find out who he worked with?"

"I want to know," Karen said sharply. "As soon as I have the information, I'll forward it along."

Joran raised an eyebrow at her. "She's on the hunt."

"I'm not getting in her way," the CEO said. "In any case, despite not being a full conclusion to our issue, you have brought us some good news. Any chance you happened to have recovered a list of who he dealt with?"

I shook my head. "Not at the moment. They're looking to see what they can recover."

"Recover?"

Silver put his hand on my leg and I shut my mouth. "Gregory fought and his equipment was damaged in the process. We have some leads, but nothing we can guarantee. At present, his system is on its way to our cyber team."

"Sounds like we're in good hands." The CEO stood along with Joran. "We'll not keep you any further. Karen?"

She kept scribbling down information. "I need to speak with them for a little longer. I want to make sure I get them the correct information."

We shook hands with the men who quickly left. They seemed unconcerned about the details, just the end result. Was it something from having a financial background?

Karen rubbed the bridge of her nose. "As embarrassing as this is, this situation falls under me. I just can't believe I never caught wind of any of it. Especially if it's been going on for over a year."

Silver stroked the patch of hair on his chin. "They were likely cautious to not get caught. You think this one might be a team effort, Ketayl?"

I nodded. "It makes the most sense as they employed the aid of someone within the company. We need to get Gregory to speak again so we can find out who he got directions from and exactly what he did." I hoped Silver's misstep was not the end of it.

She sighed. "I'll see if I can't piece together something from my end. Movie night may be going through security footage if nothing makes sense through the personnel files."

"If you want help, let me know," I said. I had lost my place within the group - no need for an arcane investigator.

Karen smiled at me. "I will. And please, feel free to come back for another class. You were a pleasure to have. Too many of them are way too serious."

I got up and bowed to her.

She laughed. "And thanks for not telling the guys."

13

I sat tapping my pen on the table. Where to start in tracking down this group while Silver and Frank looked into the places used on the death certificates? There was little I could do without more information from First Union.

Unless I could see if we were possibly dealing with an actual necromancer. There was usually a pattern. What exactly the pattern was, I had no idea, but it would show itself eventually.

I picked up my tablet and dove back into the case files to see if there was some common thread between them. As I found commonalities, I scribbled down notes on the pad of paper next to me.

Lexi giggled.

I paused, turning to look at her.

"Sorry, it's just funny to see a mix of tech and old school." She gave me a soft smile.

I shrugged and returned to what I was doing. "I only have one screen and I don't want to jump back and forth between programs. What are you working on?"

"I'm trying to see if I can follow back where the high-grade account death certificates came from, though I'm not holding out much hope at this point. Still running facial recognition. Got a few more from the struggling accounts. Sola's going to be busy if they keep picking up these people for us."

I bit my lower lip. "I feel bad for these people. They just wanted to get back on their feet."

"Not all of them," Lexi argued, "Besides, there are programs out there to help people struggling with debt."

"I'll admit it's a gray area, but..." I trailed off and bit my lower lip. All I could think about was what I had witnessed with Patrice. Someone desperate enough to give up her life with her family so they could be in a better position.

Lexi let out a long breath. "Ketayl, it's not like I don't understand. Silver and Frank may be dead set about Gregory having broken the law and so have these people, but I agree he did some good. It just wasn't the right way to do it. He had to have known he would eventually get caught."

I sighed. Part of me hoped the data from Gregory's system was lost.

Silence fell between us for a few minutes until she asked, "Is there something I can help you with?"

I glanced back at Lexi. "Not likely. I'm searching for a pattern for a necromancer."

"Yeah, that's out of my area of expertise." She turned back to her system.

"It's about all I can do at this point." Even I could hear the sadness in my voice. I hated feeling useless.

Lexi hummed for a moment. "It's still important. I mean, you found the one who was threatening our pack. Even before you came out to us, you had found evidence of one."

I huffed lightly at her wording. I did not think she still thought of me as part of her pack. While I had been nearby in Ghost Forest was one thing. They had basically adopted me into the pack, but we were thousands of miles away and I had not been in contact with them for months.

I stiffened up as I heard her approach me from behind. "Hey, let's take a break. Both of us need to get out and get some fresh air. And lunch couldn't hurt."

Shaking my head, I explained, "I've got to have something before they come back."

"Come on," Lexi whined, "They'll be gone until late tonight with as much traveling as they have to do."

I frowned. "Go ahead. I'll be fine. Just bring me something back."

"Don't make me pull a Silver on you."

I stopped and looked up at her, my eyes wide. "What's that supposed to mean?" *I know he left her with orders to not let me go out alone, but what else?*

Lexi cleared her throat. "You're too close to be able to see the big picture." She tried to mimic not only Silver's voice, but also his inflection.

"Ugh." I hung my head. "Okay, okay. You win. Please don't try to sound like him again in the future."

Lexi laughed so hard tears streamed down her face. Once she calmed, she said, "I didn't think it'd work so well."

I frowned. "Did he tell you to do that?"

She shook her head. "I've overheard him enough to know his patterns."

Cleaning up what I was working on, I grabbed my bag, tossing my tablet and pad of paper in there.

"Hey, don't bring work." Lexi reached for my bag.

I held it away from her. "It's only if inspiration strikes."

"You better leave it at that or I'll pull out more of his lines," she warned.

I shook my head and shooed her out the door.

JUST WHEN I thought I found a pattern, I found a break in it. Accounts for property, accounts for businesses, accounts for personal assets, they were a variety of different professions... the list went on.

Silver and Frank would be back soon. Hopefully they found something, though it sounded like a dead end again. The morgues and hospitals had no records of the deceased.

"Hey, Ketayl, can you come here for a minute?" Lexi said.

I got up, leaving my tablet and pad of paper behind. "What is it?"

She shifted in her chair. "They reported that the buildings were nothing special, right?"

I raised an eyebrow at her behavior. Rarely had I seen her squirm. "That's the short version I got. I'm hoping they have more, but not likely. Why?"

She pointed at a map she had up. "Is it possible we were looking in the wrong place? I mean, Gregory used a fish market to hide where he was."

"Are you telling me you were able to trace them further?" I leaned forward. Did she have something?

"Not exactly. I've found my way out, but I'm still bouncing around from hub to hub. Whoever it was hid their tracks well, but not as well as Gregory. It's long and tedious." Lexi blew the loose strands of hair out of her face.

I put my hands on my hips, waiting for more.

"So, out of curiosity, while I wait for my algorithms to run, I triangulated each of the positions to see where they converged because they were so evenly spaced. I mean, there are other morgues and hospitals closer together, but..." She sounded unsure.

I tilted my head, considering what she was attempting. "Were they using the closest one to the deceased?"

Lexi shook her head. "It's been mixed if they're close or farther away. Not to mention we'd see more than three."

"And the location of death is their home." That had been the one solid pattern.

"Plus, the locations for the morgues and hospitals are all in lower income areas. These people are rich. Like insanely rich. I can't see a reason all of them would be sent to one of these." Lexi kept squirming.

"Okay, you've got my attention. Where does it converge?" I had to give her something otherwise she was going to drag this out.

"An abandoned church," Lexi said flatly.

I pursed my lips. "Irony at its finest. You think there's anything there?"

Lexi shifted and bit her lower lip. "Maybe. I wanted to run it by you before I started searching for footage in the area. The church itself likely won't have anything inside, but I can check."

"Go ahead. It may be far-fetched, but I'll take whatever I can get at this point. If you find anything suspicious, I'll go over there and see if there's anything arcane related. I'm hoping we're dealing with another hacker with a terrible sense of humor." I frowned at the idea, but it was better than dealing with an actual necromancer.

She over-exaggerated a shudder. "Same here. The last necromancer we encountered still gives me the chills. Oh, and you're not going alone."

I sighed. "I know. I'll take Silver with me so he can see if there's anything divine."

Lexi pouted. "Awe, I wanted to go."

I bit my lower lip for a moment. "That's actually not a bad idea. You have another set of senses that would complement ours."

"Yay!"

I raised an eyebrow at her enthusiasm. "That means we'll have to take Frank too."

"Awe..."

I heard the lock on the door open. Silver strode in with Frank. Both appeared weary from the day.

"Anything at all?" I asked.

Silver crossed his arms and leaned back against the counter, his head bowed.

Frank shook his head. "I don't know how all of this stuff works, but they had nothing in their system and no one remembers the names. These are pretty small places and they see a lot of unidentified people, but someone fancy like the people we're looking for would've easily been remembered. Granted, I'm pretty sure a few were trying to rush us out, but it could have been for other reasons."

I turned my attention to Lexi. "Looks like we're down to your idea for now."

"What idea?" Silver asked, standing up.

Lexi looked at me for a moment before explaining. "The places you guys went were all in low-income areas, correct?"

Frank raised an eyebrow at her. "Yeah, slums and poorer neighborhoods, why?"

"Why would a rich person go there? The areas cross over an abandoned church. I've still got to pull footage, but it's all I've got," Lexi said.

"Really, we're going with this half-baked plan?" Frank spat.

I stood up and faced him. "Have either of you got something that you're not sharing? I don't. I've been searching for patterns of a necromancer and every time I think I've got one to follow, the pattern breaks."

Silver stroked the small patch of hair on his chin. "There may be something in that. Can I look at your notes tomorrow?"

"Yeah." I paused and turned my attention to Frank. "While Lexi follows up on her idea, we'll all keep searching for other leads. She'll keep on her other trails as well and enlist the cyber team as needed to help with the workload. Frank, I think even you can accept that."

Frank snorted. "Sure. It's late so I'm going home to crash. Not a one of us here is going to be able to think straight right now."

I nodded and he let himself out.

"Hey, Ketayl." Lexi said softly.

I turned to look at her.

She gave me a small smile. "Thanks. I'm never sure when to push for dominance when it comes to dealing with things like that."

"I'd just do it when he gets argumentative. Might make him listen," Silver muttered.

I shook my head. "Frank has a point. Both of you go get some rest," I ordered.

Silver stood over me. "Don't count yourself out of that order."

I hated being so much shorter than him. "I'll be fine - I can keep going for a while."

I caught Lexi mouthing "big picture" from behind Silver and pointing at him. I frowned at her.

"You're going to be too tired to see the big picture," Silver argued.

I rolled my eyes while Lexi laughed. Silver turned to glare at her.

I tilted my head to the side to see around Silver to our werewolf companion. "You've been paying too much attention to him," I whispered, knowing she would hear me.

She cracked a large smile at me. Her behavior confused me. One minute she was fighting with my partner and the next she would follow his requests.

Silver looked back and forth between the two of us. "I think you two have been cooped up together for too long. Ketayl, go rest now. We'll work on this in the morning."

I rolled my eyes. "Fine." It was not worth the headache arguing with Silver over this. Lexi would probably help him also.

"Is there a pattern with the breaks in the pattern?" Silver asked.

I shrugged. "I haven't looked for one, but it's an idea." I was willing to try just about anything at this point.

We had been at this for hours going over my notes and searching though the case file. Both of us had our tablets out and were attempting to make sense of the information pertaining to the high-grade account holders. Frank had come to check-in before heading to the Sola office to talk to the people they had brought in for us.

Silver's phone rang. He stood up and went to his room to answer it.

"You two are so cute," Lexi commented. "At least when he's not being a complete jerk."

Her comment caught me off-guard. "What?"

"You and Silver. Though things have obviously been strained between the two of you." Lexi's eyes never left her screens.

I took a deep breath, thinking through how I wanted to word it. "It's complicated. Things have been off for both of us since the beginning of the year."

Lexi frowned and turned her gaze toward the floor. "I know about that. I got pulled out of training to try and help find you guys. Wish I could have been more helpful."

I shook my head, refusing to look up at her. "It's fine. I'm sure you did all you could, and I appreciate that."

Silence fell between us for a few minutes.

"Do you want to talk about it?" Lexi asked quietly. Her typing had stopped.

I shook my head. "Thanks, but right now I've got too much to do. We really need to find who is targeting the high-grade accounts."

"Ket, I'm worried. You haven't been getting enough rest," Lexi whined.

"It's just the case. Happens a lot. I'll be fine." I forced a smile for her.

She eyed me for a minute. I wanted to turn away and get back to work, but I knew she would take that as submission and I did not want to let her know that she was right. Given her ability to detect lies, it was probably a wasted effort on my part.

Silver thankfully came out of his bedroom before she could push the issue. "Karen has something for us."

Immediately I packed up my things. I needed to get away from Lexi before she pried further. I was tired of talking about that series of events.

My partner stayed silent until we got into our loaner vehicle. "Why did you turn Lexi down?"

"Huh?" My mind had already switched gears back to the case.

"When she asked if you wanted to talk."

I pinched the bridge of my nose. "It's just a distraction at this point. You were listening?"

"Yeah, sorry. I didn't want to interrupt you two. I didn't know she had also been tasked with helping find us." Silver tugged on his braid.

I crossed my arms and frowned. Good thing I had stayed silent on the matter. "Did Karen say what she had?"

Silver tugged on his braid. "No. Probably the identity of the person who worked with Gregory."

"I wonder if they found someone else to take his place. They could be in danger."

"If they aren't a willing participant," Silver said.

I sighed. "Must you suspect everyone?"

"I'm keeping my options open, which is unusual for the two of us." His words were becoming more clipped. What was going on with him now?

I rolled my eyes. He seemed pretty narrow-minded, but I had no idea what was going through his head.

14

____

"I managed to find out the name of the person who reported the struggling accounts," Karen said.

I raised an eyebrow. It was not the information I expected.

"Is it related to who worked with Gregory Cummins?" Silver asked.

Karen nodded. "Same person. Financial advisors never go down to talk to the techs. They call the help desk and wait for someone to come to them."

"Is there a reason you haven't given us a name yet?" Silver asked.

"I take it you won't accept that I wanted to build up the suspense." Karen sighed when neither of us said anything. "Initially I thought she was down there because she had started dating Christian Henderson. Vanessa Westerly is a quiet woman. I would even go so far as to call her timid."

I wrote the names down on my tablet.

Karen crossed her arms and sat back. "I pulled her personnel file. She's not someone I would suspect of being involved in something like this. She barely makes her numbers and doesn't push for advancement. She dresses neatly, but definitely frugal and conservative in her choices. Always brings a lunch. Nothing screams she's been receiving some kind of pay-off that I can gather."

I tapped my finger on the side of my tablet. "How often does she go down there?"

"Once a day at lunch time," Karen said.

Silver raised an eyebrow at me. "What are you thinking?"

I bit my lower lip, contemplating the problem before us. "If we approach her directly, she might be too skittish to give us anything or worse she'll alert the others that we're onto them. Is there any chance we could put someone down there to listen in?"

Karen tapped the end of her pen against her chin. "I don't see why not. I'm sure we can set up a dummy terminal nearby. We'll get some techs coming in for training or whatnot from other locations at odd intervals. I'll see what I can set someone up as."

"Who do you want to put in there?" Silver asked.

I folded my arms and looked up at my partner. "Lexi. She makes the most sense - she can carry on a conversation with anyone who might be suspicious of her presence. Plus, she doesn't need to be right on top of them to listen in."

Silver raised an eyebrow at me. "Didn't you give her a full workload?"

I nodded. "I'll take over and do what I can in the meantime." I might not have Lexi's skillset, but there had to be something I could handle.

"I know we're in a dire situation here, but this is rather exciting," Karen said with a smile. "Perhaps I chose the wrong line of work."

"It's not as exciting as you might think," I said. "I usually get myself into trouble."

Silver snorted.

I threw a sidelong glare at him.

Karen frowned. "Now, I'd hate to go around William and Joran, but they can be pretty orc-headed at times. I'd rather not chance them messing up your investigation. Could we meet at my studio for the time being? You both already know where it is."

Silver shrugged. "I don't see a problem with it."

I nodded. When she made the request, I thought I would have to convince Silver it was the better path.

"It'll also give me a chance to talk to... Lexi was it?" Karen looked between the two of us.

"Yes." I bit my lower lip for a moment. "I'm assuming you want the change of venue to make it less suspicious."

Karen nodded. "I'm going to bypass Personnel. The less people who suspect her, the better. I'll call you with when we can meet. I want to get some of this started before then."

This whole thing was new to me and Karen did have a point about it being somewhat exciting, though I was more concerned about making sure Lexi stayed safe.

<hr>

LEXI BIT her lower lip and looked at me. "Are you sure you want me to do this?"

I sighed. We had gone over the plan with her multiple times now.

Karen had been able to set us up in a very short period of time. Apparently, a temporary transfer needed less paperwork. "Yes. You'll be fine. This is your area of expertise, right?"

"Well, yeah, but..." Lexi shifted in her chair again. "I mean, I don't know if I can pass as a normal Human anymore."

I raised an eyebrow at her. "No one seems to notice when you go out."

She fidgeted in her seat. "Okay, I'm not sure about this undercover thing."

I took a deep breath. I knew nothing about undercover either. "Well, he's not the best source, but Silver might know something. He reads those kinds of books."

Lexi sat up straight and stared at me. "Silver? 'Mr.-I-don't-lie' reads books about people living lies?"

That was not something I had contemplated before. "I never said it made sense."

"We're also talking fiction here. I don't think that will translate well into the real world," Lexi argued.

"It's better than nothing. You can also check with the Sola branch." This argument was getting us nowhere.

Lexi sighed dramatically. "I'm not setting foot on Frank's turf again if I can help it. Way too much going on in there for my senses. Go on, message Silver. If it seems hopeless, I'll suck it up and talk to Ayda."

I let out a long breath. *Finally.* I pulled out my phone and messaged Silver to meet us back at the hotel.

"What about the workload you gave me?" Lexi asked.

I raised an eyebrow at her. "I'll take over where I can. I may enlist Spark's help."

Lexi raised an eyebrow at me. "Sparky? Isn't he a lab tech?"

"He's fast at analyzing footage," I pointed out.

Silver walked in with Frank. "What's going on?"

"That was fast," I commented.

Silver folded his arms and looked at me. "We were on our way in."

"I need you to help Lexi. You're more familiar with undercover than I am." It was a long shot, but there had to be truth behind the fiction.

My partner snorted. "I'm not sure fiction will help here."

Not him too. I rubbed my temple. "Just try, okay? Were you coming back with something?"

Frank looked at each of us. "Just dead ends. We were hoping you might have something. Guess I'm flying solo now."

I shook my head. "I'll swap places with Silver." Until I said it, I had not realized how much I needed to be out and searching like they had been.

"Ketayl..." Silver's voice had a warning tone to it.

I put my hands up. "I'll behave." I quickly grabbed my bag and signaled for Frank to head out before Silver could try to change my mind.

We were both silent until we got into his car. "Should I ask what you meant when you told him you'll behave?"

My lips formed into a thin line. "I've lost Silver before so I could follow a lead. I had been trying to keep him out of trouble."

The older man laughed. "I like you, kid. Seems like you're a quiet one also. Your partner there doesn't ever shut up."

I rolled my eyes. "Tell me about it. So, where are we going?"

"While I think it's far-fetched, but I do want to check out that church. Figured it was better to do it without him."

I raised an eyebrow at Frank. "Silver would be able to detect any divine usage."

"Yeah, and the place is probably soaked in it from the years of being a place of worship. Arcane, not so much," he pointed out.

I raised an eyebrow at him. "You have a better grasp of magic than I thought."

Frank laughed. "Life was easier when it was actual magic users I was chasing instead of these high-tech wizards. I can do basic stuff on a computer, but I'm getting too old to keep up."

I smirked at his candid words. I was glad I brought him back on-board.

"Besides, my old partner was divine sensitive. Unfortunately, Tef got hurt and had to transfer to a new job if he wanted to stay with the TIO. Was a right pain-in-the-ass fairy, but he was my brother."

I clenched my teeth at that word. "You do like your racial slurs, don't you?" I wanted to avoid letting him know how much it affected me personally.

Frank laughed. "I got too used to it. Especially with Tef. He'd toss them right back. This sensitivity training is a load of crap."

I took a deep breath. "I'll try not to take offense then." No matter how close to home it hit.

Frank put his hand on my head. "I like you, fairy girl."

I rolled my eyes and shifted away from him. At least now it sounded more like a term of endearment.

"You know, I initially put up with that partner of yours because I thought it might be like my days of running with Tef," Frank admitted.

"I assume Silver's personality doesn't match."

"That's just the start of it. He's got a good sense of the divine from what I can tell. Just not much sense otherwise. Start to wonder why he chose this line of work."

I let out a long breath. Silver was not suited to the work he had been tasked with.

He tapped a finger on the steering wheel. "I've got to ask: Why has that jerk of a partner kept you locked up in the hotel? Think you're going to be more useful in searching than him."

"He's overprotective. And he hates desk work." I stared out the window as Frank drove.

"Your previous limited duty got anything to do with it?"

I hesitated answering. "Probably a good amount, but he's always like this."

"What's Silver to you anyway? I mean really. Don't give me he's your partner crap, because it's obviously more personal than that." His words began to feel like an interrogation.

I bit my lower lip, thinking through the complex answer to his question. "He's my closest friend. We've been through a lot together. I trust him more than anyone else." Despite the recent conflicts between us, it remained true.

"Hm, thought you might say something different," Frank muttered.

I raised an eyebrow at him, but refused to inquire further. "Just don't let him get bored. At the minimum you'll end up with pens in your ceiling."

"Oh Hells. How do you put up with him?"

I shrugged and changed the subject. "Why do you think the church is a lead now?"

Frank hesitated. "I'm not entirely sure. Thought it over last night and at this rate I'm ready to try anything. Just don't tell that asshole partner of yours. I'll never hear the end of it."

I smirked. "I'm not about to tell him. Wish we could have brought Lexi. Her senses would help."

"Let's just do a reconnaissance of the area and see if there's anything suspicious first. Heard you have her going undercover."

"I'm hoping that lead pans out. There are two individuals we're hoping to get information from. One was the person who was likely working with Gregory and the other is his replacement at First Union."

"You don't say. You're after the whole damn chain. Man, I miss having a partner, but these young ones think they know everything. It's been a long time since I felt like part of a team." There was a hint of sadness in his voice.

I smiled knowingly. The months of working alone had gotten to me.

"Anyway, I haven't properly had the chance to tell you that I'm glad you brought me back on-board. Can't help but notice it was when the transfer of lead happened."

I bit my lower lip, thinking through my words first. "Silver and I had a disagreement. He decided he needed to transfer lead over to me. I'm normally lead when it's more than just the two of us."

"Didn't think he had any sense. Crap, where is this place? I can see the steeple, but these roads keep leading me in circles." Frank ran a hand over his hair.

I pulled up the navigation program on my phone and located the church. "Take a right on the next street."

"Damn, I need to learn to use one of those. I know most of Sola, but this area is not one I ever come to. Nothing ever falls under our jurisdiction over here."

I directed Frank to the church. As we got closer, I saw more and more homeless people out on the streets as the buildings appeared further run down and abandoned.

He pulled up across the street from what looked more like a cathedral. The large steeple towered over the multiple story building. The building itself spanned the length and width a normal block with overgrown grass and bushes around it. A smaller building sat off to the side.

"Why would this be abandoned? I would think some group would want to take over something this grand," I commented.

Frank crossed his arms and looked up at the building. "From what I was able to gather it used to honor all of the Gods before the split happened. Some groups had already focused down on one or two Gods, but not to the extent it is today."

I raised an eyebrow. It seemed like he had already done some research. "I honestly don't know anything about the split."

He waved me off. "You're probably too young for it. Happened about the time of the Racial War. Likely no one wanted some place they considered tainted. Either that or the conversion would have cost too much. Granted, this whole area looks pretty run down so the neighborhood likely plays a part. Might find homeless inside."

I was not about to mention I was about his age. Granted, I worshipped none of the Gods. This subject I would have to defer to Silver.

Following Frank out of the car, we walked up to the entrance. Something arcane was barely on my ability to sense. It was difficult to make out. I discreetly held my hand up in front of me, keeping it against my stomach as we walked, reaching out with my power.

"You got something?" Frank asked.

I tilted my head, trying to make sense of it. "I'm not sure. There's something at the edge of my senses, but it's too hard to tell."

"I probably should've asked more about your arcane abilities. My old partner could tell from quite the distance."

"I've got a longer range than anyone else I've met." I bit my lower lip. That had sounded boastful though I only meant to provide fact. "I don't see anything out here though - it's all coming from inside."

"See?"

I took a deep breath and remembered that he knew next to nothing about me. "I can see the arcane. Enough to make out signatures and what spells were used. I should've brought my camera. It has an arcane filter on it."

Frank shrugged. "Eh, that would've tipped off your partner. I'll rely on your senses."

"You've got a lot of faith in someone you hardly know," I commented.

Frank laughed. "Like I said, I like you, fairy girl."

I rolled my eyes at the nickname.

"We shouldn't go in though. We're not prepared for that."

I nodded. "We would need the other two. Especially Lexi. She'd be able to smell if there was decaying flesh."

"Well, that's morbid." Frank made a face.

I shrugged.

"Probably plenty of dead animals in there. Maybe a few homeless who died of one thing or another. I doubt the local law enforcement even bothers checking it out. This area doesn't seem too well patrolled."

We moved closer to the church, staying on the sidewalk.

I shook my head. "There's still something there, but I can't make it out. Whatever it is also feels off. It's as if it's not pure arcane, but I shouldn't be able to sense that."

"Necromancer?" he asked.

I pursued my lips. "Possibly. The first case I ever worked with Silver on, I could make out an emotional response which came through from the divine side. I might be too far to make it out clearly." I stepped toward the church, needing to get closer.

Frank grabbed my shoulder. "No. We don't go any further. Ain't risking you on a far-fetched idea. Let's go back and see how the other two are doing."

"Don't pick up on Silver's habits," I commented.

"Don't insult me like that. I just ain't taking a chance on my partner."

I laughed lightly at his words. "Okay, let's go. You need me to direct you out?"

"Yeah, the faster we get out of this thrice-damned level of Hells, the better."

As we walked back to his car, the hair on the back of my neck rose and I whipped my head around, scanning the area.

"What is it?" Frank asked.

I tilted my head, reaching out with my power toward it, but it was gone. "I'm not sure. Possibly someone watching us."

"You ever sensed something like it before?"

I bit my lower lip, matching up the sensation from another in my memory. "It's been a couple of years, but something similar."

"Alright, let's get out of here. Probably should find something else to tell that nosy-ass partner of yours," Frank grumbled.

I got into the car and asked, "How have you two survived working together?"

"Let's just say you ain't the only one who's managed to shake him. I just happen to know when not to get in over my head. From what I hear, you're still working on that."

I groaned. *What has Silver told him about me?*

15

"YOU TWO WERE GONE FOR A WHILE," Silver said. I thought I had imagined the accusing tone until I saw his face. He had narrowed his eyes at me.

"Like me and you haven't been gone for hours on end," Frank threw back. "Not to mention she's Hells of a lot more useful than you are. And definitely quieter."

Silver growled at him.

I stepped between them. "Enough." My power unintentionally bled into my voice again causing both men to stop and stare at me. I turned to Lexi. "Are you better prepared to go undercover at First Union?"

Lexi had been gaping at me. Her mouth moved for a moment with no sound. "I... I... Maybe. I'll figure it out. Maybe no one will really talk to me."

I glared at Silver.

His shoulders slumped. "Okay. I've told her what I could, and we pulled up what we could find in the TIO database on it."

I raised an eyebrow at him.

Silver looked away. "Did you manage to get anything?"

Frank spoke before I could organize my thoughts. "Nothing we can confirm. Possible leads, but I think we'll hold off until your girl here reports in." He thumbed at Lexi. "My partner here is chasing the chain and I think that's a better use of our time than just going for the top." He put his hand on my head and I stepped away, smoothing my hair.

"Hey, she doesn't like to be touched," Silver barked, grabbing Frank's wrist.

Frank tore himself away. "Seen you do it often enough."

I was letting my power build when an oppressing dominance filled the room. Not as strong as it had been in with the Alpha Prime and his Beta, but still powerful enough to make me pause. I looked to our werewolf.

Lexi stood up growling at them. Both men turned their eyes to the floor. "Would you two grow up? We need to work together and the only thing I ever hear from you is bickering. And when you're not throwing insults at each other, the tension between you is still unbearable."

As soon as she sat back down and stopped pushing for dominance, the two men let out a long breath.

"Damn, the women on this team are powerful and scary when they're mad," Frank said quietly.

"Yeah," Silver replied.

"Hey, they agreed on something." I smirked at Lexi who was still staring them down.

Lexi let out a short laugh. "Well, I'm hungry and I need to get out of this room. Ketayl, want to go to dinner?"

I put my hands on my hips, staring at Silver. I did not let go of his gaze. "Yeah. They might figure themselves out by the time we get back."

Silver looked away. "I'm in deep," he muttered.

Without another word, I followed Lexi out the door.

Once we were on the elevator, she spoke. "Haven't seen you that level of mad at Silver since the first time you came to the estate with Holly."

"He's so hot-headed at times I don't think he knows what he's saying," I grumbled.

Silence fell between us through the rest of the ride.

"Hey, can I ask you a favor for tomorrow?" Lexi asked quietly.

I raised an eyebrow at her. "Hm? For when you go into First Union?"

She turned her eyes to the ground. "Yeah. Can you be on the line with me? I'd feel better with you having my back."

I nodded. "Of course. Not like I planned to put either of them on it. By the way, I didn't expect that dominance push out of you."

"Was it too much?" She fidgeted with her hands.

I shook my head. "It was needed. Thanks."

We walked in silence for a few minutes.

"Is it impolite to ask how dominant you are?" I asked quietly.

Lexi shook her head. "I have always tried to keep it contained, but in terms of the Alpha Prime's pack, I was just under Sasha."

I blinked and looked at her. "I never would have guessed."

"You've got some power too."

I shrugged. "I probably shouldn't do that. I hadn't meant to this time."

Lexi smirked at me. "It was needed."

I let out a short laugh at having my words turned around on me.

"I hate to admit it, but Silver was right, you two had been gone a while."

I sighed. "This stays between us, okay?"

She smiled broadly. "This has to be good."

"Frank wanted to go to the church without Silver," I said quietly.

Lexi stepped in front of me and stopped. "Why? He didn't like my idea."

I sighed. "Even you admitted it was a stretch and he's willing to try anything at this point."

She shook her head and returned to my side. "I'm assuming nothing."

I bit my lower lip for a moment. "Maybe not. We were too far away for me to make out what was on the edge of my senses."

"Does that mean I'm off the hook for tomorrow?" Lexi sounded hopeful.

"No."

"Damn."

SILVER AND FRANK left the next morning without a word of their plans. Lexi was on her way to First Union.

"Ketayl, please tell me you're there," Lexi whispered. There was a lot of background noise, so I was surprised I even heard her.

"I'm here. What's going on?" She did not have a video piece so I had to rely solely on sounds.

She whined slightly. "This is nerve wracking. I'm about to go in."

I bit my lower lip trying to think about how to make her less nervous, but a memory came to mind. I had remembered Retanei's words to me when I went out with her on my first field assignment. "'Nothing I can say or do will make you stop being nervous.' I'll be here to direct you as best as I can. You're not alone."

"Well, that's not much help, but I'm glad you're here. At least in my ear. I'll get you a visual when I can."

"Are you still going to patch me into Christian's microphone?" I asked. It had been thrown out as an idea, but we never solidified that part.

"If I can do it without him noticing. He's good. I might not be able to. How are my algorithms doing?"

I glanced at the screen they were running on. "Still bouncing around. I think they're circling through some of the same hubs." At least that was what I could make of it.

"It's a lazy way to do it, but most people would have given up thinking it's hopeless. Okay, I better stop chatting."

"You've got this." It sounded a little more positive than telling her good luck.

I spent a few hours listening. Occasionally Lexi would check to see if I was still on the line. While we waited for Vanessa to arrive, I spent most of my time piecing together what I could about the breaks in the patterns. She had left me nothing to take care of, automating all of her tasks for the day. No wonder she had time to come up with the idea to triangulate the locations - she had the time to kill.

There was one man in the office who seemed entranced by Lexi. He would stop by every time he got up to get a printout. She had been politely getting him to leave her alone, but I could hear her patience growing thin. Once he left, she would gripe quietly afterward. At least she had been seated fairly close to Christian and had set up her video feed to face him.

"Can I leave after lunch?" Lexi asked, her voice low.

I gave a short laugh. "You don't like your printing friend?"

"Ugh..." Lexi rolled her eyes. "I really want to assert dominance to get him to leave me alone, but that'd tip off everyone here."

I sighed and picked up my phone in case I missed something from Silver. They had been silent all day. After the argument between Silver and Frank last night, it worried me.

The biggest thing was I hoped they stayed away from the church. Something still felt off about that place. I tried to convince myself that if it had been a place of combined worship, then maybe there were mages who went there in order to explain the strange sense of arcane. I knew better, especially when I felt like someone might be watching us, but I could hope. Not to mention any traces of arcane would be long gone. The general nature of the arcane would not allow for something to be running long term.

"She's here," Lexi said quietly.

I turned my attention back to the video feed. Several seconds later Vanessa came into view and sat down next to Christian at his station. She held her lunch in her lap.

"Did you manage to tap into his microphone?"

I caught Lexi shaking her head on the side of the camera, never looking away from what she was typing. A screen popped up next to the video feed. "I'll transcribe it here," she wrote.

C: Do you really have to come here every day?
V: Do you have to ask that every day?

There was silence between them for a bit while Vanessa ate her lunch. What if there was nothing here? I would have ordered Lexi into an uncomfortable situation for no reason. Either way I owed her for this.

C: You haven't given me a name for a while.
V: She doesn't like it, but we have to keep quiet. I've got some people lined up for when it's safe to move again.
C: Why?
V: Heard the TIO is involved.
C: Hells. Does that mean you'll stop coming down here?
V: No. It would look weird if I didn't.
C: You should have said something sooner instead of coming down here and eating your lunch in silence like a creep.

The interaction between them was... strange. I bit my lower lip, concerned that they knew we were involved. How much they knew was going to be important. That would impact how we moved.

C: Anyone I should look out for?
V: There's an Elf with silver hair that's been poking around.
C: Anyone else?
V: Heard he's been seen with some older Human guy recently.

I breathed a sigh of relief. Lexi and I had likely gone unnoticed. It sounded like Silver was right that Christian was a willing party.

At least there was something, but nothing to act on. I tugged on my bangs. This whole thing was infuriating. There was a long pause between the two we were listening to.

C: Do you know what the TIO is doing?
V: No. They'll give up eventually. The others have as long as we play it safe.
C: What does the boss think?
V: She doesn't like it, but she agrees.
C: Glad I don't have to deal with her.
V: I wish I didn't.

With that, Vanessa packed up her lunch and left. While more would have been nice, I was willing to take what we got.

"He's calling her not nice things," Lexi said quietly.

I sighed. "Didn't sound like he liked her much, but I think he's more of a willing participant than Gregory was."

Lexi hummed in agreement. She glanced at something on her screen and rolled her eyes.

"What?" I asked.

"Printer guy," she muttered.

I shook my head. "I'll try to make it up to you."

"Chocolate?"

If that's all it was going to take, I got off easy. "We're going to have to get better proof of Christian's involvement. It sounds like it'll be easier to catch Vanessa. I'll have Silver and Frank follow her." Where were those two?

"Can I leave now?"

I glanced at the time. "Give it a half hour. Don't want to make it too suspicious. If anyone asks, just tell them you have an appointment."

"I'm hugging you when I get back."

"Duly warned."

Lexi had come back hours ago and there was still no word from Silver or Frank. I rapped my fingers on the arm of the chair.

"You could always message them," Lexi said.

"I know, but at the same time I don't want to interrupt them if they're in the middle of something." I got up and paced.

She tapped her finger on the table for a moment. "That's why I said message. Silver will respond when he's got a moment. I don't know if Frank knows how to respond to messages or cares to."

I sighed.

"Come on, let's head out for a bit. You obviously need some fresh air." Lexi tugged on my hand.

I bit my lower lip, debating if I should stay and wait for them. "Alright." If I stayed, I would just worry. Even going out I would worry, but at least there were distractions.

"I guess I could track them."

I raised an eyebrow at Lexi.

She made a face before returning to her computer. "Get ready to go. This'll just take a minute."

"Actually, don't bother. They can take care of themselves." I tried to sound confident about it, but it did not stop my worry.

As we left the hotel, we crossed paths with the two in question. They were laughing and chatting with each other. It was a nice change from them arguing, but I did not appreciate the communications silence.

"Where have you been?" I asked, keeping my voice as neutral as possible to hide my aggravation. Getting worked up over something this small would do no one any good.

"After last night, your boy and I decided we should take a day and get to know each other. Can't have you playing referee for us. This case needs to be solved," Frank said.

Silver tugged on his braid. "Sorry we haven't actually been working on the case."

I put my hands on my hips. "It's late so tomorrow I want you two to start looking into Vanessa Westerly. Be careful though, she knows you're both with the TIO."

"Wait, you got something?" Frank looked at us with wide eyes.

Lexi and I both nodded.

Silver crossed his arms and looked at us. "Where are you headed?"

"I need food. Werewolf metabolism and I'm stressing," Lexi said sharply. "Definitely want chocolate."

Silver turned to Frank. "Want to join them? We need to form a plan of action."

Lexi hung her head back. "Ugh, I want to say it's girl's night, but he has a point."

I took a deep breath. I remained unsure if I was ready to deal with them, but I needed to see this change for myself. Maybe even find out what they did.

I hung at the back of the group. Silver fell in line beside me.

"Hey," he said quietly.

I glanced up at him.

He tugged on his braid. "Sorry I've been unhelpful. More of a hindrance really."

I shrugged.

"Can we go for a walk later to talk?"

I nodded. Silver and I also needed to sort things out between us. It struck me as odd that he had been the biggest problem.

As I watched Lexi's messy bun bounce lightly in front of me, I contemplated Silver's behavior. I ignored the case in Ocean's Edge because there was a necromancer spell messing with both Silver and Rathal. However, when we first arrived in Ghost Forest for the case, he acted the same. But when it was just us in Sandpoint, we worked well together. Did he not know how to deal with being a part of a larger team? He did seem to get overprotective to the point of being belligerent when there were other people involved.

I bit my lower lip. This train of thought would get me nowhere. Until I was certain of the cause of his behavior, a plan to deal with it would be pointless.

Silver taking my hand broke me out of my thoughts. I looked up at him to see him smiling gently down at me.

I pulled my hand away and shook my head. Then I pointed at the two in front of us with my chin.

He mouthed the word "later."

"Oooh! That sounds good!" Lexi turned around and grabbed my hand, tugging me toward a restaurant.

I stumbled for a few steps before I coordinated my feet. She still moved faster than I could consistently keep up with. "Hey, slow down!"

Lexi wove us through the crowd with ease. We were in front of the restaurant before she stopped. "Sorry, got carried away."

The men were catching up to us, but they were having a harder time getting through the crowd.

"Did you just want away from them?" I kept my voice low and shook my hand to get some feeling back into it.

Lexi looked down sheepishly. "Yeah, even if it's just for a moment. The tension is gone, but it still feels awkward."

I gave a short laugh. Perhaps we should have left them to their own devices.

"Besides, it smelled like you wanted away," she said.

I formed my lips into a thin line. Lexi was right, but I had ignored the feeling.

"Geez, Lexi, don't take off like that," Silver said.

"I need food," she said firmly.

I let them bicker while I considered if we should all be seen together like this. Soon enough word will get out that all four of us were working together. That was if someone had not figured it out already. With the number of people around it had become next to impossible to determine if anyone was watching. With any luck, they would have lost us in the crowd.

"Ketayl?" Silver asked.

I shook my head. "Let's feed her before I get dragged through the crowd again."

My partner laughed and put his hand on my back, leading me toward the door.

I stiffened up at his touch, but remained silent. Saying or doing anything now would draw attention.

Frank had gotten ahead of us and spoke with the host. "There's four of us. Wanted to take my niece and his girlfriend out for dinner."

My face heated up at his words. *Why? Why does everyone think that of me and Silver?*

Though I paused at how he referred to Lexi. It could wait until we were seated. Lexi and Silver glared at each other over who would sit with me. Eventually Silver won by pointing out that Frank called me his girlfriend.

I sighed. Lexi I had come to trust and would rather have had her. Unfortunately, Silver made sense for the story Frank had spun.

"Hey," Lexi said just loud enough to be heard over the bustle of the restaurant. Her attention was on Frank. "Why did you call me your niece?"

A question I had wanted to ask.

Frank smiled. "If they can put two and two together that I'm working with Silver then I might as well drop some potential misinformation since we don't know who could be involved. Might keep them off your tails for a bit. Besides, at my age, the best I can get would be to take my niece out."

His words made me feel slightly more at ease with how he had referred to me. I wished he had come up with something different though.

"Alright, now spill," Frank said, leaning forward.

I glanced up at Silver and his attention was on me. I looked over to Lexi who waved her hand at me. Right, I was lead.

"While there was no direct statement that they were working with a necromancer," I paused. Silver had wrapped his arm around my waist. I frowned and forced myself to continue. I was supposed to be his girlfriend after all. We would have words about this later though. "There's enough to follow the lead. I'll show you Lexi's transcript later."

"They definitely don't like each other, but it sounds like Christian is a willing part of this scheme," Lexi added.

"And Vanessa is the only one who deals with the boss. No name at the moment," I added.

Silver stroked the small patch of hair on his chin. "I doubt we would have come up with anything even if we hadn't taken the day for team building."

"Seriously, what did you guys do? You were at each other's throats last night," Lexi asked, beating me to it.

"Had a long conversation. Got to talking about cases we've worked on. Figured out where our strengths are," Frank said.

I sighed. Getting further into it would not solve this case as much as I knew I should solve our personality issues. The problem we faced now is the uncertainty about this being an actual necromancer or not. If Christian was the person in charge of dealing with the electronic information, I doubted whoever the boss was also did the same work. What was she? Someone who was just greedy?

Maybe she was an investor. It would make sense for the whole scheme. I pulled my tablet out and jotted the idea down.

Silver rested his chin on my shoulder. "I should give you a hard time about working, but that's a good idea."

I shrugged the shoulder my partner rested on hard, trying to shake him off. He stayed firm.

Lexi smiled. "You two are adorable."

"Don't start," I snapped. I made a mental note to have Lexi pull footage from the area of the church when we returned to the hotel. She would hopefully have something by the time I got back from dealing with Silver.

Silver walked silently next to me. I wanted to question him, but held my tongue. He usually filled the gaps with small talk so I hoped this would lead him to talk about his actual problem instead of skirting the issue.

I knew my partner would never lie to me, but he was quite good at avoiding things he did not want to talk about.

We walked along the waterfront. I watched the sunlight sparkle on the waves. At least this area was quiet. I still felt on edge though. My eyes darted about. Even a peaceful place could prove dangerous.

Silver put his hands over mine.

I had clenched them tightly together to keep from fidgeting. Too often had we found ourselves in predicaments in seemingly safe places. I moved away from him, crossing my arms. This was not the time for big brother mode.

We walked a few minutes longer down the path until we came upon a small park.

"Um..." Silver started. "Apologizing isn't going to change what has already happened."

"Explaining why you border on belligerent around others would help," I countered.

Silver walked to the fence along the water. "If I knew that, I would tell you. Then I could also do something about it."

I frowned. Then something occurred to me. "Maybe your necklace?" It affected me when he had made me wear it several months ago. What had been only a desire to be closer to him may have evolved into something more with how long he had worn it.

He turned sharply and stared at me with wide eyes. "I..." He pulled his necklace out from under his shirt and looked at the golden sun pendant on it. "We never really got a chance to talk about what happened with you and it, did we?"

I shook my head. "And I would rather not." I was still embarrassed about how much it influenced me to behave differently. I certainly would not have kissed him. "Is it a possibility?"

Silver tucked his necklace away and then flipped the end of his braid back and forth. "Maybe, but you said you figured out how to split yourself from it, right?"

"The influence I got from it started as an external source, but it was too strong to ignore. There were times when I couldn't tell if what I thought was genuine or being influenced." Even the times I had figured it out, I would still allow it to influence my actions, but I never could determine if I was weak willed or simply too exhausted from what the pirates had put me through.

My partner frowned. "Not likely then. With as long as I've worn it, I would have noticed by now."

I sighed. There went that theory. And one I was more comfortable accepting. It was far simpler to deal with an external source.

"Kela," Silver said quietly as he stood over me, brushing my bangs back.

I stayed still. I could admit at least to myself that I had missed these gentle moments with him. Even with his actions recently, I still trusted him. I also needed the moment of calm. To confirm that the person I knew was still here.

Silver took a deep breath before speaking again. "I can't promise I won't get possessive, but I'll do my best to think before I react."

Possessive? I had not even considered the word. Overprotective, yes, but possessive was more accurate given more recent events. "What I need is for you to stop arguing with everyone." *Stop putting me in the center of it.*

"I know. I'm trying," Silver said, his voice sounding desperate. "That's why I suggested the idea to Frank of taking today for team building. You made your anger well known last night. Lexi can be scary, but I never want to be on the receiving end of you being that mad again."

I let out a soft huff. Now I was scaring not only my team, but my partner who knew me better than the others. "It would have been nice to know your plans," I muttered.

Silver let out a long breath. "I wanted to, but Frank suggested we hold off until after. Partially because we had no idea if we could work out our differences. Mainly because we didn't need you and Lexi worrying about how we were doing while she was undercover."

I rubbed the bridge of my nose. This incident was not worth arguing about. "At least you seemed to have worked out your differences with Frank." I would take the victories I could at this point.

"Yeah. He's really dedicated to the job. You probably have no idea how grateful he is that you thought to bring him back on. To give him something to utilize his skills on." Silver shifted from one foot to the other. I could not recall ever seeing him do that before.

"I have a rough idea," I muttered. Now Silver was trying to change the subject. "I need to know if you can be part of a team."

"If not?" He tugged on his braid again. He had been doing that a lot more lately than I remembered him doing it. There had to be something else going on, but was it worth prying? After this case was over. Right now I needed to deal with the immediate problems.

"I don't know, but I'll find something to keep you busy. Should I start doing that?" My words were clipped. I bit my lower lip when the thought that we had reversed roles so completely crossed my mind. "I'm sorry. I shouldn't have said that. It was too far."

Silver shook his head and leaned on the railing. "Having my own words thrown back at me has given me an appreciation for the patience and restraint you have."

I raised an eyebrow at him. "I threw a fireball at you. I could have killed you."

He laughed. "I finally got you to raise the difficulty level for me."

I pinched the bridge of my nose. *That's definitely Silver.*

16

It was the first day of the weekend, and with the administration offices of First Union closed, Lexi could not go in undercover again in hopes of getting more information. Instead she searched for either Vanessa or Christian through the camera network from our hotel suite.

Christian was likely still home, but she could not confirm due to the heavy curtains.

Vanessa was a little easier, eating breakfast at a small cafe near her apartment. She was the one we were more interested in anyway.

After how Karen described her and Vanessa's own words about saving money, her spending like this seemed off. From the light meal she ordered, perhaps this was simply a small splurge. I had been known to do something similar from time to time.

"By the Gods, I didn't need to see that," Lexi said, suddenly covering her eyes.

"What happened?" I was out of my chair in an instant.

"Christian opened one of the curtains and he was naked," she whined.

I laughed lightly. "I'll buy you some chocolate for having to put up with that."

"I've been traumatized for life," she said dramatically, leaning over the back of her chair with the back of her hand to her forehead.

"It couldn't have been that bad. I thought you were used to shifting around the others." And I knew they needed to be naked at the time or they would tear their clothes. I had not been warned about that particular detail ahead of time so it had been a shock for me the one time I had been around for a hunt night.

Lexi sat up and returned to her watch. "That's different. Those are my brothers and sisters. Christian was a complete creep. Flashing people like that should be illegal." She made a motion with her hand to signal that he had a common male morning affliction.

I hummed for a moment trying to recall the local laws. "I think it is."

"Can I report him anonymously?"

"I think his involvement in this case will be sufficient."

Lexi started typing and clicking. "And adding the footage for more damning evidence."

"You're vindictive."

She smirked. "He assaulted my eyes first."

I shook my head. "What about Vanessa?"

"Still sipping her tea and reading a book. I'm not sure if she's just enjoying her morning or if she's waiting for someone. She doesn't post much on social media other than cute little pictures from other people so I can't get an idea of her routine."

I frowned. Neither one was doing anything. With them spooked about us, we could be waiting weeks for them to make another move. I hated the idea of sending Lexi into First Union for that long.

"What's your instinct on who the boss is?" Lexi asked.

I shrugged. "I really don't know. I can't see why a necromancer would want to get involved in some huge financial scheme, but you haven't located any of the high-grade account holders so I'm not ruling it out."

Lexi squirmed in her chair. "I hate to say it, but maybe Karen. She's been extremely helpful and secretive."

I pursed my lips. "A possibility. We have been taking her at her word and she could be directing Vanessa. Is there anything other than working for First Union that connects them?"

"I can look, but she could be doing it within the company - that might be harder to track now than their personal lives."

"Suspecting her may be off-base. Vanessa knew about Silver and

Frank, but not you or me. I don't know if Karen has met Frank or if she has, she likely doesn't know he's back on the case," I countered.

Lexi dropped her head back. "Ugh, why does this have to be so hard?"

"We'd be done if it was easy. Something tells me it's an outside source. Could be another who used to work for First Union or maybe an investor." Those made more sense, but then I was completely out of my element as I had no financial background.

"Well, Gregory was greedy and wanted it all for himself so he set out on his own," she commented.

I bit my lower lip for a moment - given how uncooperative he was, it was an easy assumption, but not necessarily true. "He did say he figured out what was going on and decided to leave. I think the people he was doing work for scared him."

"An opportunist then. He may have not wanted to get involved in this scheme, but he certainly used the idea to his advantage."

I sighed. This was getting us nowhere. "Has facial recognition returned any partials of the people with high-grade accounts?"

Lexi shook her head. "Just the struggling ones. The cyber team has better processing power and has a much broader search going in case they skipped the territory."

"They could be dead then. Have you provided Silver and Frank with a list of survivors for them?" I returned to my seat.

"Yeah, and they've returned with nothing other than they haven't seen or heard from them since before the time of death. Dead or alive."

I groaned and tugged at my bangs. "I'd say that we need to go to that church, but Frank had a point that there are probably deceased homeless people in there. It was a pretty run-down area - many vacant buildings and I thought I saw some people living in some."

"You're not making this easy. And dammit, I'm hungry, but I can't leave," Lexi whined.

"Want me to go get you something?" I was getting hungry as well. We had started this quite early.

She pursed her lips for a moment. "Well, Silver never said specifically that you couldn't go out for food runs on your own. I'll assume he meant out only on case-related excursions."

"Thank you for that," I said and gave her a soft smile.

"Besides, I still haven't forgiven him yet," she said sharply.

I rolled my eyes. "Should I also bring back chocolate?"

"Yes!"

I laughed lightly, grabbed my bag, and headed out. The men were busy with keeping an eye on the two. Since Vanessa had a better description of Silver, we had him follow Christian. Granted, he had an idea also, but I had a feeling Vanessa had seen my partner.

It took only a few minutes to get to where the shopping area was. I had not thought through how busy it would be. Just find something quick, get Lexi's snack, and get back as fast as possible. I needed to learn to deal with crowds.

Gripping the strap on my bag tightly against my chest, I wandered, reading the shop signs. *A sandwich? Something warm?* I should have asked Lexi what she wanted.

I could sense the people behind me and hustled to put some space between me and them. Not that there was much room to do so.

I ducked into a bookstore to take a breath from the crowd. There were only a few patrons in here. Maybe I should browse for a few minutes before heading out again - give myself a break.

The books were mixed with organization only by topic or genre and appeared fairly worn. Used bookstore? Maybe I would find something unique.

I lost track of time as I browsed the arcane books. Some of them were old, dusty tomes that likely weighed half as much as I did.

"Looking for something in particular?"

I jumped at the voice.

The older Human woman stood near me, wearing something that more resembled the long robes I wore as a Researcher at the Arcane College.

I forced a smile. "No, just looking."

The woman hummed for a moment. "Something tells me you're more experienced than most who come to this section."

I remained silent, neither confirming or denying her suspicion.

"I might have something of interest to you." She signaled me to follow her.

I hesitated, unsure if this was a good idea. *It's a bookstore. It's just a bookstore.*

She led me to the historical section.

I raised an eyebrow.

"I know what you're thinking, but I doubt I have any arcane books that could satisfy you. A forgotten history about arcane casters, I do." She pulled out a thick brown, leather bound book. She handed it to me.

"How...?" I trailed off, uncertain how she knew what I would be interested in.

She gave me a soft, warm smile. "Well, it is my job to read people so I can find good homes for my books."

What's the harm in looking? I gently opened the cover, it creaked in protest.

The woman patted me on the arm. "Take your time. If you want, there's a chair in the corner."

I smiled and nodded. "Thank you." I found the chair she mentioned and rubbed my arm to get rid of the sensation. I still disliked most people touching me.

Settling in, I paged through the book, skimming the entries. There was information going back centuries. Descriptions of the use of both traditional mages and arcanists in battles. Granted, it used the old terms for both classifications.

Sorcerer. It's still such an odd term to hear for Arcanist. Traditional mages went through more variations.

Descriptions of curses and other darker magic popped up. A lot was attributed to the fae races who avoided interacting with the rest of the world. It was assumed they were defending their territory.

My watch tapped me. I looked to see what it was and Lexi had messaged me to see if I had run into a problem. I switched back to the time and I had been here for far longer than I had planned. I quickly pulled out my phone and messaged her back with an apology about getting distracted. I made a mental note to get her extra chocolate for making her worry.

I tilted the book. There was no way I would get through all of it. I took it to the counter to purchase.

"Ah, it caught your attention, did it?" the woman asked. "I've been looking for the right home for that one. Not many are willing to accept the harsh realities."

I nodded. "It's certainly interesting."

The transaction finished smoothly and I returned to my hunt for food. I held out hope that maybe this would hold a key piece of information about necromancers.

"It's about time you got back," Lexi said as soon as I opened the door.

I put the bags down on the counter to separate them. "Sorry, I got distracted. I might have found more information."

"You weren't supposed to be working," she warned.

I rolled my eyes. "It's not a lead, just more information."

"Still work."

I handed her one of the bags. "I bought a book. Does that work better?"

"Much."

I shook my head and grabbed my bag of food and the book.

"So, why did you buy the book?"

"It's a history on arcane casters. Maybe there will be something we can use. If nothing else, it should provide a good reference outside of this case," I justified. My own curiosity was not a good excuse.

Lexi laughed.

I raised an eyebrow at her.

She smirked. "Only you would go out for food and come back with reference material."

I rolled my eyes and shook my head. "Has there been anything with Vanessa or Christian?"

"Not a whole lot. They're going about their weekends. Christian seems to be holing himself up in his apartment. He's only come out to get a food delivery. You passed pretty close to Vanessa. She's out shopping, but I haven't seen her purchase anything."

"Is there anything going on in the stores?"

Lexi shrugged. "No idea. Maybe Frank knows something. I've been noting the stores she's gone into."

"Hm." I tapped my fork against my lips. "Karen said she was frugal, but I'm going to follow up on that later."

"Not without someone else," Lexi said quickly.

I rolled my eyes. "You're really going to keep following Silver's request?"

She turned to me. "Look, I still haven't forgiven him, but I'm not going to let you go off on your own if it's case related. I watched you take off on your own once in Ghost Forest and that was frightening. I had no idea if your crazy plan would work. I had no idea if those werewolves would tear you apart."

I dropped my gaze to the floor. "I'm sorry." How often had I made others worry with my recklessness?

"That's a huge book," Lexi said after a minute.

"It goes back centuries, but a lot of the information is summarized."

"Does that mean you'll be still for a while and I don't have to worry about you wanting to go out?" Lexi sounded hopeful.

"You'll want me to go get you supper, right?"

"Okay, except for that. And thanks for the extra chocolate."

"Does that make up for being late?"

Lexi smirked. "I'll let it pass this time." She paused. "Ooh... ooh... There might be something."

"On who?"

"Christian."

I got up and went to go see what was happening, but it looked just as it had before. "What?"

"He greeted a woman at his door."

"I thought he didn't deal with the boss."

"Circumstances could have changed. Though she looked more like a prostitute."

I balked at Lexi's description. "Isn't prostitution illegal in this territory?"

"I'm not sure, but I think so. I was already planning on adding the footage to the case file."

"I guess if nothing else, we can get him on indecent exposure and hiring a prostitute," I grumbled.

Lexi hummed in agreement. "I wonder if he makes enough to hire a prostitute to come to his house with his salary or if he's using whatever money he's making off the scheme."

"Can you check his bank records? See if there are any abnormalities?"

She shook her head. "I already did and there's nothing out of the ordinary. I haven't been able to find out if he has another account somewhere. If he does, it's not under his name or ID number."

I was about to ask Lexi to see if she could find out how he was paying for the prostitute until I realized we were assuming the mystery woman's profession. "We need to figure out who she is."

"On it."

I went back to my meal while Lexi got to work. I lost time reading through the book. It spoke briefly of dark magics used, but nothing definitive. I started flipping forward in time, looking for more recent entries which would hopefully provide more information. The longer I read, the more I curled up in the chair.

"I'm hungry," Lexi said, breaking me out of my search.

I glanced at my watch and it had been hours. "What do you want?"

She shrugged, never turning from her screens. "You pick."

I rolled my eyes and grabbed my bag.

Before I could get out the door, Lexi tossed at me, "And don't take forever in a bookstore."

"Yes, ma'am."

I had not realized how late it was until I saw that the sun was going down. I shivered at the cool breeze. I wished I had brought a jacket.

Focus. Get food and get back. There had to be something I could use in that book. It was interesting so it was worth buying, but I worried I was wasting my time.

I ducked down an alley to avoid the crowds. I would come back to the main street as I got closer to where the restaurants were located.

Something pulled at my senses after a couple of blocks and I turned, looking for the source. It was arcane. I put out my hand, searching further with my power. Nothing.

I sighed. The sensation of being watched was similar to when I was with Frank outside of the abandoned church.

Shaking my head, I continued on my way. I had only made it a few steps when it came back stronger. My hand immediately went out so I could follow the spell back to the source. It dissipated before I got out of the alley.

I searched for a few seconds longer. My phone going off stopped the attempt to find the source.

"Ket, are you okay? What's going on?" Lexi asked, her words coming out rapidly.

I rolled my eyes. "Are you watching me through the camera network?"

There was a pause. "Yes."

I sighed. "I'm fine. I caught something arcane. It's gone."

"I don't like this. You should come back. We can have something delivered."

"Lexi, I'm fine, really." Everyone was being far too overprotective.

"Please."

I took a deep breath. "I'm already out this far. I might as well get food. I'll be back soon."

"Can you at least go back to the main street?" she begged.

"When I get closer to where I need to be. I don't want to deal with the crowds," I countered.

"Ket..." Lexi whined. "I can't pull a Silver on you through the phone to get you to listen."

"You've been following me through the camera network. Isn't that enough?" Why did I have to have this argument with her?

There was a sharp blow of air into the line. "Okay, but be careful. Vanessa is nearby again."

"I will. I..." I paused, the sensation was back even stronger this time.

I spun, looking for the source. It felt close this time. I clutched my head, dropping my phone, as it turned into an attack. Piercing and pounding sensations came from all directions at once.

A ghostly voice said, "Don't interfere."

"Ket? Ketayl!"

I used my power to push back against the attack, getting some breathing room. The sensation disappeared. I shivered as a chill ran up my spine. Whoever it was, they were powerful.

"Dammit, Ketayl, answer me!" Lexi shouting through my phone snapped me out of it.

I bent down and retrieved my phone, dusting it off with a shaky hand. "I'm here," I said quietly.

"I'm going to get one of the guys to come get you," she said firmly.

"No. No, I'll come back. Go ahead and order something." My mind was as far away from food as could be, but Lexi still needed to be taken care of.

"Stay there. I'm sending Silver. If you don't, I'll leave my post and come get you," she threatened.

I took a deep breath. I needed Lexi to stay on her task. "Fine."

17

WHILE I WAITED FOR SILVER, I remained on alert: constantly scanning the alley with my eyes, listening for something out of the ordinary, and stretching my senses for the arcane. He was taking a long time to get here, but he had been keeping track of Christian and the man lived on the outskirts of Sola.

I paced. Who was the woman that left the message to not interfere? Someone obviously knew I was involved and part of the TIO. They definitely knew now that I was an arcane caster also.

Loud footsteps hurried quickly down the alley. I turned on my heel to see Silver running toward me.

"Lexi called me in a panic. What happened?" he asked once he got closer enough.

I sighed. "It's really not as big of a deal as she made it out to be. I was on my way to get us food."

"Why are you in an alley if you were getting food?" It was impossible to miss the accusing tone in his voice.

My shoulders slumped. "Avoiding the crowd. Lexi got worked up over something and she was about to leave unless I waited for you."

"You need to tell me what happened. We're not leaving here until you do. I'll determine for myself if she was overreacting." Silver's voice was firm.

Great, he's going to be overprotective now. "It's nothing. I sensed something arcane a few times and heard a creepy voice." No need to mention the attack.

"And you were jumpy when I got here. Give me the details."

I rolled my eyes and crossed my arms, not looking up at my partner. "I sensed something arcane like someone was watching me. Similar to when we were in Ocean's Edge." I purposely avoided telling him about my encounter with it while I was with Frank. "It happened three times. Each time getting stronger. The last one whoever it is left a message to not interfere." I continued to avoid mentioning the attack. It would only make things worse.

"Kela..." Silver said softly. He shook his head. "How can you think a threat is nothing?"

I remained silent. Silver put his hand on my head. I kept my gaze to the ground.

"Hey, I'm here and you know I block scrying. We should probably stay together."

I had forgotten he blocked scrying. He never did explain how, but now was not the time to ask. "No."

"Don't argue with me over this. Your safety is at stake."

I took a deep breath. "We can't have the entire team hiding under your cover."

"I'm talking about you. You were the one targeted." He kept getting louder.

"Lexi and Frank aren't arcane sensitive. They might never have noticed if someone was watching them," I argued back.

My partner stepped closer, standing over me. "I'm not taking a chance with you!"

I jumped at the volume of his voice. I kept my eyes down and clenched my jaw. I had not thought my plan of action reckless.

Silver pulled me against him. "Can't you just accept that I can't lose you?"

I sighed, moving away from Silver. "I need you to understand that we're in a team of more than just us right now. I have to think of the safety of everyone."

He pulled me back into a hug. "I know. And that's one of the many things I love about you."

I stiffened up at the word Silver used. He tossed it out as if it was a natural thing to say. I questioned if he truly meant it. He had never said he loved anything about me before.

"We should get back." I had no idea what else to say. I knew I would end up obsessing over his wording when my focus should be on the case. I managed to get out of his hold.

"Okay, do you want to get food first?" He seemed calmer at least.

I paused to think about it. "Um... yeah... we probably should. Lexi has to be starving by now."

"We can pick her up something sweet."

We walked in silence for a couple of minutes until I found a new topic. "Was there anything with Christian?"

Silver shook his head. "The best I could make out, he spent his day in his apartment playing video games. Ordered food. Ordered a prostitute."

"She was a prostitute?" Lexi and I had figured, but I wanted confirmation.

"Yes. I overheard the conversation. They talked about prices and services before she went in. Money changed hands as soon as she was inside. They joined where someone could see them. It was on the alley-side of the building, but still quite visible to anyone over there."

I sighed. There went that possible lead. "Lexi did complain about Christian showing up naked when he opened the window."

"That was not something I wanted to see. Even less watching him join with a prostitute," Silver grumbled.

"Apparently I'm needing to make this up to the entire team." We had gotten lucky prior in not having to deal with things like this.

Silver shrugged. "It's part of the job. Though I wouldn't mind if you still decided to make it up to me somehow." His tone shifted to mischievous.

I rolled my eyes. I wanted to threaten him with desk work, but held my tongue.

He took my hand as we approached the main street. I let him, knowing better than to argue over something so minor.

"Do you know if there's been anything with Vanessa?" Silver asked as we approached the busy street.

I shook my head. "Not as of when I left. She's been going about her day: eating out and shopping without buying anything. I'm hoping Frank was able to get more than we have through video. Last I heard she was in this area."

"You been working on anything interesting?" Silver had my hand kind of tight. Not painfully so, but definitely more than normal.

"Reading. Not getting anything else to follow as a lead yet."

Silence fell between us for a few minutes.

"Have you felt like you're being watched at the hotel?"

I looked up at Silver who was focused on where we were walking. I bit my lower lip and paid attention again to the crowd. "No. I haven't sensed anything arcane at least."

"I doubt much would get past you."

"You put too much faith in my abilities," I muttered.

Silver snorted. "Faith, yes, but I've also seen what you're capable of firsthand."

I remained silent. He still overestimated my abilities.

"So, where are we going?"

I blinked. "I'm not sure. I planned on coming to the general area and figuring it out when I got here."

"Okay. I'm picking then." Silver tugged me along toward a restaurant. "If I can get off babysitting duty, I plan on going to the branch office to use their physical training facilities later."

I pursed my lips. Christian was likely a dead end. We could keep video surveillance on him. "Go ahead."

"You're going with me."

I shook my head. "I've got to keep searching."

"I'm not taking no for an answer."

I rolled my eyes. Was it even worth arguing with him over?

"I noticed you didn't bring your violin so this is the next best thing to get you away from the case for a little while both physically and mentally."

My shoulders slumped and I sighed. "Can't I just go to Karen's studio again? Or down to the pool?"

"No. I need someone to spar with."

"Take Lexi. I'm sure she could use a break by now."

Silver laughed. "I'm not taking on a werewolf even in their native form. I may be crazy with the fights I get into, but I'm not stupid. Frank really isn't an option either as I could accidentally hurt him."

"The last time you hit me with your shield it hurt," I pointed out.

He frowned. "It was part of making you angry. I feel bad about it, but at least I healed the injury afterward. You need to get some practice in if this turns into a fight."

That made me pause mentally. I had learned to listen when he started gearing up for one. "Are you getting that impression?"

"Not quite, but I'm not ruling it out."

I took a deep breath. "Will this make us even?"

"Sure."

I hung my head. Training with Silver it was then.

SILVER LEANED against the wall with his arms crossed while he waited for me.

"Let's get this over with," I said. I never looked forward to his training sessions.

He smirked at me. "We'll start with your favorite: running."

I groaned. This was going to be more painful than I had estimated. Was this payback for having him follow Christian?

For the next hour, Silver dragged me from one thing to the next. By the end, I lay on the floor, staring at the ceiling, trying to catch my breath.

He knelt next to me. "If I knew you were going to keep running away from me during sparring, I wouldn't have started with running."

"Don't come at me like that then," I shot at him. I refused to move from my spot. I was fairly certain my back had melted to the floor.

Silver laughed, taking a seat next to me. "You've gotten better with your tactics."

I rolled my eyes. Now I was hungry. I would not admit it though.

"Why did you run so much?" he asked.

"I've only had Lockonis to train with for several months." And she liked fireballs. Running was the only thing I could do to keep from getting hit.

Silver laughed. "Okay, I think I understand. Come on." He took my hand and peeled me off the floor.

I wobbled, my legs protesting with having to support my weight. I needed a long, hot shower badly.

My partner brushed at my back. I must have picked up some dirt. It was something he used to always do after we trained together. Right now, I could use a little normalcy. Especially after the warning I received earlier.

At least now we had confirmation that the necromancer was female and had the ability to wield the arcane. Whether or not she was an actual necromancer remained to be seen. I needed to get back to that book. I remained unsure if the attack was on purpose or not. It could have been something that occurred when using that spell, whatever it was. If only I had paid more attention when it was happening.

I glanced at my partner. He usually liked to train to think through things. "Come up with anything?"

Silver stroked the small patch of hair on his chin. "Yes and no. We should have Lexi see if she can run the financials on Christian. I want to see if he's outliving his income from First Union. The prostitute was not cheap."

I contemplated his idea. "We're putting a lot on her. We should send that request to Sparks." Sending it to the Halfling in charge of the lab at the main office might not be the best option, but I could not ask more of Lexi.

"Yeah, you're right. He probably needs something to do," Silver commented, handing me a towel.

"Give him a call and tell him what you're thinking." I wiped my face and neck down.

My partner raised an eyebrow at me. "What are you going to do?"

"Take a shower." I threw my towel in the bin and walked away.

I was clean, fed, and curled up on the couch with my arcane history book. I had tucked my bare feet underneath the pillows. Lexi left when we got back to go find something to eat and get some air. Her messy bun appeared more frazzled than usual.

Silver moved my feet so he could sit down.

I shoved my feet under his leg where they would be warm.

He laughed. "Haven't done this since we lived together in Ghost Forest."

I shrugged and continued reading. I had still only found vague references to necromancers. I flipped a few pages forward, uninterested at this time about politics.

The book disappeared from my hands.

Silver flipped it over, holding my spot with his finger. "I didn't think anything could tear you away from the case. What's this about?"

"Arcane History. Can you give it back? There might be something in there about necromancers." I held my hand open, waiting.

"Oh, it's work. No, you need a break."

I rolled my eyes and reached for the book. "I can take a break when I go to rest."

My partner put the book down on the table in front of the couch, open to the page I was on. "No, now. We should talk."

I hung my head back over the arm of the couch. *Of course he wants to talk.*

Silver laughed. "You are so much more expressive than when we first met." He pulled one of my feet out from underneath him and pressed his thumbs into the bottom, massaging it.

I squirmed and tried to pull my foot away. He held onto my ankle with one hand. "Let go," I whined.

"No, you're tense."

"Lexi and Frank will be back soon." If it was just the two of us, I might gripe at him for a bit, but I did not want to be caught like this.

"Frank is staying out for a couple more hours and Lexi said she planned to take her time. I think by now you've noticed she and I don't exactly get along."

I sighed. He was too determined and I remained unsure if I should fight him on this.

He dug both of his thumbs into the sole of my foot, releasing tension I had not realized was there. It was instantly relaxing, and I sank further into the couch. "Believe me now?" he asked, grinning.

I sighed and gave up. Fighting him when he was in overprotective big brother mode was rarely ever worth it.

"Kela," Silver said quietly. "We need to figure things out between us."

I groaned. "There's nothing to figure out."

"*Yes, there is.*"

I stopped and stared at Silver. I had never heard him speak my native dialect back to me. "*How come you've never spoken in it before?*"

"*I wasn't confident I could. I had some downtime and Lindale pointed me to the general area she thinks you and Kitteren are from. Took some time to learn it.*"

I gave him a soft smile. "*You didn't have to. And just so you know, you still have an accent.*"

Silver shook his head, turning his attention back to my foot. "At least you didn't hear me in the beginning. Apparently, I was unintelligible. I'm still unsure about holding full conversations."

I laughed lightly. Sometimes he was too sweet.

The smile disappeared from his face. "I'm not sure what to do. I know I've continued to make a mess of things. You keep saying you're the one who isn't necessary here, but the truth is, it's me. I'm good for a fight, but that's about it. This searching for clues thing isn't exactly a strength of mine."

I shrugged. "It doesn't matter. You can't gain experience without doing it."

He frowned at me. "I think you're missing the point here."

"You'll have to explain it then. If I could read minds, we wouldn't be having this conversation."

Silver stared at me for a moment. "It's too bad. It would make all of this easier."

I let out a soft huff in agreement. It would make dealing with him a lot easier. Though I had a feeling being in his head was not somewhere I wanted to go.

Silence fell between us for several seconds.

"You're probably right in that there's nothing to discuss. Not right now," Silver said quietly, his attention on my foot in his lap.

I raised an eyebrow at him. He had gone through the trouble of cornering me and now he was backpedaling.

He clenched his jaw for a moment before obviously forcing a smile. "Given the last several months, I assume words would mean little to you. No matter how much I tried to express otherwise. I'll have to work on my actions."

Is he right? I paused and contemplated his observation. Words had become empty to me, especially lately. I had been trying to ignore it, but he was right. "Okay."

"You're just agreeing to get out of having a conversation," Silver said, his tone teasing.

I rolled my eyes. "I'm sure you'll be wanting to talk again at some point."

"We can still talk about things now. The highlands in the Northern Isles are really beautiful."

I took a deep breath. Idle conversation was not something I enjoyed either.

"How come you never talk about it?"

I rolled my eyes and dropped my head back again, groaning. This was possibly more torturous than whatever it was he wanted to talk about before.

"Oh come on, it can't be that bad."

"I hate small talk," I said, not bothering to move to look at him. "Besides, you probably know more about the area than I do."

"We could always take some time off and go there."

I sat up and shook my head. I managed to get my foot away from Silver, but he took the other one. "What about where you're from. Why don't you look into that?" I shot at him.

"Yours is much more narrowed down. All I have is somewhere along the northern coast of the Inner Sea region. I really don't have anything more than that. Not without going back to the Central Seat and seeing if there are any records."

"You never looked before?"

Silver shrugged. "I admit I was always curious, but my master would always change the subject when I brought it up. None of the others would speak of it either. I spent most of my time in the library studying scriptures. My stubbornness at showing the others I could become a paladin overrode any curiosity about where I came from."

"You could always take some time off and go to the Central Seat. I don't mind."

Silver froze then. I could see the muscles in his face tense up and it continued through his body.

"Ow!" I struggled to get my foot out of his tightening grasp.

His grip loosened immediately. "I'm so sorry!" He held my foot gently, examining it. "That path is no longer open to me."

"Why?"

"Kela..." Silver said, his tone warning. His attention was still on my foot.

I glared at him. "No, you pester me endlessly. You can answer this."

He let out a long breath. "When I left the church to join the TIO, I thought I had made my intentions clear to the Order. The Central Seat has been requesting my presence and I will not give in to their demands."

I hissed when he touched a particularly sensitive spot on my foot.

"Damn, I did injure you. I'm such an idiot," Silver muttered.

"I'm fine," I argued.

Silver gave me an exasperated look out of the corner of his eye. "You need to stop using that phrase."

I scrunched up my nose at him.

As I felt his power wash over my foot, my partner sighed. "I'm fine with not knowing. Can we leave it at that?"

"Only if you grant me the same."

He glanced at me out of the side of his eye. "I could, but you're such a fascinating puzzle."

I rolled my eyes. "Then you should also figure out your own puzzle."

"Kela..." Now he sounded exasperated. "I already told you that the information, if there even is any, is out of my reach."

"I could go."

Silver stopped and looked at me. I immediately hated that look. It was as if he thought I was stupid. "Do you have a death wish?"

"Enough people seem to think so." And perhaps they were right. "When we first met you said you had some mage parishioners. I don't see the problem."

"That was Ocean's Edge, not the Central Seat. I think I also told you that they were far less tolerant of arcane casters. Hells, they dislike non-Humans for the most part."

I shrugged. "Wouldn't be the first people to have a problem with me. Won't be the last either."

"Kela, no. Just no. I'm not putting you at risk for something that might not even exist. How did you even turn this conversation around on me?"

"Seemed only fair. You poke into my past frequently. Apparently even without my knowledge." That last part bothered me most. Though I remained impressed that he went so far as to learn to speak my dialect of common back to me.

Silver gave a short laugh. "I guess I was due."

Silence fell between us for a few minutes and I simply stayed curled up on the couch, thinking through what I had read so far. It was infuriating that the book held no real value for this case. At least to where I had read, but I had not yet gotten to the Racial War. It could be possible that the necromancers had not organized until that point. They obviously had not received backing from the governments, often being the subject of hunts.

Ironically that was exactly what Silver and I were doing now. It made sense that being hunted would splinter larger groups and send them underground. Likely many lived as normal members of society and kept their dark practices secret.

"Who couldn't you let go?" Silver asked quietly.

"Huh?" I looked up at him.

"In the park after you followed that woman, I overheard you say something about if you weren't sure you could let them go."

I shrugged. "It should be obvious." He was smart enough to figure it out and I found myself too embarrassed to say it aloud.

"Why won't you say it?"

I eyed Silver. Why did he switch to my dialect? "I don't want to. Can I have my book back now?"

"No, you're done with the case for today."

I scrunched up my face at him. "I thought I was lead."

"You are, but I'm still to keep you from running yourself into the ground."

"It's just reading." Surely that was not considered taxing.

Silver gave me an exasperated look.

Smirking, I reached out and levitated the book back to me.

"Oh, come on. That's not fair." Silver snatched it out of the air and held it. "I said no. How about I read it for a bit? I might have a different perspective."

"And what am I supposed to do?"

"Rest."

I glared at him. *"Pain in the ass."*

Silver smirked at me. *"You know it."*

18

LEXI DRAGGED me out of the hotel room bright and early while Silver was still performing his morning rituals. She yawned broadly and moved sluggishly.

"We didn't have to leave so early. I know you were up late last night," I said quietly.

"More like I haven't gone to bed yet. I wanted to get you out of there while Silver was distracted." She yawned again. "It's fine. I used to be a morning person, but being a werewolf means I'm a night prowler now. We don't do mornings. That's why all of the rooms for us at the Alpha Prime's estate face west. Unless someone pissed off Nikolai or Sasha."

I laughed lightly. Though the problem with the team still nagged at the back of my mind. I needed them to at least tolerate each other. Being a moderator between Lexi and Silver would only distract us. Well, really, Silver and either of the other two. That was what I really should have talked about with him last night.

"What's wrong?" Lexi asked.

I looked up at her, startled out of my thoughts. "Sorry, just thinking about things."

"I might be able to help. You don't need to take on everything yourself."

I sighed. "It'll upset everyone."

Lexi frowned. "If it's what I think it is, you need to voice it."

I glanced over at her out of the corner of my eye and bit my lower lip for a moment. "We need to be able to function as a team. I'm not sure how much more I can be a moderator between everyone."

"Yeah, I figured. Look, I can get along with Frank, but Silver keeps rubbing me the wrong way. And it's not directly between us either - it's how he treats you. I know I called him over Frank yesterday, but he made more sense since Christian wasn't doing anything other than eating, playing video games, and screwing a whore."

"Playing video games?" I vaguely remembered Silver saying that.

"I pulled up his internet usage last night after you went to rest. He was also showing his naked self to random strangers online and watching porn."

I cringed. Those types of people made me lose faith in our society.

Lexi yawned. "Yeah, he could use some better hobbies, but at least I figured out that he was outspending his pay without any other recorded source of income. The cyber team has taken over tracking down any other bank accounts he has."

That task was supposed to have gone to Sparks.

"What about Vanessa?" If she wanted to talk about the case, then I was happy to oblige. Especially after Silver interrupted me last night.

Lexi shrugged. "Frank reported the same thing as what we saw. She talked with some people, but it seemed like nothing outside of random conversations. He wasn't able to overhear what was said."

I bit my lower lip. "I probably should have sent you."

"Nope, I think I have enough if I have to go back into First Union again."

"It would make it look less suspicious and we might be able to get more information," I pointed out.

"I might kill Christian. Or printer guy." The grin on her face said more than her words.

"Okay, okay. I get it, but it would still look suspicious if you didn't work at least part of the day. There might be more they can give us. And no killing our suspects or other employees." What kind of team were we?

Lexi laughed.

There was a long silence.

"I can't promise to not take Silver down a peg or two when he's being an outright jerk, but I'll do better to tolerate him and continue to make fun of him. He didn't seem so obnoxious when the two of you were in Ghost Forest. I guess I just never dealt with him enough."

I shrugged. That was a different time and I was not about to go into details with her. "So why did you pull me out so early in the morning? Nothing is even open yet."

"You needed to get away from the hotel. There are very few people out at this hour, plus I'm also here. Not to mention that if anyone starts anything, I'm tired and cranky."

I shook my head - my teammate was odd. "We should head back so you can get some sleep." I also did not need to be babysat.

"I'm good. Gives me a chance to rethink my strategies. I'm still bouncing around hubs to backtrack where the high-grade account death certificates originated from. I'd directly hack Christian's house, but I don't have enough evidence to go for it and there was nothing in his account at First Union as far as I could tell from a quick glance."

I bit my lower lip. "Seems like he went to great lengths to hide his tracks."

Lexi sighed. "I want to give him credit for his dedication, but it's the same damn thing. It's just long and tedious. With any luck there will be something by the time we get back."

I opened my mouth to order her to rest when we got back, but was stopped by a sudden arcane attack. I clutched my head and clenched my teeth as a sharp pain shot through.

"Ketayl?" Lexi stepped in front of me, grabbing my shoulders.

I shut my eyes tight as it continued. The sharp pain became more intense. I managed to focus my power to create enough of a barrier to mitigate the onslaught.

"Come on, talk to me," my teammate begged.

Tears rolled down my cheeks as the pain intensified rapidly. I could not hear anything over the pounding in my head. I needed to push back. Something, anything to get it to stop.

I lost track of time as it continued, struggling to hold on to consciousness. Suddenly the pain coming in stopped.

Cracking my eyes open, I took stock of my situation. I was sitting on the ground up against a building. It looked like we were in an alley. Lexi knelt in front of me. Frank and Ayda stood nearby. Ayda was casting a barrier around us.

"Oh, thank the Gods," Lexi said, relief plain in her voice.

"It's not over yet," Ayda said, her voice strained. "I won't be able to keep this up for long."

I struggled to my feet. "I can take over." Now that I could think again I could help. My legs shook to the point where I was unsure if I could stand.

"Don't even think about it. That was Hells of an attack you just suffered," Ayda ordered. She took a step forward suddenly, her eyes darting about. "Well, that works too. Glad it stopped. Hopefully they won't be back."

"We're closer to the office than the hotel. Let's get the kid there," Frank suggested.

Had we really wandered that far? It was difficult to hold onto any one thought right now.

Lexi got under my arm, holding me up.

Ayda nodded. "My car is nearby. I'll bring it around."

"Why are you here?" I asked, my voice shaking.

"I happened to be coming to see you guys when I saw the start of the attack," Frank said. "I called Ayda. Figured we needed an arcane caster."

"Thank you," I said softly. The pounding in my head had yet to subside, but it was just a matter of time now.

"I'll be right back and then we can talk more," Ayda said and left quickly, jogging out of the alley.

"How am I supposed to defend her against an attack like that?" Lexi asked quietly.

"Once you find the caster, a bullet works pretty well," Frank replied.

ONE COULD EASILY CUT the tension in the Sola Branch's media room with Silver's sword. My watch had betrayed me again, sending an alert about a high heart rate to my boss. Since Silver had not been with me, Lockonis had to track us down via the location chip on my devices so he could tell her what was going on. By the time he caught up to us, we were at the branch office.

And he was none too happy about not being contacted by

someone nearby. Ayda's involvement was likely the only thing holding him back.

Ayda and Lexi were currently talking to Lockonis who had insisted on a video call. Her picture on the screen was large and bright and I could not look at it for long. My head still swam. Sitting back in my chair was as bad as leaning forward. No matter what I did, I was nauseous.

I was glad I had not eaten anything since early yesterday evening. It would likely have come out the wrong way by now.

Frank knelt down in front of me. "You going to make it, kid?" He kept his voice low.

"Unfortunately."

He smiled softly. "Sorry, you can't leave before this old monkey. How about I get you to the crash room so you can rest?"

"Frank, you still need to give your statement," Ayda reminded. Her voice was gentle and she glanced over at me.

"And I intend to be here to hear all of it," Silver said sharply. His arms were crossed and he continued to glare at all of us.

Lockonis rolled her eyes. "Ket, I can catch up with you later, okay? I don't think you're in any condition to give a statement right now."

I nodded and groaned, leaning forward, pinching the bridge of my nose to get the dizziness to pass. It only made the nausea worse. After a moment I said quietly, "Just tell me where it is and I can get there."

Ayda gave me directions and I made my way out of the media room slowly. Walking on my own was far more difficult than I had been prepared for with the hallways swaying. I kept telling myself to put one foot in front of the other, making it down the hallway far too slowly for my liking.

I stumbled to the side and used the wall to help keep myself upright. As soon as the swaying slowed down to a manageable rate, I continued, keeping a hand on the wall.

It took a while, but I made it to the crash room. I reached for the door and the world went black.

"Hey, come on!" an unfamiliar female voice said.

Someone shook my shoulder.

I groaned and cracked my eyes open. *Why am I on the floor?* I was on my side, staring at the door I had been reaching for. At least the world stopped swaying.

"Thank the Heavens."

Multiple footsteps thundered closer. The sound and vibration echoed through my head and I closed my eyes tightly.

"Thanks, Lacura, we've got it from here," Ayda said.

"You sure?"

"Yeah, you need your downtime badly. Go give your little girl a hug for me." Ayda's voice was gentle.

Footsteps moved away from me.

I got one hand on the floor and attempted to push myself up. I managed to get my other arm under me when the dizziness returned. I rested my forehead on the floor.

"Hey," Silver said softly. "I've got you."

I assumed it was my partner who picked me up. The movement was too fast and I curled up, groaning. The nausea returned with a vengeance.

A familiar whine sounded through the hallway. What could have Lexi upset?

I shut the world out to wrestle back control. Until I was set down on something soft, I paid no attention to what had gone on amongst the others.

"You stay here with her," Ayda ordered. "I should have sent you with her to begin with."

"Yes, ma'am," Silver said quietly. "When Ketayl is ready, I'll ask her if it was another attack."

"Wasn't," I muttered.

"Wasn't what?" Frank asked. "Wasn't another attack or wasn't prepared?"

"It wasn't another attack," Ayda said quietly. "I didn't think it was. I would've sensed it being so close. Get rest, Ket. I'll keep them in line for you for now."

A door closed with a quiet click.

"I'm always the fool, aren't I?" Silver asked softly after a few minutes. "I knew you were suffering and I was being stubborn about being left out."

Laying down made the nausea go down. I cracked my eyes open to figure out my surroundings.

Silver sat on the floor next to the couch I was on. More couches lined the room along with cots folded up off to the side.

"Just rest, Kela," he whispered. "You're safe."

"I know, but there's too much to do right now to rest." I pushed myself up to an elbow and the dizziness returned. How was I supposed to work like this?

"No." Silver gently pushed me back down.

I attempted to fight, but I had nothing.

"Stay down," Silver ordered, but his voice was gentle. "From what I gathered from their reports so far, you suffered Hells of an attack. You need time to recover before you can get back to work or you'll be down for even longer."

"Stop being logical about this," I muttered.

"Someone has to since you're not doing it. Not that you ever are when it comes to taking care of yourself," Silver said, his words clipped.

Mustering the energy, I went to get up again, and again Silver pushed me back down. "I need to write my report," I argued.

"No, you need to rest. Give me a minute." Silver left the room.

Now was my chance. I forced myself to a sitting position. The room spun in a blur. I could work through this. I had not even fully stood when I fell to my hands and knees.

"Dammit. I told you to rest," Silver said harshly and picked me up off the floor. "Keep this up and I won't even entertain the thought of helping you work while you recover."

I grunted at him. I would keep trying when I had the chance, though I wondered about his suggestion of help.

Silver sat down on the floor next to me with a pad of paper and a pen. "When you're up for it, I can write down what happened."

I sighed. Talking about it was the last thing I wanted to do, but no matter what I wanted, someone was going to make me talk about it. A report had to be filed and I was the primary source of information. Even Lexi, who had been there from the start of the arcane attack, had only been an observer.

Looking back though, something bothered me. "There's no way for one person to wield that much arcane energy. Certainly not enough to override my barrier like it wasn't even there."

Silver brushed my bangs out of my face. "You don't need to push yourself to do this now."

I rolled my eyes and batted his hand away. Laying down helped and if this was how I was going to get work done then so be it. At least something was getting done.

"Geez you're stubborn." Silver ran a hand over his hair before scribbling on his notepad. "What about being connected to a ley line? You wielded way more power than I've ever seen out of you before when we were in the middle of a concentrated one."

I hummed for a moment. "I never wielded power outside of what I'm fully capable of. Having an unending supply of arcane energy is not the same as this... as if they were using something to amplify it." I got to my elbows and hurried to get up, but my body reacted sluggishly. I had to write the idea down. Break it apart in theory.

A hand pushed down on my back and held me there.

"Knock it off or I'll sit on you to keep you still," Silver warned. "Sun watch over me, you are pushing my patience."

"Good, now let me up. I can't explain arcane theory to you."

Silver moved away. Finally.

I had only begun pushing myself back up when he sat down so his legs were over my back. "Let me up." I struggled to get out from under him.

"No."

"Silver..." I warned.

"My answer is still no. I know you're in no condition to escape."

I growled at him.

"By the Gods you're infuriating sometimes." He gently touched my head. "What the...?"

"What? Let me up. Whatever it is will go away soon." I kept getting louder. I hated being pinned like this.

There was a comforting warmth emanating from his hand, which told me he was using his power. "Actually, it won't. Not without help." Silver's voice was low. "Damn, I should've looked deeper before now."

With the way we were situated, I could not turn to look at him. "Can you get off me?"

Silver remained silent, paying attention to whatever it was he was doing with his power.

I squirmed to get loose, but nothing seemed to work.

"Dare I ask what you're doing to Ket?" Lexi's voice had a warning tone to it.

Please, not now.

"Keeping her still," Silver answered flatly. "She keeps trying to overdo it and I was tired of picking her up off the floor. I've got an idea of what's still affecting her, but I need time to figure out how to counteract it."

"Nothing is affecting me. Let me up," I ordered.

Lexi sniffed audibly. "I think I need to start listening to my nose when it comes to magic. I hate to say you're right, but there's something off about her scent."

I sighed. I was apparently getting help from no one. "I feel fine."

"Until you try to get up again," Silver shot at me. "Lexi, I was going to write Ketayl's report down, but she wouldn't stop moving. Do you mind doing that? It'll keep her occupied while I figure this out."

"I'm right here." I attempted to pull myself out from under Silver. He was right that I was unable to concentrate enough to teleport, but there had to be something. "Dammit, get off me. You're heavy."

Lexi sat down on the floor next to me. She leaned her head on the couch. "I know. Silver's being a jerk about it, but you need time to recover."

"I heard that," Silver grumbled.

She stuck her tongue out at him. "Wasn't trying to hide it."

I growled at my partner. "Silver, get off of me or I swear when I get free, you're going to live to regret this."

He laughed. "Now I don't want to move. I kind of want to see how this plays out."

I glanced at Lexi who was laughing softly.

"Joking aside," Silver said, "there's something divine leftover from that attack. I'm almost completely certain it's the reason you haven't recovered yet."

I dropped my head to the couch in defeat.

"What is it?" Lexi asked.

"I'm not sure. Unfortunately, I do have to let her up."

"Finally," I muttered.

"I need a stronger connection to figure out what is going on," Silver said softly.

Oh no. I groaned into the couch. Last time he needed a stronger connection, he kissed me.

"Not that much stronger. Give me some credit that I can accurately judge what I need and know your limits."

His weight shifted and soon enough I was free again. I took the opportunity to breathe. He may not have sat directly on me, but just his legs over my back were heavy.

"Come on. I need you to sit up. It won't be long." Silver tugged on my arm.

That he refrained from moving me to where he wanted me said something, but damned if I could figure out what. I struggled to a sitting position, swaying as the world spun again. I closed my eyes, hoping it would ease the building nausea.

Silver gently cupped my face and rested his forehead against mine. This I knew. This I was okay with, but not in front of others. I squirmed, knowing Lexi was still in the room.

"Ket, just stay still," Lexi said softly. "I mean, I love watching you give him a hard time, but I don't want to see you hurting anymore."

My face got warmer as we sat there and I had lost track of time - all of my energy was spent on staying upright and not getting sick on Silver.

"Can you give Ket a break? If she gets any more pale, she might pass out," Lexi asked softly.

"I need a little more time. It's a simple spell, but there are a lot of components. I don't want to miss something," Silver replied.

"You're fixing it?" Lexi asked.

"I'm trying to make sure I know exactly what's going on before attempting it." There was a pause for a few moments before Silver moved away. "Go ahead and rest, Ketayl. I'll need some time to figure out how to unravel that mess."

I curled up in a ball on the couch. It helped none.

A hand touched my hair. One too small to belong to Silver. I cracked an eye open to see what was going on. My werewolf teammate sat on the floor next to me. "Why are you here?" I asked.

Lexi wore a strained smile on her face. "I came here to crash, but I'll wait and see if he needs help." She thumbed over at Silver.

He sat on the edge of another couch, scribbling on the notepad. "Go ahead. This might take a bit."

"She's really hurting. There's got to be something I can do."

Silver paused his scribbling and stroked the small patch of hair on his chin. "There really isn't. Until I undo that spell, she needs to rest. It's messing with her equilibrium so even sitting up is going to be hard."

I pushed myself to my elbows again. "Then I can work through it until you're ready." No sooner had I finished speaking, but I found myself flattened on the couch again.

"I think I found how I can help," Lexi said, her hand on my back.

Silver laughed lightly.

"You need to rest and I need to work," I warned.

Lexi moved so she sat with her legs over me as Silver had, but somehow, she seemed heavier. "Since you work in your head all the time, I'm not interrupting you. And don't worry about me, I'm fine here. I'm sure I'll be spending a full week with printer guy at this rate."

I dropped my head onto the couch again and groaned. Nothing was going to stop my two stubborn teammates.

I WOKE WHEN LEXI MOVED. I had not thought I would have been able to doze off with the weight of her legs over my back. At least I felt better for it. I rubbed at my eyes, groggy. In a minute or two, I would get up and get back to work.

"How long do you think it will take?" Lexi asked softly.

Silver hummed for a moment. "I'm not sure, but if you could keep people out until I'm done, I would appreciate it. I know she definitely will."

"Appreciate what?" I asked and shifted to sit up.

Silver put his hand on my back to hold me still before I could get far. "I'll explain shortly, but I have a plan to dismantle that spell."

"I'll be waiting outside. Let me know if you need anything," Lexi said.

The door opened and closed with a soft click.

My partner sat on the edge of the couch I rested on. "You're not going to like this."

I rolled my eyes. "You tell me that a lot. Might as well say it."

"The best plan I can come up with is to reset your pathways like I did when I had to keep breaking you free of the control of that orb." His voice was soft and gentle.

It did not stop the heat of embarrassment rushing to my face. I was glad I was laying down. He referred to the orb that had caused the rift between us. I supposed the real blame remained with the pirates who held us prisoner. They had needed someone who could operate the offensive and defensive ship systems with the orb and I was the only one who could do it.

Silver was both hostage and the only one who could break me free of my connection with the orb. I still had not sorted out my emotions on what had occurred between us. Also being influenced by his necklace at the time had only complicated matters further.

I closed my eyes for a moment. He referenced that time period, but was skirting what he needed to do. "Elaborate."

He stroked my hair. "I'm trying to say I need the same intimate connection with you again to do it. If you want me to go back to searching for another solution, I can, but this will be the fastest way I can think of to get you back on your feet. Even then, you're still going to need recovery time."

"Fine." I struggled to get to my elbows. It was just a kiss, right? It meant nothing more than getting back to work faster.

Silver put his hand on my back, but did not push me back down. "Hey, no. Don't force yourself to do this. Take your time to make a decision."

"I've made a decision. And whoever did this is going to regret it," I said sharply.

"Well, you're in a mood." Silver helped me sit up. "Are you sure? Kela, I need you to be sure. This isn't as life or death as it was back then. I can find another way, but it's going to take time."

"We don't have the luxury of time." I swayed. The dizziness was slowly returning. "You should know my stance by now."

He brushed my bangs out of my face. "Yeah, yeah. I better get to whoever it was first. I might be more merciful. Just... don't slap me for this, okay?"

"I won't."

Silver knelt up and cupped my face. "One of these days we should try this without it being an extenuating circumstance."

Before I could reply, he kissed me. I froze.

"Relax, Kela," Silver muttered against my lips.

As the warmth of his power washed over me, I followed his physical lead while focusing on what he was doing magically.

Like this I could sense the divine and I tried to make heads or tails of the spell he was detaching from me. It weakened with every hook he released. The problem was it was the remnants of a spell so I could not get a clear picture of what the necromancer used.

I chewed on the information about the spell I gathered and the attack itself. It seemed like what was causing me problems currently was not intended. Likely it was part of the attack and not meant to be used after like this. I would have to run the thought by Silver when he was done.

Something else made its presence known the longer I kissed him. A strange pleasurable tingling sensation. It had happened before when he had to perform his magic like this. A side effect? Previously I had contributed it to the influence I received from his necklace.

Eventually the warmth of his power faded and that sensation remained. Silver also had not broken our physical connection. Was it beyond my ability to sense?

I hesitated and Silver pulled away, looking down.

He tugged on his braid hard. "Sorry, guess I got caught up in the moment. Kissing you is addicting."

I tilted my head at him. I closed my eyes and pinched the bridge of my nose when the world turned farther than I expected. "You should find yourself a romantic partner if that's the case."

"I'm taking applications." He gave me a lopsided grin.

I sighed - he was impossible to deal with sometimes.

Silver gently pushed me to sit back on the couch. "Okay, you need to rest here for at least an hour. Light duty until at least after lunch. Speaking of, you haven't eaten yet today, have you?"

"No," I said quietly. At least the nausea was gone.

"Alright. I'm going to leave Lexi with a schedule for you and I know she'll make sure you adhere to it."

"Damn straight." Lexi's voice came muffled through the door. "Hey, can we come in now?"

"Yeah," Silver said.

Lexi and Ayda entered.

Ayda folded her arms and looked down at me. "Sounds like your attacker left a nasty parting gift."

I shook my head. "I don't think it was meant to be an after effect."

Silver toyed with the end of his braid. "I got that sense also. The attack itself was meant to kill. Since it had both arcane and divine components, I think it's safe to say a necromancer is involved."

I rolled my eyes.

"Get your reports together and you can use the media room to contact Lockonis again when you're ready," Ayda ordered.

"What do we do now?" Lexi asked.

I sat forward on the couch, the world still swaying, but it was nowhere near as bad as it had been. "We find the necromancer and stop her." When I moved to get up, a hand on each shoulder held me down.

Silver and Lexi stood over me. Each of them had the same reaction to keep me in place.

I rolled my eyes again. "I'm fine." They fought with each other often and yet they could coordinate when it came to keeping me from getting anything done.

"You will be. Give it an hour before trying to get up. Wait until this afternoon before doing anything more than desk work. And for the love of the Gods, eat something," Silver ordered. He walked toward the door.

"Where are you going?" I struggled to get up, but Lexi would not budge. Dammit, I needed to get back control of the team, not have them treating me like an invalid.

"I have a report to file." My partner left before I could respond.

"Hey! We don't have a plan yet!" I went to go chase after him, but Lexi continued to block my attempts. "Let me go. I need to get everyone coordinated again."

"No. He said don't get up and you keep leaning to the side every so often so I'm actually going to follow his request." Lexi sat down next to me. "It'll be okay. Anyway, I'm hungry so what do you want for breakfast?"

Ayda laughed lightly as she headed for the door. "Well, I've got my own work to do so let me know if you need something."

I rolled my eyes and flopped back against the couch. This team was impossible.

19

My messages to Silver remained undelivered. My calls to Frank went unanswered. It had been hours now.

"Ket, quit pacing," Lexi said. "Geez I thought werewolves were bad when we got hurt, but you've got us beat."

I turned sharply on my heel. "I'm fine. I've been fine for hours. Something isn't right. I need to know where Silver and Frank are."

"You know those two. They'll come back when they're ready. Not to mention they're probably stuck in traffic. Rush hour doesn't really slow down until late in the evening." She sounded unconcerned.

I growled and continued pacing. I voiced a thought that crossed my mind. "If they were in traffic then at least my messages should be showing delivered, right? My calls wouldn't immediately go to voice message. I doubt there's a hole in the communications network."

Lexi hummed for a moment. "I'll see if there's an outage somewhere. Wouldn't surprise me if parts get overloaded from time to time."

While she worked on that, I tried calling Frank again. It went directly to voice message. I squeezed my phone, snarled at it, and considered throwing it in frustration.

Suddenly the typing behind me increased. "Odd, the network has been running fine all day. Their phones are off. I'm trying to boot up the location chips now."

I bit my lower lip and stared at the phone in my hand. Why would they turn their phones off?

"Oh, come on," Lexi said, typing faster. "This isn't that hard. I know I have the clearance to do it."

Before I could register the thought, I was standing over her, watching her screens. "You can't get them on?"

Lexi shook her head. "It's like there's nothing there to receive the commands. The chips should boot up even if the main battery is dead. I'm going to send a help request to the cyber team and see if someone else has an idea. The last location update from their phones says they were near the abandoned church you and Frank went to. That was hours ago. They probably aren't there anymore. Maybe they're in a building that's blocking their signals. It's the only reason both of them would appear down at the same time."

I grabbed my bag and headed for the door. I would check one more place and then go to the church myself.

"Wait, where are you going?" Lexi sounded panicked.

I paused, not turning around to look at my teammate. "I'm going to check with the Sola office and see if they've heard from them."

"We could just call them and ask."

I turned enough to shoot her a glare from over my shoulder. Her suggestion was reasonable, but I was not in the mood for it.

"Or we could go there. You definitely need out of this hotel room. Cool your head." Lexi set about locking her system. "Silver is getting an earful for this," she muttered.

I rolled my eyes and yanked the door open, not stopping to wait for Lexi.

<hr>

AYDA EYED both me and Lexi. "I haven't seen them."

I felt the blood drain from my face. Lexi had been unable to track them since their phones were turned off and could not force the location chips to turn on. We had no idea where they had gone.

"Did either of them come in at all after we left? Maybe one of them said something to someone." Lexi spoke quickly, her voice higher pitched than usual.

Ayda shook her head. "I haven't seen either one since they left this morning. Frank's been logging into the system remotely, which is a new one for him. Let me see if he's been on recently." Her attention turned to her computer.

Lexi and I looked at each other. Her hands were clenched tightly at her sides and she bounced lightly on the balls of her feet while we waited.

Ayda pursed her lips. "He checked in this morning at the same time he has been since starting to work with you guys, but hasn't been on the system since. You can't reach them otherwise?"

I shook my head. "No, their phones are off and Lexi can't force them to turn on enough to give their location."

"With no word, I'm assuming the cyber team back at the main office isn't having luck either. It's a simple process, but..." Lexi trailed off. "Something could be blocking their signals."

Ayda folded her arms. "Now I'm concerned. There isn't much that can block our phones."

Whatever else Ayda said was muffled as suddenly a spell hit me for the second time today. I spun, searching for the source. It was the same signature that had attacked me this morning. I had to follow it back. It might lead to our missing team members.

"I warned you not to interfere," the same voice from the alley said. Pain increased from the spell.

I zeroed in on the window, putting my hand on the floor to create an anchor before using my power to follow the spell back.

The city flew by and I found myself heading directly for the abandoned church before a wave of arcane energy hit me, knocking me back to the Sola office. The wave pushed me even into the physical realm, sending me sprawling.

Lexi was at my side, pulling on my arm before I had even regained my orientation. "What happened?! Was it another attack?"

Ayda was on my other side only moments later. "There was something arcane, but that's all I could make out."

I groaned and held my head. Between hitting the floor and the blast of arcane, my head hurt. "There was someone watching. I managed to follow the spell almost all the way to the source before whoever it was knocked me back."

"You back-hacked an arcane spell?" Ayda asked. "I didn't know that was even possible."

"I can follow a teleport line to the destination. It's the same concept," I said off-hand while the pain in my head slowly subsided. "Haven't been knocked back before. That hurts."

"Did you see who it was?" Lexi asked. She still sounded panicked, but she was attempting to control it.

I shook my head and regretted the gesture. "No, I was approaching the abandoned church when I got hit. She reminded me she had warned me not to interfere."

Ayda hummed for a moment. "I don't like this theory, but is it possible Frank and Silver were captured by whoever it is?"

Lexi spoke before I could. "The last we got of their signal, they were in the vicinity of that church. They've got to be there. We need to get there fast!" She pulled me to my feet and I stumbled.

Now she believed me. I pinched the bridge of my nose, the last of the pain dissipating.

"I agree, but you're going to have Hells of a time getting over there at this time of day. Not unless one of you can ride a motorcycle through traffic. The general populace is slow to react to lights and sirens if they respond at all," Ayda pointed out.

I bit my lower lip for a moment. It seemed taking those riding classes out of boredom through the summer was about to pay off. "I can ride."

"You can?" Lexi stared at me.

Ayda was back at her computer. "I'll be damned. You do have clearance. Come with me." She led us down to the underground garage. A few motorcycles were hidden behind their larger vehicles. "Ours aren't outfitted like the local law enforcement because our primary goal is to get someone to the scene quickly while the rest follow. They don't have much in the line of equipment loaded on them."

While the head of the Sola branch went over to a closet, I inspected the dashboard and control layout. Similar enough.

"Ketayl," Lexi said softly. "I'm going to be too heavy to ride with you and I don't know how to operate one."

I turned to my current partner and bit my lower lip, tilting my head for a second. I had an idea to lighten her. Maybe even enough that there would be no additional weight for me to have to balance.

The arcane presence was back again. "DO NOT INTEREFERE!"

I clutched my head even as the presence disappeared. I remained unsure which hurt more that time: the pain accompanying the spell or her yelling.

"Ket? Ketayl!" Lexi grabbed me by the shoulders.

I shook my head. "I'm fine. Our observer took a moment to yell at me about interfering again. If she's not attempting the same attack as earlier, I doubt she has the capacity to do it again right now, but she is loud."

Ayda had come back with some gear. "I don't like that whoever it is can do that so easily. You won't be able to ride like that."

"If Lexi can keep me focused, I'll be fine. As I said, it's not an attack like earlier," I sounded far more confident than I was. Obviously, this person knew how to boost their power.

"Ketayl..." Lexi whined.

I turned to my teammate. "I'm going to need you to talk to me. I assume the helmets are outfitted with an intercom system." I tossed the last part at Ayda.

"Yes. I already activated them. We can monitor you. Also, you'll want these for when you get there." Ayda held up a pair of earpieces with cameras. She tossed me a jacket before putting the remaining gear on the floor next to us. Then she went and got one of the motorcycles out.

For some reason, I expected an argument from her. Not taking her agreement to this plan for granted, I quickly put the armored jacket on.

"But I'm still too heavy," Lexi pointed out.

I quickly touched her, casting a weak levitation spell. Just enough to make her lighter.

"Whoa!"

"Problem solved." I grabbed a helmet and put it on, leaving the visor up to make it easier to talk to the others for the moment. I got on the motorcycle and had been reaching for the lights when I noticed Lexi holding the helmet in her hands, biting her lower lip. "We've got to go now. If they're there with the necromancer, we might lose them if we're not already too late."

"I know, I know. But I don't want to lose you either. I'll be fine if we crash, but you're..." she trailed off.

"Easily hurt or killed, yes. Get on, hold on, and keep your feet on the pegs," I ordered.

Lexi hustled to finish getting her gear on, tucking the earpieces Ayda gave us into the inner pocket on her jacket.

Ayda stood in front of me. "I'll get as much of the team as I can manage over there as soon as I can."

"Wait for our signal to enter. I'm not risking anyone else," I ordered.

Ayda nodded. "Understood. Bring our boys back safe."

I nodded, slammed my visor shut, and took off as Ayda stepped out of the way.

20

LEXI'S SQUEAKS and whines as I wove at high speeds through traffic was distracting. Our observer had yet to give me grief again about interfering, but it was only a matter of time. If I could remain focused on the road through Lexi's noises, I should be able to keep my head when the necromancer next decided to speak.

I swerved hard around a pedestrian who was crossing in the middle of traffic. One would think the bright flashing lights would be a clear indicator to get out of the way. I grumbled to myself that they were less than 20 yards from a crosswalk.

My passenger clung tightly to my back. "For the record, I'm never riding with you again."

"I ride different when it's not an emergency," I said flatly as I drove between vehicles.

Silence fell for a moment as I hit a clear stretch. I took the opportunity to increase my speed, shifting to a higher gear.

The arcane presence came hard and fast. "If you come, I'll only claim another prize."

I grunted at the hit, slowing in order to maintain control.

"Ket? Did she contact you again?"

"Yeah. Something about if I go, she'll claim another prize. I think she's been quiet because it's hard to target us while we're moving." It was the only explanation I could think of.

"Well, if that isn't ominous..." Lexi said sarcastically. Her tone turned serious. "What if they're not at the abandoned church?"

"With as much as she's telling us to not go, I think we can be fairly certain they're there." We were getting into the streets where I would have to weave again. "Hold on."

"Oh Gods..."

Never had I thought I could make a werewolf so uneasy.

I maneuvered us through the thinning traffic, sometimes between vehicles. I took the wrong way down one-way streets. Anything to get there faster. Lexi complained the entire time.

No sooner had I pulled up in front of the church, but Lexi jumped off and tore the helmet off of her head. "You're insane!"

"We're here," I pointed out.

"Somehow. If it was just me, that would have been a wild ride, but... how can you be so reckless?"

"Just in my nature, I guess," I muttered. Now someone other than Silver had called me reckless. "I'll buy you chocolate later."

The arcane presence I had sensed when I came with Frank before was stronger. It also seemed to be more than arcane, but I had nothing to compare it to in order to figure out what.

I set the bike, got off, and took the key, leaving the lights going. I shoved it into my pocket as I ran, pulling my helmet off in the process. Lexi was on my heels.

"It smells like they've been here," she commented.

"The arcane presence is stronger." I paused in what I was saying, my feet still carrying me up the grand steps. "It feels like Silver is here, but I could be imagining things."

"You have taken a few hits to the head today," she commented flatly.

My mouth formed into a thin line. She had a point.

Lexi got ahead of me and shoved the doors open, breaking any lock that might have been on them. She continued at her speed through the large vestibule, getting to the next set of doors where one was already broken off. She stopped dead.

Once I caught up, I saw her eyes were wide and her mouth open. I rounded the corner to see what caused her reaction.

Bodies lay scattered about the grand main hall along the outer perimeter. Pews had been removed and stacked to the sides. Tall statues of Gods and Goddesses lined the walls. Some were broken, adding to the debris on the floor. The later afternoon sun came through where parts of the roof had collapsed, illuminating the dusty area in an eerie light.

Silver and Frank stood to the left near the altar, surrounded by a translucent pink bubble.

Focusing on the living, I let out a breath of relief. They were alive. Trapped, but that was something we could work on.

I drew the shrunken staff attached to my thigh and extended it, waving for Lexi to follow.

"Hey!" she said in a hushed voice, grabbing my arm. "This has to be a trap."

"I know," I replied flatly, "But I can't do anything about that bubble from here."

Frank turned to us and backhanded Silver's shoulder. Our Sola team member made a gesture I could not make out from this distance.

"Do you know what he's trying to say?" I asked.

Lexi shook her head. "Probably for us to keep away."

Silver turned as if he was going to give Frank a hard time until he saw us. He shook his head.

"Yeah, pretty sure they don't want us in there," Lexi said, "We should wait for the others."

"No," I said softly. "I won't risk anyone else. You should wait outside. I don't want her to claim you as a prize."

"Oh, no. Hells no. I'm not letting you do this alone. We're pack. We stick together," she said firmly.

I smiled softly. It would be a losing battle with her anyway. "Alright, but don't do anything reckless. That's my job."

Lexi gave a short, strained laugh.

We ran toward the men. Lexi bolted ahead and punched the bubble, creating a wave, but it showed no signs of breaking.

"Get out of here!" Silver yelled. His voice was muffled.

I knelt next to the bubble, ignoring my partner.

"Report." Ayda's voice came through the headset.

As soon as Lexi started to respond, I ripped the earpiece off. I handed both it and my staff to the werewolf next to me so I could focus on figuring out the spell used. There had to be a way to break it.

No sooner had I placed my hand on the bubble, I was knocked back, flying several yards before hitting the hard-wooden floor. I landed next to one of the corpses and scrambled to my feet to get away from him.

Lexi was next to me. "What happened?! I didn't get knocked back."

"I... I... I don't know." My eyes were still locked on the dead Human man I had nearly collided with.

She grabbed my shoulders and made me look at her. "There's nothing we can do for the dead. It's creepy as all Hells, but let's get back to getting our team out of here. Preferably before they get added. Some of these people look familiar. I think they might be the high-grade account holders."

"Yeah, you're right." I forced myself to not look back and followed her to the bubble. "We'll have to identify them later."

"Are you insane?" Frank asked as we approached them again, his voice also muffled by the bubble. "Get out of here. She'll be back anytime."

"You were insane for coming here without backup," Lexi shot at him.

I held my hand a few inches from the bubble and got zapped. I yanked my hand away, shaking it. "It has to be reacting to my arcane energy."

Silver knelt down to be at my level and put his hand against the wall of the bubble. "Leave, please."

"Not until my team is safe." Interesting the bubble showed no reaction to Silver's divine presence. There was a chance that it reacted differently depending on if one was inside or outside. "Have you tried anything?"

He tugged hard on his braid. "Everything I can think of. I can't make sense of it."

"What about..." I trailed off as I noticed movement. I spun, seeing the bodies getting up off the floor.

"Oh Gods..." Lexi whispered. "I think I'm going to be sick."

Something hit me, knocking me away from Lexi. I hit the floor hard and rolled. This was getting old fast.

When I got up, my teammate was now inside of the bubble with Silver and Frank. She had dropped my staff and headset, but both were inside with her. The bodies were still slowly getting to their feet. I was in the middle of a morbid puppet show.

"Despite my warnings, you brought me another prize. She'll be as useful as the two I claimed. Too bad they'll have to wait a few days before joining my army," a familiar female voice carried through the main hall.

At least it was not in my head.

A Human woman, wearing a silky burnt orange top and brown pants stood on the altar. How had I not noticed her? Now that she was out, I could sense strong arcane presence coming from her and something more, but even at this range I still could not determine what. Even so, it was safe to assume she was an actual necromancer. I quickly glanced at my team members in the bubble. I was the only one out here. A cold sweat ran down my back. This time I was likely outmatched.

"Too bad you're useless. Not even worthy of being fodder, and yet still too dangerous to be left alive." She tapped her chin for a moment. "No, dangerous isn't the right word. Annoying - that fits better."

I bared my teeth at her, gathering arcane energy in my hands at my sides. Outmatched or not, I was getting my team out of here.

The necromancer gave a short laugh. "You're rather funny, thinking you can take me on. You're not even worth my time. Do try to give my army a decent fight. They could use some training."

The standing corpses started coming at me, though slowly. This was right out of one of those horror movies my sister had made me watch.

"Dammit, Ketayl, run!" Silver yelled with similar shouts from Lexi and Frank.

I raised my hands in front of me, palms down. Violet electric-like bolts came out of the floor, surrounding me. The horde halted.

Separating my hands, one above and one below, I cycled them to the sides before bringing them together in front of me. I threw my hands out, a violet staff of arcane energy forming. I grabbed it from where it floated and readied for the fight.

No sooner had I collected the wild arcane energy into the staff, the necromancer's army came at me again, faster this time. My swings and thrusts quickly became a frantic dance to keep them away. Each hit dropping one, but they would slowly get back up several seconds later.

As soon as I created an opening, I took off running to get the horde to come at me from one direction instead all around. I dissipated my staff in the process, switching tactics. I needed to hit them and keep them down. I could not keep this up forever and I refused to leave my team. Worse was knowing time was limited before Ayda and the other Sola agents came in after us. I had no way of telling them to keep away from here.

Once I had them trailing behind me, I turned, throwing ice shards at the ones closest to me. They dropped.

I kept running, I had no time to stop and see how effective my tactic was. I would keep changing spells and see what worked as I circled around the hall.

Forming a fireball in my hand, I spun and threw it at the slowly thinning horde. Bodies lay further back, but they could still get back up at any time.

I continued my race. The horde had mostly formed a line behind me. I cycled it back to the center of the hall, reforming my arcane staff again. Having them coming from one direction made the fight a little easier, but I was still frantically working to keep them away.

I used a spell to jump back and give myself room, breathing heavily. It put me near the bubble holding my team. The undead on the floor remained there. I dissipated my staff and unleashed lightning at the group coming for me.

It chained from one to the next, taking out at least half of the remaining horde. It was not enough.

"Ketayl, you can't take them on! Run!" Silver yelled at me.

"*I'm not leaving,*" I told him in my dialect of common. I did not want to let the necromancer know what I was saying even though it was not important.

A strong arcane build up from behind me caught my attention. I whipped around in time to get my shield spell up to block the onslaught of power directed at me. I clenched my teeth, fighting to keep it up, but I knew if the necromancer did not stop soon, I would be in trouble. Her attack earlier today had drained me more than I cared to admit.

I glanced at my team. Silver and Lexi's presence reminded me of how I had used the energy of an existing spell to fuel my own spell to keep my partner temporarily safe. *Of course, use the power of the spell directed at me.* As I worked through the manipulation, a violent swirl of colors danced around me. I turned the onslaught of power to my advantage.

I floated in the bubble of energy surrounding me. It helped restore my own depleted reserves and then some. The horde surrounded me, but could not get through the barrier. In here it was peaceful, and I could take a moment to catch my breath.

The necromancer stopped feeding my bubble and I huddled into myself for a moment before pushing outward, knocking the remainder of the army away from me.

Several seconds ticked slowly by and they did not get back up.

I glared down the necromancer who was looking at her fallen army with wide eyes. It was just me and her now. "Let them go," I said flatly. "This is between us."

She snarled at me and waved her hand. I flew through the air, hitting the wall of the upper level with a loud crack. I fell, rolling along the hard wood floor. I came to a stop with my back to the bubble holding my team. Searing pain coursed through my body - I could not tell if I had broken anything. I stayed where I was, unable to move for the moment. Maybe the necromancer would come closer. It would give me the advantage in this fight.

The team was shouting my name.

"Dammit, Ketayl, get up! I've seen you take a harder hit than that and keep fighting!" Silver yelled. "Get up, dammit!"

I heard footsteps coming toward me despite the yelling. The sound of her high heels echoed loudly through the hall. Each slow step of hers allowed me to pull myself together.

The necromancer stood over me. "It looks like this is all she is. Though she did cost me quite a lot. It'll take time to rebuild my army. At least I know what I need to do to improve them next time," she said.

I cracked my eyes open. My hair hid my face from her. As soon as she lifted a foot and moved to kick me, I grabbed her leg, sending electricity up it.

She fell and struggled to scramble away from me. She muttered something under her breath before she had gotten back up. Whether it was a spell or simply cursing at me, I could not make out.

I forced my way back to my feet, holding my ribs. I tasted blood in my mouth. I was unsure if I could counter another spell. I sank lower, unsure if I could even muster the strength to dodge.

"Dammit, kid, run!" Frank yelled. Silver and Lexi were busy frantically attacking the inside of the bubble.

"Not leaving," I said quietly. "Not losing my team." I took the necromancer's muttering as a chance to catch my breath. I felt a stabbing pain with every inhale. I wondered if I had broken a rib. The motorcycle jacket likely kept it from being worse.

"This ain't a time for heroics. Get out and get backup," Frank argued.

I ignored him - there was no backup. Not against someone like this. I could not risk the necromancer getting her hands on more people to have as hostages. More who she would convert to her army.

The necromancer finished casting. I clutched my head at the pain. What in the Hells was this spell?

As the pain lessened, a shadowy form took shape and soon enough I was staring at a sneering version of myself. I squinted, unsure if I was seeing right. What kind of spell was this? She wore the same clothes I did, but did not look as beaten up as I felt. Her dark auburn hair hung loose around her, brushing the back of her calves. Then I realized my own hair elastic was missing.

"Look at you, barely standing," my copy said. "You should give up now."

I bared my teeth and shook my head. I needed to ignore the taunts and figure out how to take down the necromancer. She stood on the altar with her arms crossed, watching her spell play out. I growled at her. *What can I use?*

My copy walked around me slowly. "Always putting the people you care about in danger. Pain, suffering, and death follow you wherever you go."

Ignore her.

"Look at the girl who can't even figure out how to put a puzzle together. Some Researcher you were. You know they're only stringing you along - you'll never be assigned a rank. You're not even useful to the TIO."

"Don't listen to her!" Lexi shouted. "You know what she's saying is a lie."

I closed my eyes for a moment. *Not a lie. It's all things I know to be true.*

My copy stopped in front of me. "Face it, you'll never have a normal life. No one wants to be around a monster like you."

"*Shut up!*" I spun a kick around at her head. I grabbed my ribs again when I got both feet back on the ground. I was pretty certain now that I had broken something.

She easily dodged my attack, jumping away from me.

I narrowed my eyes. Normally I would have used magic to give myself more breathing room. Did my copy not have my abilities?

She laughed mockingly. "You've got no fight left. No life left. You should have died decades ago."

Why was she not responding in the same dialect? I glanced over at the necromancer. The puppet master must not be able to duplicate it. There had to be something within the clues I had been given that I could use to my advantage. She could use things in my head to taunt me, but it was somehow limited.

It was hard to breathe. I was uncertain if my vision blurred with held tears from the exertion or from the words I knew to be true. *"Shut. Up."* If only she would so I could concentrate. There had to be a way to break the connection.

My copy kicked me and I fell to the floor. "Can't protect yourself let alone the ones you care about. Irony that you're doing this to yourself."

I wiped the corner of my mouth with my hand. *Physical and psychological attacks, but not magical. If I can stay focused on the facts, I might get through this.*

"Didn't expect that, did you?" My copy smirked maliciously. "Never could see what was right in front of you." She turned her head to look at my trapped team.

My hair raised off the back of my neck as I let my power rise while I struggled back to my feet. *"I told you to shut up."*

Behind my copy the necromancer smiled broadly. To my left, the others were shouting, but I could not hear them. All that came from that direction now was white noise.

I closed my eyes for a moment, letting my power rise further. This spell should have no hold over me - I did worse to myself on a regular basis. Still, she was infuriating.

Opening my eyes, I took a step forward and purposely stumbled to the side in order to line up my copy and the necromancer. I would only get one shot.

"Just end it. You'll be doing everyone a favor," my copy sneered.

"I will." I instantly gathered my risen power to my hands and

unleashed it. The beam of raw arcane energy consumed my copy and hit the necromancer.

My tormentor disappeared and the necromancer was sent backwards. A loud crash accompanied her collision into the podium behind her.

I glanced to the side, waiting for the bubble to dissipate. It held strong, but I could hear the others again telling me to run. There was no running - it was hard enough to stand.

The necromancer pushed herself up. "I am sick of you! You come into my church and destroy my army. I will take these three and everyone else you care about."

My shoulders slumped. I had hoped that last attack was the end of it. Now she was done toying with me and I had nothing left. *I failed...*

No, I had one option left. This was going to be it, but I was taking her down with me.

Standing tall, I gathered arcane energy to my hands. My hair gently floated around me.

The necromancer stood once more on the altar. She began casting another spell.

I raised a finger to my lips. "*Silence,*" my voice echoed with my power.

An iridescent band of arcane energy wrapped itself around the necromancer's mouth. It would only hold her for so long. I only had one card left to play against someone this powerful. The spell which killed my biological mother. I might be able to fix it on the fly.

I glanced at my team. "Thank you," I said softly, forcing a smile for them. Regardless if I fixed it or not, they deserved at least that much from me.

"No..." I heard Silver say, though it was still muffled. "Don't you do it."

Ignoring my partner, I turned back to the necromancer who still struggled to pull the band silencing her free.

With my hands by my sides, I held them palms up, releasing my power from its normal confines. An iridescent storm of arcane energy surrounded me. I thought it would be frightening to let go of control, but instead it was calm and peaceful despite the raging torrent around me.

The necromancer got herself free and threw spells at me as fast as she could cast them, but nothing could break through the storm of arcane energy.

My hair whipped around me, lifting off the back of my neck. This was one spell I could not cast without the incantation to be able to remember the manipulations I needed to perform. Not that I had ever cast it before.

I brought my hands together in front of me and struggled to pull them apart, the swirling ball of black and white formed that would be my focus for the spell.

> *"One of dark, one of light*
> *The road we once walked*
> *Is now lost in the flood"*

My voice boomed with my unchecked power. I had switched to my dialogue of common, needing my native tongue to help me focus. Silver would be the only one who would be able to understand my words. It was better that way.

"I've never heard her cast a spell before," Lexi said.

"Neither have I," Silver replied. "This can't be good."

> *"One of dark, one of light*
> *Soul forged in the fury of fire*
> *Tempered by the coldest of ice"*

My feet left the floor, the spell lifting me up. I brought the chaotic swirling black and white ball of energy over my head. I shifted my hands as it grew larger.

> *"Want for nothing*
> *Nothing brought to bear*
> *I am the dark, I am the light"*

The strain of holding the spell tore at me. Just a little longer. A little more power. Blood soaked my shirt and filled my mouth once more.

"Dammit, Kela! Stop before it kills you!" Silver shouted. Out of the corner of my eye, I saw him punch the bubble before attacking it with his sword and shield.

Despite his use of that name, I ignored him. I had already come this far. I was done at this point and there was no turning back.

"Chaos"

I threw the spell at the necromancer, using my whole body to launch it.

She screamed as it hit her. Her body convulsed before she collapsed to the floor. Her eyes remained open, her face frozen in horror.

A shadowy figure appeared, claiming an orb from the necromancer's body and leaving just as quickly. I blinked, wondering if I had actually seen what I thought I had.

My feet touched the floor as the pink bubble holding my team dissipated. I stood there staring straight ahead. My clothes were soaked and not from sweat. Every inch of my body seemed to be screaming in pain. I knew what came next.

"That was amazing!" Lexi shouted excitedly, jumping as she jogged toward me.

My legs gave out and I had not even the strength remaining to brace myself for the impact with the hard floor. I sent a silent apology to Kitteren and our adopted parents. I failed to fix the spell.

The impact never came as someone caught me.

"Ket?" Lexi asked, her voice next to my ear. She must have been the one to catch me. "Ketayl!"

Other footsteps hastily approached.

"Agent down! I repeat, we have an agent down!" Frank called. "Dammit, someone get in here!"

"She's bleeding badly. There's something else off about her scent, but I don't know what. What do we do?" Lexi shifted, adjusting her hold. I grunted as a sharper pain overrode the rest.

"It's okay," I said quietly. "I knew the risk."

Silver growled. "No, it's not okay. You should have run."

"Couldn't leave my team." It was getting hard to talk with blood in my mouth.

"Lay her down. I need to see how bad it is," Silver said.

"Report!" Ayda called. She sounded like she was a distance away.

I managed to open my eyes enough to see Frank leave. I closed them again. It was too hard to keep them open.

Lexi was incredibly gentle putting me down. It was opposite to how fast my jacket was opened.

"By the grace of the Gods..." Silver whispered.

"Cel, over here," Ayda called. "Help Silver out. The rest of you clear the building." There was a pause as footsteps approached. "Celerin is our healer and has a background in modern medicine. He should be able to help."

"What happened?" a male voice I was unfamiliar with asked.

"Between the beating she took and that last spell..." Frank trailed off.

Silence hung for several long seconds before who I assumed was Celerin spoke again. "She's strong enough, but there's no way to heal this much damage. I'm sorry."

"Dammit, Celery, don't say that. We've got to do something for the kid." Frank argued.

Did he just call him a vegetable? I needed to focus on something to keep from submitting to the pain.

"It's okay. I knew," I managed to get out. They had the right to know that I understood and accepted what I was getting into.

Large rough hands grabbed my face. *"Look at me,"* Silver ordered.

I pushed myself to answer his request. It was the least I could do seeing as he went through the trouble to use my dialect of common and I wanted to see him one last time.

Silver's face changed from tight to his eyes wide and his mouth open. He backed away a few inches. "What...?" He shook his head. "You're not leaving. You know there's another option."

I closed my eyes and groaned. "Kill me now," I muttered.

"That's not funny," Silver shot at me.

"What option?" Celerin asked.

"A restoration spell. I've used it on her before," Silver said quietly. "I need a couple of things in preparation, but we have to hurry."

"What do you need?" Ayda asked.

"A blanket large enough to wrap her in and people to hold her down."

"Cel, go find him a blanket," Ayda ordered.

Someone knelt at my head while a heavy weight pinned my thighs to the floor.

"Hope I'm not hurting you," Lexi said softly.

I did not have the energy to tell her I barely noticed over the white-hot stabbing sensation still traveling through me.

"What should I do?" Frank asked.

"Talk to her," Silver said. "I don't know if she'll hear you, but I can't do it while casting the spell."

"Right here," I managed to get out. "Let me go." I wanted to see my biological family again. Until now I had not really accepted that one desire.

"*You don't get a say in this,*" Silver snapped at me.

"Let's get started. Cel will be back soon and I don't want to risk her not being strong enough to survive this." By her voice, Ayda was by my head. Thin, strong hands held my shoulders down.

A larger rough hand took one of mine. "Ain't letting someone who can put up with this old monkey go." Frank's words were quiet.

"At least you get a warning this time," Silver said. He took a deep breath. "*I'm sorry about this.*"

Pain overrode everything my body had been through. I thought I had hurt before. I arched my back and twisted, trying to get away from the source.

While I held back a scream, I could not stop the whimpers at what Silver was doing.

Hands struggled to hold me in place.

"Damn she's strong," Ayda said.

"Come on fairy girl, you can make it. This is nothing compared to that fight," Frank said. "You can't check out on this stupid old monkey."

My insides felt as if they were being torn apart for the second time today. Tears streamed down the side of my face and I could not stop them. I could not even manage to tell Silver to stop.

Why would he not let me go? He did not need me. I only held him back.

I continued my struggle to get away from the source of the pain.

I stopped hearing anything over the pounding in my head. The torture continued. *Please stop*, I silently pleaded.

The pain went on for so long. I had no idea how much time had truly passed.

By the time I could start making out my situation again, I was wrapped in a blanket and being held by someone.

I curled up against whoever held me. I had missed my chance to see the family I had lost. I let out a shuddering breath.

"*Shh, you're safe,*" Silver said softly. He stroked my cheek with his thumb.

It was the last thing I remembered.

21

<hr>

SILVER HAD BEEN STROKING my hair for a while. I knew it was him by the fingerless leather gloves and the occasional sigh. I had remained still with my eyes closed since I woke. I was still wrapped in the blanket, but had no idea where I was. Lying here, breathing was the most I could manage at the moment.

At least my team was safe. I managed to get them out of there.

I heard a door open.

"How's she doing?" Lexi asked.

"The same," Silver said quietly. "I think Ketayl is through the risk of healing shock, but I won't know for certain until she wakes up. What's with the towels?"

I heard Lexi's footsteps move into the room. "I thought I'd help her clean up and change once she was ready. No reason to keep her in those blood-soaked clothes."

Silver stroked my hair again. "It might be a while. She lost a lot of blood. My restoration spell may have sealed her wounds and put broken bones back into place, but she'll have to recover much on her own."

Silence fell for several seconds.

"Go on. You need to give your report. I'll stay with her," Lexi said.

"I can't leave. Not until I'm completely certain she's through the risk of healing shock," Silver argued.

Lexi sighed. "I'll let you know if there's an emergency. Go."

"But..." Silver trailed off.

"Go before they come down here and haul you upstairs," Lexi ordered. She pushed her dominance, but it was only a fraction of what she had put out before.

Silver let out a long breath. "Alright. The second there's a change, let me know."

"I protect my pack," Lexi stated firmly. "At least when she'll let me."

The door closed with a quiet click.

After several seconds Lexi spoke again. "You don't need to pretend to be asleep with me."

"Not pretending," I mumbled. "Can't do much else."

"Well, Silver did put you through a few Hells." The sound of something being wheeled closer filled the room. "Other than weak, how are you feeling?"

"Fine." It was my default answer. I was still alive somehow, so I was fine.

"Uh huh. Try again."

I sighed. I should have known better. "Everything hurts, but don't tell Silver."

Lexi snorted, something I had not heard from her before. "I think he knows. I think we all know without having to ask. Though I am worried that your scent is still off."

I made a noise that I hoped would be understood as "I don't know." The world through her perspective was different than mine. "It's really quiet."

"Quiet?"

"Something is missing. Something that's always there." I yawned, pulling the blanket up to cover my mouth. "It's hot too."

Lexi hummed for a moment. "Silver never said we couldn't take the blanket off."

The cool air of the room hit my heated skin as soon as she lifted the blanket and I shivered.

"Cold?"

I gave it a couple of seconds to adjust to the room before I answered. "It was just the change in temperature. I'm fine."

Lexi whined. "You look like you've been through a war zone,

though I suppose that is accurate. Think you have enough energy to get changed?"

I struggled to get myself to my elbows. My shirt felt stiff in places and wet in others. Changing up would be nice.

An arm was under my shoulders. "Hey, I'm here to help, remember? Why don't we just cut this off? It's beyond saving anyway."

I could not force my eyes to open to see what she was talking about. "I can clean it later."

"No, even with your power I don't think you could get all of this blood out. Lay down, I'll get it off." She pushed my shoulders gently to signal that I should rest.

I behaved for the moment. Not that I had the energy to argue. I forced my eyes to crack open and watched Lexi rummage through drawers. Something was off. It was like the world had dulled.

"Finally. I thought I was going to have to go upstairs to get scissors. I don't want to let them know you're awake or you'll have a bunch of visitors all of a sudden." She walked over and drew the curtain near the door. "And let's add a little privacy in case someone forgets to knock."

She had not knocked though I did not bother to point it out.

I struggled to get to my elbows again and cracked my eyes open enough to see how caked with blood my clothes were. She was right - there was little left that was not covered in blood. I could do it, but it would take a long time to get them completely clean. I was not that attached to this outfit.

She gently tugged my shoes off.

When she suggested helping me change, it had not occurred to me until now what that entailed. "It's okay. I can do it myself."

"You can't even keep your eyes open." Lexi pushed me back down. "Naked people don't bother me. This is the least I can do for you saving my ass."

Our conversation died and I was trying not to join it from embarrassment.

I needed to focus on something other than hearing Lexi cut my clothes. It took me a moment to put her previous statements together. "We're at the Sola office?"

"Yeah. Silver was absolutely adamant about no hospitals and no medications," she grumbled.

I let out a short laugh and regretted it immediately as a sharp pain shot through my body. I took a few deep breaths before explaining Silver's actions. "They have a hard time dealing with someone like me. I have a bad reaction with medications and healing."

"Good to know. Of course, he could have explained that instead of being a jerk about it."

"You do know who we're talking about, right?"

Lexi stepped away for a moment before I heard running water. "Yeah, yeah. I should know by now. How do you put up with it?"

I hissed as a cold, wet cloth touched my skin. The contact alone was painful.

"Sorry! Sorry! Your torso is a giant bruise. I'm not sure I can clean all of the blood off without hurting you."

I took a deep breath. "It's okay. I can manage."

"Ketayl..." Lexi started. "Okay, but don't push yourself. We can find a different way."

Silence fell between us outside of my occasional grunt at the pain.

"How come Silver sometimes calls you Kela?" Lexi asked quietly.

I hesitated. I refused to give her the full answer, but I could not lie - she would smell it if I did. "He likes to use it when it's just the two of us."

"Outside of him shouting it pretty loudly back at the church, I've overheard him use it before. It seems pretty sporadic when he does." Lexi had moved away and I heard her getting the towel wet.

"Usually he wants my full attention."

"Can I call you that? It's pretty."

I could not tell her about my past, so I went with a simpler answer. "Silver might get upset."

"He doesn't have to know."

I sighed and then hissed as she touched a particularly tender spot.

"Sorry!"

Lexi made idle conversation over the next hour or so while she helped me clean up and change. She had managed to find an over-sized short-sleeve shirt that hung off one shoulder on me and a pair of exercise shorts from the training area downstairs. While she rummaged around in the cabinets for a fresh blanket, the door opened.

"Hey, what's with the curtain?" Silver asked, shoving it aside with more force than necessary.

I cracked my eyes open to look at him. He was out of his armor completely. I almost never saw him without the jacket.

"I told you to call me if there was a change," he shot.

Lexi stood between me and Silver. "No, I told you I'd contact you if it was an emergency. So, either you calm down or leave. Ket doesn't need to deal with your crap right now."

I closed my eyes. Lexi was right: I did not have the energy to deal with Silver's behavior. I mentally groaned at the thought of having to mediate another fight between them.

"Alright. I get it." Silver paused. "Can I have some time alone with her?"

There was silence for a minute.

"Fine," Lexi said sharply. "I'll go let the others know she's awake."

"Thanks. Can you also find her something to eat? You'll probably know of something better than I do."

Footsteps moved around and the door shut with a quiet click.

Silver put his hand on my head. "That was stupid and reckless," he said softly. "I'm just glad you made it."

I hummed. I was not entirely certain I was. Pain aside, I had long ago prepared myself for the end.

He held my head with his hands, stroking my cheeks with his thumbs. "Hey, look at me."

"I'm tired." Mostly I had not wanted to see his expression.

Silver stroked my hair. "I know, but a lot happened and your eyes can usually tell me how you're doing."

I sighed. He would pester me endlessly until I complied. I was not ready to go back to sleep yet, so I forced myself to look at him.

"I wasn't seeing things," Silver said in a hushed voice.

He was far too close for comfort, but damned if I could look away. Those now clouded blue eyes still haunted me. I thought he would have regained his bright blue eyes a short time after we had been rescued from the pirates, but they never returned.

"They're different colors," he said in a hushed voice.

I rolled my eyes. "That's nothing new. You've seen the color-changing thing before."

"No, one is blue and the other is green." He touched lightly under each eye with the corresponding color.

I closed my eyes and turned away. "I'm sorry, I never wanted you to see that." At least now I could pinpoint what was off. My power slept. Usually I could still sense something arcane though.

"Why not? It's incredible. I take it this has happened before."

"It only lasts about a minute."

Silver stroked my hair. "I saw it before I used the restoration spell on you, but wasn't certain if I had been seeing things. It's been several hours. Do you know the cause?"

"My power slumbers. Usually happens if I get too involved when I'm singing. It's why I don't like doing it around others or I have to be careful." I tried to find anything arcane, but there was nothing.

He hummed for a minute. "As close as the spell you cast might have been, I don't think it counts. I wonder if it has something to do with the spells the necromancer used against you."

I gave a short laugh at the idea and then groaned, forgetting it would hurt so much.

"Take it easy." Fingers gently grabbed the hem of my shirt.

I tried to stop him, but could not coordinate enough.

Silver grabbed my hands and squeezed them lightly. "I just want to see how you're doing now that you're not covered in blood. I won't lift your shirt too high."

Not that I could fight him right now.

True to his word, he only pulled it up enough to see my stomach. "You've got to be in so much pain right now. I won't risk any further healing until your divine levels go down."

Silence fell between us for a few minutes while he examined my injuries. It was only broken up by my hisses when he touched a particularly tender spot, which there seemed to be many of.

I found something to break the growing tension between us. "Now you know I'm still a freak of nature even without my power." With my eyes normally being gray, I never pursued the issue beyond knowing the term was heterochromia.

Silver grabbed my head and turned me back toward him. "Look at me!"

I cringed, keeping my eyes tightly shut.

"Come on, Kela," he said softly. "Just like you told me what your name should have been, let me in with this also."

I sighed, opening my eyes, but looking down. "There's nothing more than what I've already told you."

"Hey."

I finally looked up at him.

"Absolutely stunning. Who else knows?" Silver gave me a soft smile.

I bit my lower lip. "Just Kitteren and my parents."

He stroked the small patch of hair on his chin. "I'll have to contact them and see if maybe we can figure out why it's lasting so long."

"Please don't. I don't want them to know what happened." I could already hear the lectures my sister would be giving me.

"A little late for that." His hand went to my hair again. "The others upstairs also contacted Lockonis because we couldn't figure out what was going on with your power, but she hadn't gotten back to us last I knew. At least I have somewhat of an idea now."

There was a quick knock on the door, before it cracked open. "Is it okay to come in?" Ayda asked. "Lexi said Ket was awake."

I shifted uncomfortably - I should have sensed Ayda's presence. This was quickly turning out to be vastly different from previous times. My mind raced at the thought. What had I done? Was it me or someone else that was the cause? How long before my arcane abilities returned?

"Yeah," Silver answered and I closed my eyes again. "Did Lockonis ever get back to us?"

"She wants to talk to her as soon as she is able before discussing anything. You awake, Ket?" she asked.

"Yeah," I muttered.

"Think you're up for a quick video call?"

I kept my eyes lowered and struggled to my elbows. I hissed at the sharp pain shooting through my body. Just when I had gotten used to the constant ache...

An arm was around my shoulder, helping me sit up. "You can ask for help you know," Silver admonished.

Ayda was on the other side of me. "No need to rush. I told her you were awake, but I didn't know if you were able to move yet."

"Might as well get it over with." I kept pushing to get up. Lying about would accomplish nothing.

"By the way, your sister is going crazy," Ayda commented. "Thank goodness Savanas was in the room or she might've been on the first flight here."

I groaned. Kitteren never changed.

"And now I also have the Alpha Prime calling me personally. I think that one is Lexi's doing," Ayda grumbled.

Now in a sitting position, I hung my head. Why did people have to spread the word as soon as I got hurt?

Silver had helped get me to my feet when a man I had not met came in. I kept my eyes down at his shoes.

"Cel, what's with the bunny ears?" Ayda asked.

"Why not?" he asked. "You should see the rest of the outfit."

The head of the Sola branch sighed. "The cat ones might be better."

"But I like the bunny ones. In any case, I see Ketayl is up and moving to some extent. I was worried since her blood type is something I haven't seen before. I wouldn't have wanted to risk a transfusion."

I leaned heavily on Silver and it hurt.

Cel moved about the room. "Do you think you can teach me that restoration spell? I know of a couple of agents who could use it when they get cocky."

Silver gave a short laugh. "Yeah, it's usually a good deterrent for reckless behavior. She just hasn't learned that yet."

"We should get going," I said softly, wanting to get out of this awkward conversation.

Silver hooked his other arm under my legs. "It'll be easier to carry you. Save your strength for the calls ahead."

"Put me down," I ordered, glaring at my partner. Out of the corner of my eye, I saw Ayda raise an eyebrow at Silver.

"Good luck making me." Silver strode out the door.

I shifted uncomfortably in my seat, keeping my eyes lowered. Silver stood to my left, Frank to my right, and Lexi sat in front of me on the floor with her back against my legs. I was going nowhere.

Why they were also here for the video call, I had no idea. No one else needed to hear the chewing out I was bound to get let alone be here to watch it.

Lockonis appeared on the large screen before us and I lowered my eyes further. "I guess I shouldn't expect any different," she said. "Where did you learn a spell like that?"

I bit my lower lip. I should have known that question was coming. I guess I had not thought I would survive it. "My mother," I said quietly. There was no point in denying or trying to change the conversation. Right now, I needed to carefully choose my battles - I only had so much energy to expend.

"I'm fairly certain Lin doesn't... oh." Lockonis paused. "I assume you mean your biological mother."

I nodded.

"Why would she teach you something like that?" my boss asked.

I hesitated, staring at my hands folded in my lap. I did not want to talk about it.

"Ketayl..." Lockonis' voice had a warning tone to it.

I cringed. Why did people have to push?

Silver squeezed my shoulder and I hissed. "Sorry," he said softly.

Everyone was going to harass me until I said something. Might as well get it over with. "She didn't. I remembered from when she cast it." My volume lowered further. "I wasn't able to fix it." I pulled at the collar of my shirt - it had gotten warm in here.

"And why would you remember something as crazy as that?" Lockonis sounded upset.

I whispered, "It was the spell that killed her."

Silence fell in the room.

Lockonis sighed audibly. "Good thing Silver was there then. Look at me."

I wished people would stop asking me to do that. I shook my head. Too many people had already seen my mixed-colored eyes.

"Ketayl." A female voice I had not expected spoke my name softly.

My head shot up upon hearing Magus Engelil. I regretted the action since it made the room spin. I struggled to remain sitting upright. "Magus." Why was she on the call? I closed my eyes for a moment to clear the spinning in my head.

When I looked at the screen again, Magus Engelil's hair was a soft dusty blue, loose curls flowing over her shoulders. Her hair matched the airy dress she wore. For some reason her hair always matched her outfit.

I struggled to try to get to my feet, but Silver kept his hand on my shoulder, holding me in place. I might not have made it anyway - the attempt left me lightheaded.

"What in the Hells?" Lockonis asked. "Please tell me you have some idea of what is going on with your eyes."

I cast my eyes downward and remained silent. It was my problem to deal with.

Silver spoke after my silence stretched on for about a half minute. "She said her power is asleep. Apparently, it has happened before. I haven't had a chance to contact her family about it. It doesn't usually last for anywhere near this long."

"I'll contact Lin later," Lockonis said. "The reason I took so long to respond is because I wanted Engelil to look at what you sent. I certainly couldn't make heads or tails of it."

"Unfortunately, I had nothing to add to her observations. Though now I may be able to piece something together," Magus Engelil said softly.

I hid my face in my hands. This was both embarrassing and the dizziness had returned. It had to be the heat. Why did they keep it so warm in here?

"Ketayl, you look extremely pale," Magus Engelil noted, her voice gentle. "Are you sure you're feeling well enough to continue?"

Silver immediately knelt down next to me. He brushed my hair out of the way. "You're sweating and it's quite cool in here. Can we continue this conversation later? I should get her back to the infirmary."

"Yeah, keep me updated," Lockonis ordered. "Engelil and I will figure out what we can from here."

Silver did not even wait for the call to end before he was pulling me from the chair.

The loud voices faded over the pounding in my head.

"SILVER, I think you're right that Ket over-exerted herself," Cel said. "Neither of us has found anything else wrong. I'd do a blood test, but she's lost enough already."

I had been listening to him and Silver talk for a bit. The pounding in my head had gone down once I had been set on the bed in the infirmary.

"If you need anything, let me know," Cel said and the door closed with a quiet click.

Silver sighed, brushing my hair back. "What am I going to do with you? Why did you have to go so far?" His voice was so quiet, I nearly missed it.

The sound of a stool being wheeled over filled the room. Then silence.

After a few minutes, he spoke again. "Every time you do something like this, I know I should tell you, but I don't want to possibly lose you to my words..."

Tell me what? What could possibly make me leave? I considered asking Silver, but remained quiet, hoping he would elaborate. He probably thought I was asleep anyway. Not that I had the energy to move right now. I hoped this weakness went away quickly.

He kissed my forehead. "And after what I've done, I have no right."

Can't you just say whatever it is? I debated yanking his braid until he answered. I filed the idea away for later. It was childish and stupid, but he could be as infuriating as he claimed I was.

Silver lightly ran his fingers over my hair. The movement made me sleepy. Before I could muster the strength to tell him to knock it off, he said, "That necromancer... she was really scared of you. That you could ignore her commands and survived that attack. That you might be too much for her to combat. Guess in the end she had a right to be. You continue to surprise me when you're pushed into a fight. A staff of arcane energy - I'm glad you figured out how to do it."

Did he know I was awake? It was hard to tell if he was idly talking or if he knew I was listening and wanted an answer. I was not up for conversation.

"You know, she watched you and Lexi tear across the city. Being in the bubble, I couldn't tell if anything she used was divine." Silver gave a short laugh. "Lexi looked like she couldn't get off the bike fast enough. I know I'd be terrified after that. You're damn crazy. I guess it's different when you're in control."

I started to drift. I wanted to stay awake to hear if he would say what he wanted to tell me.

"You know, you can be downright infuriating," Silver said. His tone was odd as if he could not decide if he wanted to give me a hard time about it or not.

If that was what he wanted to tell me, he had made it known already.

A soft click ended his one-sided conversation.

"I'd ask how Ket is, but if she's awake I guess that's a good thing," Lexi said softly.

My partner's hand left my hair. "What do you mean?"

"Ket's just resting right now. Probably not up for much again, are you?" Lexi asked.

"No," I managed to say softly.

"Oh Hells," Silver said loudly. The stool squealed loudly. "How long have you been awake?"

"Never slept," I admitted.

Lexi laughed. "Silver, your face is bright red. Say something you didn't intend for her to hear?"

There was a short pause. "Why are you here?" he demanded.

"I came to see how she was doing while I waited for the broth to finish. I knew the recipe, but asked Sasha to help me adjust it for Ket's size. Ayda gave me an earful about Nikolai calling her, but it's hard to hide that kind of information from the pack when one of them knows," Lexi said.

I was going to have more calls than I cared for once I was back on my feet. Perhaps delaying as much as I could was the better option at this point. Though I doubted my sister would wait for very long.

22

Lexi and I sat in the hotel, watching through the camera network as Silver and the Sola team took Vanessa and Christian into custody. I would have been out there also, but my power still slumbered days later so I was stuck directing them from afar. We only waited this long as to let First Union save face and get them on the weekend.

I suspected there were other reasons, but I had been left out of those meetings. Granted, I still tired easily, but it pointed out how much they had not needed me.

Most of that time I had spent holed up here, only going out when it was absolutely necessary. The world was terrifying without being able to even sense the arcane. I had no idea how vastly different the world was without it.

Every time my power slumbered previously, I had been in a confined area so I never realized it before. The world appeared duller. The vibrancy was missing. That said nothing of the colors I would see passing by on occasion. That was all normal to me. Now shadows seemed darker, people became more threatening. I had no control over the world around me. I was at the mercy of it.

Silver and Lexi made it a point to drag me out at least once a day. Lockonis and Magus Engelil had not come up with any solutions of how to wake my power up. I certainly had no idea either. I had been scouring every source I could think of, but there was no information about it. Arcanists tended to be a quiet bunch, not giving up much about their experiences. Given how history had treated them, I could not blame them for taking their secrets with them to the afterlife.

More than once I kicked myself for being envious of my teammates still having their abilities to sense things a normal person could not. I had done this to myself. How long had I wanted to be normal? Now I had it and immediately I wanted to go back.

"Well, that's it," Lexi said. "Want to go to the Sola office and watch the chaos?"

I shook my head. It meant going out. "I'm fine here. I'd only get in the way."

"Okay, let me rephrase that. We're going to the Sola office." Lexi dragged me to my feet.

I pulled away from her. "Really, I'm okay here. Let me know how it goes."

"No, you're the team lead. You need to be there," she argued.

I took a deep breath and closed my eyes for a moment before I explained, "I lost that title after I lost my abilities. If I was team lead, they would have demanded I be out there for the arrests."

Lexi sighed, grabbing my arm. "You would have been here directing them regardless. Especially with Vanessa and Christian being so far apart. Going after both of them at the same time was a good idea. It didn't give the other one time to disappear."

I got my arm free from her.

"You're going. No more fighting." Lexi grabbed my arm again.

I managed to snatch up my bag and my sunglasses as she dragged me out the door. My odd-colored eyes had me self-conscious enough that I made the investment to hide them. I found a pair with mirrored lenses and would wear them even if I was out in the evening.

As we made our way through the city, I stuck close to Lexi, even more unsure of the crowds. Was anyone watching us? How would I be able to defend myself never mind keep my friend out of danger?

Lexi sighed. "I can hear your muttering. You know you're safe with me, right?"

"Yeah, but I shouldn't have to rely on you," I said quietly.

"Ugh!" She took my hand and dragged me along faster. "Silver was right - you can be downright infuriating."

I STOOD in the corner with my sunglasses on and arms crossed, listening to Frank interrogate Vanessa. Silver had Christian in another room with Lexi observing. I only hoped they could tolerate each other long enough to get something.

As it was, Vanessa had complained extensively and refused to cooperate if we kept her tied to the table. Seeing as her threat level was low, they decided to try it, but that meant two of us needed to be in the room now.

"Look, all I know is her name is Colleen Richards and she's an investor," Vanessa said. She had repeated this information a number of times. "Can you get her to stop staring at me like that?" She motioned at me.

"No," Frank said.

"Lady, you need to take the damn sunglasses off. We're inside you know," Vanessa spat. She had turned to glare at me.

I shrugged. I could care less where we were, I was keeping them on. It bothered me more and more that I could not sense the arcane. What if Vanessa was a caster? I reminded myself that Ayda would have noticed and said something. I would not be in here in that case. There were enough people who could take care of what I normally did.

Frank slapped the table. "Hey, you're talking to me. Keep your focus right here."

"She's creeping me out. She hasn't said a word." Vanessa seemed to like to use complaining to keep from cooperating.

"Oh, honey, you have no idea." Frank gave her a slow smile. "And I'll let her show you if you don't answer my questions."

I raised an eyebrow at him. What was he dragging me into? He knew I was nothing without my power. This was as much as I was going to be able to do to unnerve her.

"How did you meet Colleen?" Frank asked, starting the same line of questioning over. This was getting ridiculous.

"She sought me out at First Union. I wasn't the first advisor she approached. Look, she creeped me the Hells out, but she had a really good proposal." Vanessa turned to me. "You're still creepier."

I frowned. She was avoiding Frank again.

Vanessa sighed and turned back to Frank when I ignored her jab to get me to talk. "Like I said, Colleen is extremely creepy, but I never figured her for a necromancer. We're not the first people to have done this in the system so I never thought the killing was literal."

"And what about Christian?" Frank asked.

She sat back, crossing her arms. "He got the idea pretty quick that I was using him for something bigger and demanded to be fully brought on-board. He wanted a cut and I figured it was easier to keep him quiet and working."

At least she was talking now, though she had wanted a deal right off. I supposed it was better than feigning innocence. No one was willing to even consider discussing a deal without getting information first. It had taken Frank hours to get her to this point. Between that and the fact no one had told her Colleen was dead probably prompted her to finally give in.

I wondered how Lexi fared observing Silver and Christian. She had gone of her own volition. I think she still held a grudge against the man though likely against both of them. She seemed to be at least tolerating Silver for the moment.

"And you had no idea these people were ending up dead? It's awfully hard to believe." Frank remained calm while he questioned her.

Vanessa ran a hand over her hair. "Colleen dealt directly with the clients. I just got names for particular accounts. If I knew she was creating an undead army, I would have backed out of the deal. No amount of money is worth that. And now you have to protect me from her. Look, I can give you the name of the tech guy I initially worked with also."

"Gregory Cummins," I said flatly. "He's already in custody."

Vanessa jumped and stared at me with wide eyes. "Holy Hells, lady."

Frank smirked. "You were the one to point out the struggling accounts who had people dying off also. Only difference is he didn't actually kill anyone."

Ignoring Frank, Vanessa got up and stood in front of me, getting in my face. "You have some nerve."

"Sit down," Frank ordered. "You've got quite the list of charges already. Do you really want to add to it by threatening my partner?"

Vanessa grabbed the metal beaded cord of the badge hanging around my neck and pulled me closer.

Just as Frank got out of his chair, I grabbed Vanessa's hand, pulling her free. I twisted her arm, spinning and shoving her face-first against the wall, holding her there with her arm behind her back. I used all the bodyweight I had to keep her there. The movement caused a sharp pain to shoot through my body and I grunted at the effort. I still had not recovered from the fight with Colleen. I refused to budge though.

She tried to get out of my hold. "The Hells?! Let me go!"

Frank leaned against the wall to look at her. "I warned you." He turned to me. "Okay, I think she gets the idea."

I backed off and moved away as Vanessa got herself back together. My movements were sluggish. It felt hot in here all of a sudden and I had gotten lightheaded again. *Just when I finally started feeling better.*

"Let's take a break." Frank got behind me. "Give her time to think it over."

I nodded, the movement making me dizzy. I managed to put one foot in front of the other and strode out as normally as I could manage. Frank kept himself between me and Vanessa as we left.

Once out, I closed my eyes and leaned against the opposite wall holding my ribs. Silver reminded me frequently to stop pushing myself so hard.

"Didn't know you had that in you, fairy girl. Let's get you somewhere where you can rest." Frank hooked my arm around his shoulders.

"I'm fine, you old monkey," I tossed back. Over the last few days I had given in and started throwing insults back at him, much to his delight. If only he knew it was because I was tired of everyone coddling me.

Frank laughed lightly and pulled me away from the wall. It had been the only thing holding me up and I swayed as the world spun, leaning too heavily on him for my liking.

Silver and Lexi came out of the observation room next door to the interrogation room we had been in. Just what I did not need.

Lexi immediately got under my other arm. "Hey, that was pretty cool in there."

"I knew this was a bad idea," Silver muttered.

"What happened with Christian?" I asked through clenched teeth, now more or less hanging between Lexi and Frank.

"Not now," Lexi admonished. "Rest first, report later."

"I'm fine," I argued and struggled to pull away from both of them.

There was work to be done and they needed to stop treating me like a child.

Silver snorted. "Why am I not surprised? Come on." He led the way to the crash room. I had spent much time there between interrogation sessions.

I tried to pull away from Lexi again, figuring if I could get one to let go, it would be better than nothing, but she held firm. "I can walk."

The trio said nothing.

"It's nothing. Really. I just moved a little too fast," I said.

My protests were still met with silence.

"I may be powerless, but I'm not an invalid," I continued to argue.

No words came from the others.

I growled at them, still struggling to get free. It only made everything hurt more, but I refused to put up with this treatment without a fight.

Thankfully they did not need to parade me past the other agents at this branch to get to the crash room. Couches, which could lay flat, lined the room with cots folded up in the corner.

Lexi made me sit on one of the converted couches. I sat there cross-legged and refused to lay down. I was still lightheaded and overly warm, but I would not give in.

"Come on." Silver tugged on my shoulders. "Can you two go check on Vanessa and Christian?"

"Yeah. Let us know if you need anything," Frank said, waving Lexi out the door with him.

Once they were gone, Silver sighed and came around, pulling my sunglasses off. "You don't need to act so tough around us. Lay down. I need to check on your injuries anyway."

I cast my gaze down, still uneasy about anyone seeing my mixed-colored eyes. No one had made an unkind comment about them, but I could sense the stares.

"*Hey, look at me,*" Silver said softly.

I shook my head. Usage of my dialect of common or not, I tried not to look at anyone without my eyes covered.

He put his hands on either side of my head and tilted my head up. I looked at him briefly out of habit before I turned my gaze down as much as possible. He had seemed fascinated by my eyes ever since he first saw them. Why could he not find something else to be fascinated with?

Silver rested his forehead against mine. After a minute he said, "At least you didn't injure yourself further."

I breathed a sigh of relief. I had pushed myself too far a few times and hurt myself in the process.

My partner attempted to push me back, but I resisted in protest. "Would you rest? Just because you didn't injure yourself doesn't mean I didn't notice you're sweating and leaning to one side."

I scrunched up my face. "There's too much to do."

"It can wait." Silver brushed my hair out of my face. "I didn't know you had gotten so good at hand-to-hand combat. It'll make for some interesting sparring sessions when you're fully healed."

I turned my head away. "It wasn't really anything. Vanessa didn't expect it so I had the advantage. I wouldn't stand a chance against you." Not without my power. It was the only equalizer I had.

The hold on my emotions was tedious at best right now. I let out a shuddering breath.

Silver sat awkwardly on the bed next to me. "Kela, talk to me."

"I hate this," I whispered, tears forming. I hated hurting, hated being powerless, hated feeling useless.

My partner gathered me in his arms. "It's okay. We'll get through this. Before you know it, you'll be back to normal."

I let out a huff. "I wanted to be normal, but now..."

"It's not normal for you. You spent six decades constantly attached to the arcane. This has to be terrifying. I'm not sure how I'd handle not being able to sense the divine."

His words broke the last threads of control I had left, and I cried into his shoulder. I wanted this torment to be over.

Silver held me and rubbed my back. He said nothing more.

I noticed the pain lessened as he held me. "You better not be sharing my pain again," I managed to get out.

"You should have told me how much pain you were in and I would have done it sooner." His voice sounded strained.

"You're impossible." I had more or less gotten used to the constant pain. It was when I decided to push too much, like the incident with Vanessa, that I really felt it.

"Good. Now lay back so I can see how you're doing. You managed to hide from me until it was time to leave this morning," Silver ordered.

"Fine, but give me back my sunglasses."

"No. You don't need them in here." To make his statement stronger, he put them on a table well out of my reach.

I moved to go get them and he knelt between me and the table they were on. I rolled my eyes and did as he asked. Resting would be good. I found myself drained all the time, but it got a little better every day.

My mind drifted while he checked on how I was healing. I was unnecessary now. Easily replaced. A burden in truth. Being crippled in this manner was torture. What could I do to show I was still useful?

2 3

"I'm not sure what you expect me to do here," I said, standing next to Silver. The abandoned church loomed over us. "Even if I had my abilities, the arcane remnants would have broken down by now."

"Since you were recovering, Ayda took your place and used the camera filters since she can't see the arcane like you can," Silver replied. "You can review the images later."

"And what is it you need from me?" I was useless like this. I was team lead in name only.

Silver tugged on his braid. "Let's just go. The others are already here. Even with the help of the Sola branch, picking apart what happened when and what is related to our case has taken quite a bit of time. Ayda has already given the local law enforcement an earful for ignoring this place."

I did not want to be here. There was no reason for me to come here. "I'm not going to be able to tell you if there's an arcane trap or not."

My partner took my hand and I stumbled to not fall down as he pulled me toward the church. "You're not getting out of this. Ayda and I already went through looking for magical traps."

I dug my heels in, only succeeding in causing myself to trip. "Dammit, Silver. I don't need to be here."

"Yes, you do. Unless you want to end up off-duty," he said firmly.

I glared at him. "Don't threaten me like that. Besides, I'm already on limited duty."

"I'm not threatening it. I'm trying to keep you from ending up on it so quit arguing with me." Silver yanked on his braid with his free hand.

It seemed arguing with everyone was all I had been doing lately. I sighed and jogged to be able to walk next to him, tearing my hand away. "Fine."

Not that doing this would actually help. Being crippled the way I was, I was more likely to lose my position. I was useless as an arcane investigator without my abilities. Death would have been a mercy to this.

I let out a shuddering sigh.

"Ketayl?"

It was time to voice my thoughts. "I don't think coming here is going to change anything. I'll likely be off-duty until I figure out how to get my power back. I'm surprised they haven't pulled me yet."

Silver stopped when we entered the vestibule. He took my sunglasses off. "You're still needed even without your power." He flicked my forehead.

"Knock it off." I growled at him and snatched the sunglasses back, immediately putting them back on. "Let's just get this over with."

He led us into the main part of the church without saying anything further.

"Where is everyone?" I thought agents would still be working with as much as they had to sift through.

"Probably downstairs. There's a secondary reason I wanted you to come." My partner's tone was odd and I could not place what it was.

I took a deep breath and folded my arms. Getting frustrated with Silver was not going to get me out of here any faster.

He tugged on his braid. "I told you a long time ago that I could introduce you to the Gods, but I could never figure out a good way to do it without seemingly favoring one over the other."

"Coming to an abandoned church that used to worship all of them and had a necromancer using as a place to keep her undead army is a good method?" I gestured at the large room. I turned away from the large blood spot on the floor near the middle. I knew I had left that.

"Ketayl..." Silver tugged on his braid. "Come on. You might at least find the historical context interesting."

I mentally counted the statues on the sides of the room. "So, there are twelve Gods."

Silver smirked down at me. "Actually, thirteen, but no one likes to talk about Death. Most people these days view no gender attachment to a particular God, but when they're displayed like this, there are an even number of Gods and Goddesses."

"You said thirteen - you can't have an even number."

Silver pinched the bridge of his nose. I had not seen him do that before. "For the twelve displayed here. Again, few like to talk about Death."

"I'm surprised that you don't just want to talk about the God of the Sun," I muttered.

He scrunched up his face. "Just because I was a paladin of that Order doesn't mean that's my only worldview." Silver paused, stroking the small patch of hair on his chin. "I would consider giving you that one because most of the other paladins only accept the God of the Sun, but unless there's something you're not telling me, you haven't met anyone else of the order."

I shook my head. "I've only ever seen you performing your morning prayers to the sun."

Silver opened his mouth to say something and then closed it again. "Okay, you have me there. Can you at least let me do this without arguing with me?"

I raised an eyebrow at him. "You apparently want to lecture instead of have a conversation."

"Only because you keep arguing with me. I didn't think you could get any more infuriating," Silver snapped.

I scrunched up my face in frustration and crossed my arms. I could remain silent.

Silver walked us from one statue to the next, giving a brief overview of what each one was attributed to. I had to give him credit for keeping it factual. It brought my mind back to dealing with the necromancers. They were once much more tied to a group that worshipped the old Gods, but I could never find much information about them. Perhaps there was a church or something dedicated to them that I could find.

I pinched the bridge of my nose as he spoke at the last statue.

There was a second reason I had stayed out of the field for the most part - I exhausted easily. I knew I got stronger by the day, but it was so incrementally slow. I could make it through this. I had to prove to the others that despite my current state, I was not an invalid.

I jumped when I felt an arm wrap around my shoulders. "I'm fine," I said quickly.

Silver came around to stand in front of me. He pulled off my sunglasses and I tried to grab for them, but he held my shoulder with one arm and my sunglasses behind him. He squatted down so he was at eye-level with me. "You're not. You were up late last night, and you've been pushing yourself again today. There's nothing wrong with saying you're at your limit. Let's do a quick check downstairs with the others and then we'll head out, okay?"

I rolled my eyes. "Fine." At least I could get back to attempting to be useful.

Silver led us down the rickety stairs to the floor below. It appeared the area used to be a hall. I briefly wondered what would go on here that would not be held in the main area of the church. Currently tables were set up in rows, dried blood coated many as well as the floor below.

"Ketayl, I didn't expect to see you here," Ayda said with a smile. Then she narrowed her eyes at Silver. "Come to see a necromancer's workroom?"

I shrugged. "I guess." It could grant me some insight.

"Actually, if I can steal you away for a moment, I could use your expertise. The notes of her work are beyond me." Ayda signaled for me to follow her.

"They haven't been collected and scanned into the file yet?" I asked, perking up. Finally, something to do. I may not be able to do anything directly with the arcane, but at least I could work on deciphering the necromancer's notes. Arcane theory did not require ability.

Ayda shook her head. "I've been holding off on that until you were better recovered. Not to mention there's been plenty to do otherwise. I can't believe they never even sent patrols through this area."

I followed Ayda silently, letting her grumble about the local law enforcement.

She paused as we were about halfway across the hall and turned to Silver. "Why don't you go see how the others are doing? I can keep an eye on her."

I raised an eyebrow at the head of the Sola branch.

She waited until Silver had left before continuing toward a room at the end of the large hall. "Something tells me he'll get fired up if he finds out what's in the notes."

"It doesn't take much," I said in agreement. He would likely need to look at the notes at some point.

Ayda opened the door for me. "I noticed. He's still pretty young so hopefully he'll mellow out in time." She handed me a set of gloves that she dug out of the bag near the desk in the small office.

I bowed and stumbled. The movement should not have made me lightheaded like that.

Ayda grabbed my shoulders to steady me. "And that's why I wasn't expecting to see you. You still need to recover. Silver's a damn fool for bringing you out here."

"I'm fine, really. Can't keep relying on everyone else to do my job." I prepared myself for another argument.

She shook her head. "I guess I should say the same about you being young also, but something tells me that you're never going to mellow out."

"Okay, enough. What do you need me to look at?" I had listened to enough opinions on my character today.

Ayda frowned at me, but flipped a notebook open on the desk and paged through it. "You'll want to go over all of this, but this one caught my attention."

I narrowed my eyes as I read the page. "This is that attack." The one that meant to kill me. The one Silver needed a stronger connection to remove the last of. My face heated up at the thought and I hid behind my hair. I had not pulled it back at all today having no time trying to elude Silver and Lexi.

"Yeah, and while I don't understand the details of the spell, you were right that she was not going to be able to repeat it again anytime soon. She sacrificed three people to gain enough power for it and still failed. I wonder if the reason she didn't keep going was that she couldn't control that much power or that she ran out of sacrifices," Ayda mused.

"Either way it hurt like Hells," I muttered.

"It certainly appeared that way, but we're all thankful it didn't kill you as intended. That was a lot of power being used against you. It's been a long time since I've seen two high level casters fighting," Ayda commented. She gave me too much credit.

I pulled my thoughts away from the horrors the necromancer performed to the theory written out in front of me. "Piecing it together, I managed to block the power from the first one. The additional sacrifices must have been the surges in power. I was wondering how she so easily overrode my attempt to shield myself from her."

Ayda let out a short laugh. "I wasn't even sure if I could block the attack. I may have been the equivalent of a high mage back in the day, but I'm way out of practice. And this right here," she said, gesturing to the notes on the desk, "This is beyond me. As it is, since you arrived, I've been struggling to learn the suggested arcane spells that have been added to the database. You and Lockonis have certainly been busy digging up useful ones."

I shrugged, not wanting to mention that some of those I created. "I can't read the divine parts so I won't understand the whole spell either. It's something Silver and I will have to review together." The words sounded far more confident than I felt. Lockonis could just as easily take my place. Ayda could just as easily take my place. I had a feeling she underestimated her own abilities.

Ayda put her hand on my shoulder, gently tugging at me so I would back away. "I don't envy you that task. No more for today though. You're pretty pale and I don't feel like dealing with that paladin's attitude."

I had come to hate Silver's restoration spell. The initial searing pain was bad enough, but the long recovery time was utter torture. If my injuries had been less severe, they would have been fully healed by now, but there was no helping what had occurred.

"Ketayl?"

I had been staring at the papers on the desk without moving. "I'm fine. Really. I'd like to go over this."

Ayda stood on the side of the desk with her arms folded. "You need to go rest. I'll put a priority on getting it into the file."

"I just need my tablet and I can get..." I trailed off and looked down at my hands. "I can't." I had spoken as if things were normal. As if I had my power and could copy the files into the system. "I can't." My shaking hands became blurry as I stared at them.

A task so minor and I could not perform it. This was part of my job and I could not do it. I balled my hands up, squeezing them tightly.

Ayda pulled me away from the desk. "Hey, breathe. It's okay. We've got the equipment at the office to scan all of this in. You'll be neck deep in figuring this out in no time. Or if you want, teach me the way you normally do it. It sounds like something that would come in handy."

Her voice seemed far away. There were even smaller things I was used to which I had been unable to do. Tasks as simple as drying my hair. I had been distracted by Lexi insisting on doing my hair lately that I pushed the inconvenience to the back of my mind.

The Elven woman with me stuck her head out the door. "Lacura, go get Silver for me." She leaned down so she could look me in the eye. "Snap out of it. You'll have your power back before you know it."

I closed my eyes and held my hands tightly to my chest. *I did this to myself. I made myself useless.* I looked at her, forcing a smile to my face. "I'm fine."

Ayda leveled a look at me. "Go. Rest. I'll get Colleen's notes in personally. You'll be too busy trying to make heads or tails of that mess to even notice your power come back."

"What's going on?" Silver demanded as he hurried into the room.

"You shouldn't have pushed her to come here in her condition. She needs to recover. Now both of you get out of here." Ayda pointed at the door.

Silver looked between the two of us before getting his arm around my shoulders. "Yeah, we should go."

I nodded. It had been a mistake to come here. I had nothing to contribute. I had nothing.

2 4

With the remainder of the case being taken over by the Sola branch, Silver, Lexi, and I were sent home. Though we were all being held in Great Tree. I wanted to go back to work, but instead we found ourselves staying at my adopted parent's house.

Since I still lacked my arcane abilities, it made sense for me to be here since it was closer to the EAC, but the other two did not need to remain with me. Having constant company had become taxing.

I watched silently as my parents and my teammates had a lively conversation over lunch. It was like this at every meal. Everyone was upbeat and happy. The one saving grace was that it was not my turn to clean up so I could disappear after I finished. I had tried to skip what meals I could, but someone would always find me. I had become powerless in more ways than one.

My food disappeared as fast as I could manage and I deposited my dishes in the kitchen sink. Before I could escape, Father caught up with me. He held a black rectangular box that was about as long as my forearm.

He smiled gently, holding out the box. "Here, I'll try to keep the others busy."

I raised an eyebrow before opening it. It was a wooden flute. Purple crystals hung from the cords tied near the mouthpiece. "I haven't played something like this in a long time." It was the same shape, but larger than the practice one Mother had started teaching me music on decades ago.

"It doesn't matter. I know you've been needing time alone. It'll help you clear your head and give you something else to focus on. Go." He made a shooing motion at me.

"But what if...?" I trailed off as Father pointed at the door to outside. I bowed my head and left.

I could not turn down the gift of some peace and quiet Father had given me so I hustled away from the house into the forest, clutching the black case to my chest. I kept my path along the lake to be able to find my way back easily.

I slowed as I came up on a large rock sitting at the edge of the forest overlooking the water. This would do. It echoed of another long-lost place of quiet.

Carefully picking my way over, I soon stood on the rock. I took a moment to breathe deeply and take in the remaining fall colors on the trees around the lake. Some people from the city were out on boats, but it was a far cry from the busy summer season.

This was nice, but it would not be enough. I sat down and opened the case, gently taking the wooden flute out. The light-colored wood showed no sign of wear, making me wonder where this had come from. Who did it belong to? It appeared to be brand new.

Questions I should have asked before leaving. Perhaps I had gotten too used to there being a wide variety of instruments available since Mother was a musician. With the black cord and the purple crystals, it gave off the sense of being something very personal. Father should not have loaned this out so freely.

I opened the case again, searching for the name of the owner. A small silver-colored plate was attached inside the lid with my name on it. I rolled my eyes. I should have known.

With that mystery solved, I had no excuse to delay what I had been sent out here for. I brought the flute to my lips and I cringed on the first note out. I knew I was out of practice, but it sounded horrible. It really had been too long.

Nothing left but to remember how to play it. Father was quiet, but he always seemed to be tuned in to what I needed.

After a while I got the hang of it again and managed to play simple melodies. I stopped as the sun started to get low. I had hoped playing all afternoon would have done something. Maybe I just needed to accept that my power was never coming back. No matter what Magus Engelil and Lockonis tried, nothing was working. I had exhausted all of my ideas as well.

I sighed and leaned forward, hugging my knees to my chest, still clutching the flute. What would I do now? I was useless like this.

"Kela?" Silver called softly.

I kept my eyes out over the water so I did not have to look at him. "I'm fine." My words were clipped. I could not bring myself to force a smile.

He kelt down next to me and brushed my bangs back. "Is your power back?"

I shot him a glare. "Does it look like it?" I spat.

Silver backed away. "With the sound of what you were playing, I thought they might be."

"It's just music. I'm not very good with this." I held up the flute. Before I gave into my frustration and damaged it, I picked up the case and tucked the flute away.

"That was not just music. How can you perform that type of magic without your power?" He knelt down next to me.

I shrugged. "It's something different and I can't control it. I don't know how to explain it. You'll have to ask someone else. How long were you listening?"

Silver hummed for a moment. "I'm not sure how long I've been here. The sun has moved quite a bit."

I rolled my eyes. "Well, it's getting dark so I'm going to head back. You're welcome to stay."

"Wait," Silver said and grabbed my arm as I went to leave.

I glared up at him. "Let go."

"Just give me a minute, will you? What's going on?" my partner demanded.

"I think it's obvious. Now let go." I pulled, but Silver held firm.

"No. Will you just talk to me? I can't read your mind." His hand got tighter around my arm.

I pulled harder. I used my free hand to try to pry his off. My chest got tighter as I realized I could not escape. Without my arcane abilities I was powerless.

Silver let go when I accidentally knocked the flute case out of my hand during my struggle.

I ran before he could grab me again. I paid no attention to which way I went. I just needed to get away.

My partner called after me repeatedly, his voice growing ever more distant as I ran. Even when I had not heard him for a bit, while my lungs and legs burned and with a sharp pain in my side, I kept running.

It had gotten too dark to see and I tripped over something that sent me sprawling into the dirt and fallen leaves. I gasped for air as the hit knocked the wind out of me. Eventually I rolled over onto my back and stared at the stars. The moon was dark tonight and I was far enough from the city to be able to see much more of the night sky.

Perhaps I should stay here for a while. I had not heard Silver for a few minutes, and it would be hard for him to spot me on the ground.

Not to mention I was sore from both the run and hitting the ground.

I shivered as the warmth I built up from my run dissipated over time. I should leave before I froze, but it was quiet here under the stars.

Why did I run? It was not the first time Silver had physically stopped me. He had previously gone so far as to pin me to the floor, and I had never felt as threatened as I had when he grabbed my arm earlier.

I hugged myself tightly. Being powerless had come with more problems than I could ever have imagined. Why was I so reliant on my arcane abilities?

As the night wore on, it got colder and no amount of hugging myself in my oversized sweater while lying on the ground looking up at the sky was going to warm me up. I sat up and looked around. It was too dark to get my bearings and I did not know how to navigate by the stars. My best bet was going to be to get back to the water and follow it back.

The moment I put weight on my right foot I hissed and fell back down. I poked at my ankle. It was swollen and tender. Wonderful. The best I could do for the moment was rest it on the cold ground.

I shifted so I sat back against the closest large tree and huddled as much into myself as possible. At least it was clear tonight. Rain would have only added insult to injury.

After a while of watching the stars, I yawned. I rubbed at my face. I needed to stay awake, but the cold made it difficult.

A flash of light caught my attention and I huddled down as much as possible. I did not see what had caused it.

"Dayko, have you spotted her yet?" It was Mother's voice and it sounded like it had come through a speaker.

"Not yet. I'm still on her trail," Father said. He sounded close. "I'll find her soon, Lin."

Did I want to be found? I stayed silent, not moving. Then I would have to not only explain myself, but also face Silver. I had acted like a fool and now here I was in the dark forest with an injured ankle.

Staying here all night would be preferable.

The light passed by me again. The source was behind me. With any luck Father would not spot me. Though he was a tracker and a hunter. My chances of him not finding me were nonexistent.

Passes of light grew more frequent as did the brightness.

"Oh Gods," Father said in a hushed voice and soon appeared next to me looking at the ground. "Where...?" He stopped his search when he turned the flashlight on me.

I forced a weak smile up at him. I was too numb for much else.

He knelt down next to me. "You are quite the escape artist. You got a lot farther than I figured you would have."

I shrugged.

Father took the radio off his belt and held it in front of his mouth. "I found her. She's safe."

"Thank the Heavens," Mother said. "Hurry back. She has to be freezing."

He put the radio away. "I assume you tripped and landed pretty hard over there."

I flinched and looked away when the flashlight shown in my face. The light revealed that my sweater was covered in dirt and leaves and my leggings had torn in a few places.

"You're certainly flithy enough for it. Are you hurt?" Father asked softly.

I nodded.

"Ketayl, please talk. Silver hadn't meant to frighten you. He was supposed to make sure you got back before it started getting dark. I'll remember not to send him next time." Father did not sound pleased. I wondered what that conversation had been.

The words I was about to say turned into a hiss when Father prodded at my ankle.

"Just this one?"

"Yes," I said quietly. My teeth chattered when I spoke.

Father took his jacket off and threw it over my shoulders. Then he got next to me and helped me up. "That's it. Just put your weight on your left leg for the moment. I'll carry you back."

"I'm fine. I can walk." I knew I should not, but I would rather push myself than be carried.

"Ketayl, no. You'll make it worse and you're freezing. Come on." He turned his back toward me, squatting down.

I hesitated. "I'm heavy."

"Ketayl," he said my name sharply, his tone warning.

I sighed and climbed on his back. I was never going to hear the end of this. I wished I had disappeared.

He walked in silence for a while. I was too busy shivering to interrupt it. When I was on the ground, it had not felt as cold as it did now. Even his warm jacket was of no help.

"Just hang in there. We'll be back soon," Father soothed. "I can take a more direct line back now."

"Don't want to go back," I muttered through my chattering teeth.

He laughed lightly. "I almost don't blame you. There are some very worried people back there who are likely going to coddle you and I know how much you despise that."

I groaned.

"At least know that there will be hot food and drink waiting. Along with a warm blanket and likely a hot bath as soon as Mom sees you."

"I'm not a child." Though I knew I might as well have been - I had been throwing a temper tantrum like one lately.

Father laughed. "You still are. Like most your age, you live and work in the adult world, but you are Elven and you have not come of age yet."

Work. Without my power I was useless. "I'm not sure if I can go back like this."

"We'll stop in the workshop and see how bad your ankle is before heading to the house."

"That's not what I meant," I said quietly. Why was I having this conversation? The mental argument did not stop the words from coming out. "I can't go back to the TIO like this."

Silence followed. I rested against Father's back. He was warm. He was safe. Like this I was still a child.

"You don't have to. If you want to stay with them, I'm sure your other skills will be of value. If you decide to do something else, Mom and I will be here to support and guide you," Father said softly. "You may not be blood, but you're my daughter, remember that."

Could I leave the TIO though? Was there anything else?

WHY ME? I thought as Lexi dragged me around Great Tree for the third day in a row. She had not had a chance to visit the city before and since we were staying at my parent's house, she had taken the opportunity. She insisted on me being her guide. Parks, shops, restaurants - she wanted to see as much of the city as she could.

I pushed my sunglasses up, worried they had fallen out of place. I knew this gate. "Why are we at the EAC?"

Lexi smiled broadly. "First of all, I hear the grounds are beautiful. Second, I was asked to bring you here."

I rolled my eyes. "You could have just told me that they wanted to figure out what's going on with my power again." Though I believed we had exhausted all of our options.

Lexi made me take her on a tour of the grounds. I avoided people as much as possible. I brought her back around to the gate as soon as I could, hoping to evade the people looking for me.

Unfortunately, a few people were waiting for us at the gate. Magus Engelil stood talking with Lockonis and Silver.

I bowed to Magus Engelil. "Ma'am."

"Enough of that," she chided gently. "You know I think of you as a peer."

I shook my head. I was powerless and thus not even in the same realm as her.

Lockonis groaned loudly. "You're so damn stubborn, Ket. Come on, let's go for a walk."

I rolled my eyes - I had just been on a walk.

As I followed the group, Magus Engelil and Lockonis chatted, discussing ideas. It was all variations on things we had tried. Silver tossed out a few comments even though he was a divine caster. His were some simpler ideas that had no connection to the arcane itself. Lockonis shot him down, focusing on the arcane.

I sighed. I would do as they asked, but I held no hope for getting my power to awaken. I agreed that when I released the confines on my power and the spell I cast were the sources of my current issues, but it had been weeks now. There was a theory that when the necromancer created my copy, it also left something behind like the attack, but Silver could not find evidence to support it.

Lexi hung next to me. "You don't think any of this will work again?"

I shook my head. "It's all variations on previous attempts. There's only a small percentage of one working."

"I thought I heard someone say you worked on small percentages of things going your way." She gave me a soft smile.

"Too small and getting smaller. I did this to myself. I don't know if it'll ever come back," I said quietly. "Might be better off this way." Like this I was a danger to no one.

"Hey, you back there," Lockonis called loudly. "If I hear you giving up again, I'm kicking your ass all over the testing bay, power or no."

I shut my mouth and glared at the back of her head. No need to add to the misery.

Lexi took my hand and squeezed it. "She's right. You can't give up."

I pulled away from her and hugged myself. I was sick of hearing all of the positive words. I would not tell her or anyone else that I already had given into the idea that this was permanent. As time went on, I became more and more numb to the world. My daily routines had become nothing more than empty actions to satisfy the people around me. Lately I did not even bother to plaster a smile on my face and pretend everything was okay.

If only they would give up. If only everyone would go back to their lives and forget about me. Maybe then I could move on. But all of this focus on my current lack of arcane abilities just kept reminding me that I screwed up.

We arrived at an area along the water that was quiet. It surprised me there were no students here relaxing below the trees and enjoying the unusually warm autumn weather to study outside. Granted, that was one thing in my favor.

Magus Engelil came up to me and took my sunglasses off. "You don't need these here among friends." She touched the side of my face.

I froze in place. What was she doing? Logically I knew she was using her power, but I could not sense it and my chest tightened at the knowledge.

She withdrew her hand after several seconds. "It's the same as I can see. Your reserves are there, but I'm unsure why they remain disconnected. Though I'm thinking blocked is a more appropriate term. It's difficult to tell."

I let out the breath I held.

"That might be why our previous attempts haven't met with any success," Lockonis said, folding her arms. "We've been trying to reconnect, not unblock. I hate to say it, but Ket was right - our ideas weren't going to get us anywhere. I guess we should rethink our strategy."

I reached for my sunglasses, but Magus Engelil walked away with them. I turned my gaze down and let my hair fall in front of my face. At least my blue eye would be covered. Silver disliked it when I did that because with only the green one showing I looked like Kitteren.

"Mind if I steal her away for a few minutes while you talk? I want to discuss some things." Silver said.

Magus Engelil smiled. "Of course. We've taken up quite a bit of your time."

He put his hand on my back and directed me toward the water. Silence fell between us as we walked the short distance. It was out of hearing range for Lockonis and Magus Engelil, but I knew Lexi would be able to hear us. I doubted it mattered. He had previously talked about needing to find a new partner and this conversation had been coming.

I took a deep breath. "I guess it's time you moved on to a new partner."

Silver turned sharply. "What? Why would you even think that?"

"You need an arcane investigator. I can't be one anymore. Not like this." Hurt started to break through the numbness. I did not want to give up working with him as much as he annoyed and frustrated me. There was simply no other choice. Like this I could not keep him safe.

"That's crap and you know it. Even without your power, I still need you. Your knowledge of the arcane hasn't left," Silver snapped at me. His hands were balled up into fists at his sides. How could he have not seen that this was inevitable?

I sighed. "I can't cast. I can't see the arcane. I can't sense it at all. I can't fulfill the role I need to when we face a necromancer again."

My partner yanked hard on his braid. "Hells, I haven't even helped since the first time we encountered one. Don't count either of us out of this. Keep this up and I'll be the one kicking your ass all over the testing bay."

"Silver..." I stepped away from him, turning my attention out over the water. "I think it's time we both accepted the reality of the situation." *Stop making this harder than it has to be.*

He came up next to me, putting his arm around my shoulders. "There's one idea I had before you had gotten back to the gate, but you're probably not going to like it."

I rolled my eyes. "I don't like most of your ideas."

Silver gave a short laugh. "I guess you're not the only one who likes to go to the extreme. Will you hear me out? The Magus seemed to think it had potential."

I rolled my eyes. "Fine." It would be better to hear it from Silver than listen to Magus Engelil calmly and sweetly explain yet another tactic. Perhaps not better per say, but at least different.

"Your power is still tied to your emotions to some extent, correct?" he asked.

I shrugged. "Was, but that's more or less accurate."

He put his hand on my head. "You've been downright depressed since it happened. I dare say to the point of being apathetic lately. Maybe we need to find something to cause a strong emotional reaction out of you to break through the block. I still think there's something I can't quite sense that's also messing with you from the necromancer."

If only he knew. One would have thought my tearing through the woods to get away from him would have sufficed for an emotional reaction.

He took hold of my shoulders and turned me to face him. "Hey, look at me."

"I'm tired of people asking me that." I was whining, but I simply wanted to leave and hide away somewhere.

"I know and I understand why. Come on." He gently tilted my

head up. He lightly ran his thumbs under my eyes. "I always loved the gray, but this is absolutely mesmerizing."

There was that word again. He tossed out something he loved about me so nonchalantly. He never used to say stuff like that. What in the Hells had happened in the months we had been apart?

I squirmed as he kept staring at me. "Can you stop that, please?"

His cheeks reddened slightly. "Sorry, I wanted to remember this in case it's the last time I get to see it."

I managed to gain some breathing room. "Don't talk like it's going to change."

"I'm probably going to regret this."

I raised an eyebrow at Silver. He moved quickly and it took me a moment to realize his lips were on mine immediately followed by a wave of his power. I shoved him away and swung an open palm, slapping him with everything I had. My hand stung and I shook it. *"What in the Hells do you think you're doing?!"* I shrieked. *"You've got... some..."* I covered my mouth with my hands as the colors I was so familiar with returned to the world around me. I ignored the shocked looks from the women not far away to take it all in.

"Ow... I knew I was going to regret that," Silver said, rubbing his cheek.

The small strips of color I always saw flying around faded back into existence. I sensed not only the two powerful casters near me, but also the students at this school. I could even feel Silver's presence again, though I never previously considered that connected to my arcane abilities.

The world had become bright and vibrant again. My eyes watered at the sight. I closed my eyes for a moment and took a deep breath, letting my power out a little to play, letting it lift my hair and move it around gently.

"Well I'll be damned," Lockonis said. Her voice was faint due to the distance.

When I opened my eyes again, I stared up at my partner.

Silver still rubbed his cheek. "I know I did that to get a rise out of you, but did you really have to hit me so hard?"

I threw my arms around Silver's neck, standing on my toes to be able to hug him. Normally I would never take such an action, but he had brought my world back to me.

Strong arms wrapped themselves around me as he took a step

back. He picked me up off the ground, spinning us around. "So, can I get an actual kiss now?" he whispered in my ear.

I kissed his cheek.

"I had been hoping for something more," his voice was teasing.

"Why break with the tradition of only in extenuating circumstances?"

Silver laughed lightly and held me tighter. I knew I should let go, but I could not bring myself to push him away. Not even with hearing the others approaching us.

"*It's good to have you back, Kela,*" he whispered in my ear.

Hearing him talk in my native dialect of common broke the last of my emotional walls and I held onto him tighter, laughing silently.

I GLANCED over at Silver who was scribbling on a notepad. He had been at it off and on for over a week now. Not one pen had been thrown at the ceiling in that time. No whining. No small talk. Not even an attempt to drag me down for extra physical training.

What was going on here? I tapped my finger on my desk. Needing a break from my own work, I got up and stood over his shoulder. "Do you want help with something?"

Silver jumped and covered his pad of paper, but not before I saw that he had been breaking down the chaos spell I had used against the necromancer. Of all things, that was what had kept his attention this whole time?

"You don't need to hide it," I said softly. "I'm not sure how useful the words are without the arcane theory to go with it."

My partner sighed, pulling his arms away from the notepad. "I don't need the arcane theory for what I'm trying to figure out."

"What are you trying to figure out then?" I went back to my desk and dragged my chair over to sit next to him.

He was tugging on his braid fairly hard when I sat down.

I took his notepad and read it over. "You have the wording wrong." I held it out to him. "I can give you the correct translation."

Silver looked at the pad of paper in my hand. "Won't that cast the spell again?"

I shook my head. "The words are merely a set of directions. I needed them to remember the order of manipulations."

He grabbed his pen and held it out to me. "Just write it down."

"Okay..." I eyed him for a moment before finding a blank page and scribbling down the incantation. "What are you trying to figure out about it?"

Silver sighed. "It's just... it sounded a lot like a prayer."

I tilted my head. I never considered the option. "Well, most incantations tend to be poetic so it's easier to remember."

Silver took the notepad and pen from me when I flipped back to start reading his notes.

"There's got to be some reason you're fixated on this outside of it sounds like a prayer," I said, sitting back in my chair.

He let out a long breath, his shoulders relaxing. "I think it might be more of a necromatic spell."

I blinked at him, not making the connection. "What?"

Silver paused, not looking up at me. "You repeated lines about light and dark. That could easily imply divine and arcane."

I sat there staring at him with wide eyes. I opened my mouth to dispute the notion and closed it. I never even considered that.

"It could mean something else. I have no idea. Maybe I do need the theory behind it," he said quickly.

I pushed my chair back and hugged myself, looking away from him. Had I inadvertently used one? Why would my mother have known such a spell? Had she been a necromancer? I could not remember her ever using divine magic and we had lived in a village of divine casters.

Silver was on the floor kneeling in front of me. He brushed my bangs back. "Hey, these are wild theories I'm throwing out. Like you said, I probably need the arcane theory to go with it."

I took a deep breath before I spoke, still not facing him. "Is that why it failed? Because I'm not versed in the divine?"

"It's a possibility, but I'm also thinking the magical energy required would be more than any one person is capable of," Silver said softly. "I could feel the sheer amount of power you were putting into it, as could both Lexi and Frank, but you were obviously at your limit. Hells, I'm not even sure what you were doing before you started casting."

"Releasing control on my power," I answer absently while I

chewed on his observation. I bit my lower lip for a moment. "Are you thinking it's supposed to be a two-person spell? One arcane, one divine?" Would it still be considered necromancy? We might need another designation.

Silver flipped the tail of his braid back and forth. "You know, you might be onto something. This is going to be hard for you to talk about, but what happened to your mother when she cast it?"

I cringed. I knew he was simply wanting to put a puzzle together. "She died," I whispered. That was all he needed, right?

"Did she die immediately after casting it?" His words were slow as if he was hesitant to ask.

I shook my head. My mind took over, sending me back to that time when I was a small child. I held her head on my lap, crying. Reddish-blonde hair cascaded over my legs, most of it caked in blood as were her robes. I begged my father for help. The other villagers held him back from coming to heal her.

I could remember his dark auburn hair flying wildly as he fought to get to us. His emerald green eyes locked with mine as I called for him.

My mother called me by the name Silver now liked to use. Blue eyes replaced her normal light gray. She smiled at me, blood dripping out of the corner of her mouth. I could not recall what she told me then.

"Kela! Kela, dammit, snap out of it!" Silver shook my shoulders.

I took a shuddering breath.

"Dammit, I should never have shared what I was working on." He wiped gently at my face.

I had been crying?

Silver pulled me from my chair onto the floor with him and simply held me. We stayed there for a while. I lost track of time. He kept whispering reassurances and apologies.

I needed to answer his question still. "She didn't die immediately," I said quietly. "It was the same." Same as what I went through, but I survived and she didn't. It was unfair. She should have had the chance to be healed also.

"By the Gods... and you witnessed it?"

I bit my lower lip. "I held her until the end. They wouldn't let my father try to save her."

Silver asked no more and simply stroked my hair.

"He was a divine caster," I said quietly, "but it might've been beyond his capabilities." Even so, he should have been allowed to try.

My partner sat back. "He was?" He stroked the small patch of hair on his chin. "That might explain why you absorb divine energy."

I turned to more recent events to help settle down. My partner had insisted on spending more time together. He seemed desperate, but never spoke of why and I never asked. I refused to pry if I could help it. Silver usually would pry, but seemed to have some sense of when to back off.

This push from him was uncommon, but I could see what he was trying to do. He only wished to understand what went on. Unfortunately, he dredged up memories I would have sooner left locked away.

However, this, this right here was more like the easy-going relationship we had before. I would not forsake it.

"We should get back to work," I said. My sense of duty overriding the desire for continued closeness.

"Actually, let's take the rest of the day off. There's something I've been meaning to give you and I haven't."

I backed away and raised an eyebrow at him. His face seemed a bit flushed. Soon enough I was following him back to his quarters.

Silver opened the door and gestured for me to enter. I took a look around. I had not been in here for almost a year. He had put his original armor up on display. His sword and shield were missing, but he still used those. He had his full plate armor set up like it was a museum piece. It certainly stood out in the common area.

His quarters were smaller than mine with less amenities having been designated for short-term stays, but the permanent quarters had been full at the time and he never attempted to move even when one opened up.

"Thought it was a better like this than in some box in storage. Anyway, wait here and let me go get it." Silver sounded off. I could not pinpoint what it was.

I shrugged. If he wanted his old armor on display in his quarters, who was I to argue? I looked around at the other new decorations. He had kept little on display previously, just souvenirs and the like, but now the room was fuller. Small statues decorated the built-in bookshelves. They looked vaguely familiar.

As I stepped closer, they looked similar to the large broken statues at the abandoned church. I counted the number and sure enough there were twelve. Two of them were at the top - the God of the Sun and the Goddess of the Moon. I tilted my head at the layout. He had not put the Sun highest.

Books sat below the display of statues that had not been there previously. It appeared most were texts regarding the worship of each of the Gods. Notebooks had been thrown haphazardly next to them. I reached for one and stopped. Prying would be wrong.

I looked back up at the statues. Why all twelve?

"Kela," Silver said softly.

I spun on my heel, trying to hide the fact that I had been studying his decor. In his hands was a small flat white box.

He raised an eyebrow at me. "I guess you haven't been in here since I added those."

I turned my gaze to the floor. Every time I thought I knew my partner, something came along to prove me wrong.

"There's something to be said about looking at the pantheon as a whole." He stepped up next to me, his eyes on his display. "I'm hoping in time maybe it will give me insight into what draws people to be necromancers since there isn't one God they all follow. Though I'm still missing information about the ancient Gods."

"I'm partially surprised it's not Death," I mused.

"Probably because Death isn't the end of life. It's a transition. Let's leave the religious lecture for another time though." Silver fidgeted with the box. "I had meant to give you this a while ago, but it never seemed to be the right time. Still doesn't seem to be the right time, but..." He held out the box to me. I swore his cheeks had reddened slightly.

I raised an eyebrow at him and took it. Gently taking the cover off and unfolding the tissue paper, the crescent moon hair clip he pointed out at the store in Sola sat there. I looked up at him, lost as to why he was giving me this. "Why?"

Silver tugged on his braid. "I wanted to. We may essentially be opposites, but we still occupy the same sky." He picked it up out of the box slowly, the chains uncoiling until the crystals at the end were taken up with it. "May I?" He gestured at my hair.

Heat rose to my face. That made no sense. It was a gift from a friend. "Um... I guess."

I stayed perfectly still as Silver went behind me and undid the elastic at the end of my hair. As he pulled the top of my hair back, I fidgeted with my hands, unable to remain completely still. What was wrong with me? My emotional state was all over the place. Apparently, I did need to take the rest of the day off so I could regain my focus.

Silver ran his fingers through my hair after he finished putting the clip in. I stayed frozen in place, unsure of what to do.

The sound of something falling got him to move away. I turned in the direction of the source which seemed to have come from the front door.

My partner opened his side of the mailbox, retrieving the envelope delivered. He frowned at it before opening the letter.

I started to walk over, curious as to what he received.

Suddenly he snarled and crumpled up the letter, throwing it in the direction of the small trash basket.

"Is everything okay?"

Silver frowned, folding his arms and staring at where the crumpled letter had fallen. "I'll deal with it later. Let's go into town and enjoy the rest of the afternoon."

"But..." I looked at the crumpled letter.

"Kela, it's nothing for you to worry about." Silver gently touched my cheek. "Let's go. I heard some areas in town started decorating early for the Winter Solstice." He grinned broadly.

I rolled my eyes. He could be such a child.

But what about that letter? Something told me I needed to pry, but I had no idea how to press him to talk about it.

ACKNOWLEDGMENTS

Joshua Jackson and Brandi Burns: not only thank you for reading this over when it was a hot mess (and being beta readers), but for keeping me going on it. The time period that I was working on this book in particular was rough for me personally with a lot of ups and downs and worries that I was never going to get this finished. There were many times I thought about scraping it because let's face it, I'm not an accountant nor do I understand it. Josh tried to help with the financial stuff and I admit that my eyes glossed over the moment he would start throwing terminology at me.

A quick shout out to my local critique groups as well.

To the people who have been reading my books and spoken with me: thank you. You guys really keep me going and I continue to hope I don't disappoint. Interacting with you online or at events is great and I love it.

ABOUT THE AUTHOR

J.C. Jackson is originally from New England and currently lives in southwestern Idaho with her husband and daughter.

On top of writing, she enjoys gaming whether that is picking up a controller or throwing down some dice in a tabletop RPG (as well as other board games). She has also been a fan of science fiction and fantasy since she was little.

Blog: https://jeicjackson.wordpress.com/
Facebook: https://www.facebook.com/jeicjackson/
Twitter: https://twitter.com/JeiC
Instagram: https://www.instagram.com/jeicjackson/

ALSO BY J. C. JACKSON

Terra Chronicles

Twisted Magics

Shattered Illusions

Twice Cursed

Conjured Defense

Mortgaged Mortality